Isabelle
and
Her Daughters

Gloria West

PART ONE: ISABELLE

CHAPTER ONE

Eloise was the real beauty of our family, with long, jet black hair, flashing grey green eyes and willowy figure. Oh, I was considered to be what I believe is often described as 'striking' but I certainly did not possess my younger sister's beauty. I was smaller in height and my hair and eyes were dark. My younger sister, Colette, was pretty too with brown hair, the lightest shade in the family and blue grey eyes. So, the Lefevre girls were often looked at twice in the street and other public places.

We lived near the Bibliotheque-Nationale, the famous library where Papa held a responsible position. He had been educated at the Sorbonne University and had ensured that his daughters had also been well educated. My poor mother had died in a typhoid epidemic when I was eleven years old. This had come as a heartbreaking shock to us all.

Eloise was Papa's favourite although he tried, sometimes unsuccessfully it must be said, not to make this too obvious. In my way I was fond of Eloise but I preferred Colette. And I wished now and again that my father would show more open affection towards me.

My sisters and I had a nursemaid called Anne Dupont. I had a clear memory of a fascinating tale she had told me when I was thirteen. "Your Papa," she said, "Before he married your Maman, Celeste," he had an affair with a dancer from the Opera."

"Really?" I asked, fascinated by a side of my father that I hadn't known existed. "What was her name?"

Anne had nodded. "It was Yvette. She had started dancing as a child. She was a petit rat."

"A what?"

1

"The petit rats were pupils of the School of Dance near the Opera where I worked as a maid to one of the instructors. Most of these little girls came from poor families. They started to train at a young age. I remember Yvette wearing faded shawls and soot-coloured hats. Her mother was bossy, she used to sit on a four-legged stool during the performance Yvette was in.

But she always threw a shawl over her daughter when she came off stage. She had a little basket with sugared water inside it. Yvette was always ready to drink this."

"I can well believe it," I had commented, knowing I would have felt the same way.

Anne nodded. "Anyway, she progressed to the corps de ballet and when she was older, some of the society gentlemen arranged meetings with the dancers through their mothers. But your papa met Yvette in the Foyer de la Danse."

"What was that?"

"A big room behind the stage with barres and mirrors all over the place. The dancers used to get together there before the performance and the men used to come in there and…" Yvette had paused before continuing speaking, "Associate with the dancers."

Anne looked pensive for a moment. "Of course, your Papa's parents wouldn't have approved of him marrying the girl he was having an affair with. What with them being the owners of a well-known grocery store. Your maman was seen as a far more suitable bride because her family ran famous patisseries. And…."

This fascinating conversation had been interrupted by Papa coming home unexpectedly early one day and overhearing. He burst into the room, his face like thunder. Anne looked scared.

"That's quite enough, Anne. You did good work as a nursemaid to my girls and now Isabelle's a bit older, her companion. But I didn't employ you so that you could gossip about our family behind my back."

Anne looked downcast as Papa turned to me. "Isabelle, go to your room while I have a word with Anne."

I had burst into tears, I cast a worried look in Anne's direction. "She's not going to get into trouble, is she? Please don't send Anne away, Papa."

"I'll deal with this, stop arguing, Isabelle. Just do what you're told," my father had snapped. So, I had done so, knowing better than to say anything else although I couldn't help feeling sad for Anne.

Papa did dismiss Anne from our service but he made sure she had been paid what she was owed and then he made arrangements for her to work for another family of his acquaintance.

I was relieved by this but I missed Anne terribly.

Anne was replaced by Blanche. Originally, I preferred Anne, I missed her sense of humour and her interesting stories. But I became used to the more discreet Blanche in time. She became a familiar, comforting sight in her laced smock cap with long streamers hanging behind. She often read to us after our high tea. I liked the sound of her voice.

Other treats were eating muffins and drinking Indian tea in an English tea shop. We sometimes attended the circus where we watched the Shetland ponies dancing on their hind legs and the dancer on horseback with one leg in the air. This was my sisters' favourite act. Mine was the ballerina pirouetting on a small platform. "Wish I could do that," I had whispered to them, earning a disapproving look from Blanche.

The Paris Exposition that we attended with Blanche was incredible. People from the whole world were there. We were enthralled at the amazing sights we saw. It seemed almost as if the whole world were present. Dark skinned men in fezzes and turbans milled among the vast crowds. Snake charmers played flutes and Colette was delighted to be given a donkey ride while Eloise rode an elephant.

Blanche hurried us past the semi-naked belly dancers. We gazed longingly at the Oriental rugs, perfumes, and ivory bracelets on sale until Blanche gave in to us and bought us a bracelet each. We put them on our wrists and admired them.

We gazed up in awe at the Eiffel Tower, resembling a huge French flag made of 22,000 gas jets, each in a blue, white or red glass globe. We rode on a Seine River boat attractively decorated with paper lanterns.

Sometimes, we were taken to the Louvre to see the pictures. The one I liked best of all was a painting by Monsieur Degas, depicting two ballet girls in the wings of the Paris Opera but I did not dare tell Papa it reminded me of the Yvette story. One of the girls was bending down to tie her shoe, the other was limbering up, her one leg lifted onto the barre, touching her ankles with her hand.

The activity I enjoyed most was dancing. It helped me to forget all my troubles. Eloise was the proud possessor of a fine singing voice but I had always shown the most promise at our music lessons. Colette could also sing but her voice was not up to the same standard as Eloise's.

When I reached the age of eighteen, I did not then know that the year 1890 would change my life forever.

CHAPTER TWO

My father, in the summer of my eighteenth year, was contemplating marriage with the widow of a journalist who had, in his time, been fairly popular as well as widely read. Her name was Louise Charpentier. She had made several visits to our house but I didn't like her no matter how much I tried to do so. I knew she disliked me too, giving me, the impression she thought I was too outspoken for my age. Her own daughter was quiet and meek. I had tried to like her daughter but occasionally I could not help wondering if she were a little sly.

Madame Charpentier had a pinched mouth, she disapproved of many things. She could be charming to my father and Eloise but I felt it to be false. I couldn't understand why my father wanted to marry her; it was not as if he needed her money. But perhaps he was genuinely fond of her. There was no accounting for taste after all.

One spring evening, Papa called me into his study as he wished to speak to me on my own. I had more or less taken it for granted that my father would probably wish to arrange a suitable marriage for me at the right time. What did he have in store for me? I wondered, hoping I would approve of his choice. But he didn't bring the subject of my future marriage up immediately.

"Madame Charpentier has left her card with us so we shall be having an extended 'at home' tonight. This, I am happy to say, gives me the opportunity to offer her my hand in marriage."

How old fashioned he sounded I thought although I remained silent.

"If she consents, I shall be so happy."

I certainly won't share in your happiness, I thought. Glancing at me, he continued. "If she does accept, we'll have a pleasant party later in the year before we make a formal announcement. We shall also be having another guest tonight."

Papa hesitated for a split second. "Do you know who I mean?"

"Suppose it's that wine merchant friend of Madame Charpentier's."

He nodded. "You know very well his name is Georges Bourbonneux."

I forced myself not to look in the opposite direction. "Yes."

Papa looked crafty. "He'd make a good husband for you."

I shook my head, vehemently.

"Don't be silly!" Papa snapped. "George's business is flourishing and you'd be able to live comfortably with him. It's doubtful he'd mistreat you."

His words made a hollow ring in my ears. I disliked Georges Bourbonneux. It wasn't only because he was fat and unprepossessing in appearance. I knew people who were fat or plain or both that I did like. My main reason for not being able to take to him was because he had a smug, self-satisfied air about him. His conversation was hardly scintillating. The last time we had seen him, he had spoken endlessly of the bad effects of the phylloxera beetle on his suppliers, the vineyards that would affect his trade. Hardly a riveting subject!

Another reason I was wary of Georges was because I had heard whispered rumours that he had been known to attempt liberties with his female servants.

I shook my head vehemently. "No, Papa, I certainly *don't* want to marry Georges. I don't wish to wed at all yet. Couldn't you let me become a *demoiselle de maison* at one of the emporiums? I'd love that and be forever grateful to you for letting me do this."

I tried to smile winningly at him while his face remained impassive. My idea seemed a good one to me. If I could join the other young women from good backgrounds and respectable homes whose parents paid for the privilege of having them trained in business skills. As I would also have been provided with board, lodging and chaperonage on the premises, it would in my opinion be a lovely way not to be in the presence of Madame Charpentier.

I loved browsing around the exclusive shops and the feel of soft, expensive fabrics. My passion after my dancing was for beautiful clothes made of rich materials.

My father, however, was not to be swayed.

He frowned. "Certainly not, Isabelle," he said. firmly. "I should prefer you to be respectably married rather than go into trade yourself. Georges is not perhaps handsome but he is not exactly ugly either. You may, if you wish, wait until you are twenty-one at the time of the actual wedding. But there should be a formal engagement between the pair of you."

I heard my voice rise to an alarmingly high pitch. "Even if I live to be a hundred years old," I screamed, "I'm not going to be George's wife. You would have to drag me kicking and screaming to the altar." I knew I was probably sounding melodramatic but at that moment I didn't care.

My father's tone had been calm but he now began to lose patience with me. "There seems to be little point in carrying on this stupid conversation. I despair of it though I can't help hoping you'll come to your senses. Let me know when you've reached a more sensible decision."

He turned on his heel and left the room, slamming the door behind him.

I ran to my own bedroom in floods of tears. I threw myself on to my bed where I lay, face downwards, totally absorbed in my misery when I heard a tentative knock at the door.

Blanche entered, I felt her lift me up with her strong arms and pull my face onto her motherly bosom. She rocked me gently almost as if I were a baby. Then she started patting my back. These motions were soothing so I began to calm down slowly.

"You must excuse me, Mademoiselle Isabelle," Blanche said, "For coming into your room without you asking me to. It was because I saw you rushing past in the corridor very upset so I couldn't help wondering what was wrong. Tell me about it." She hesitated for a moment. "Only if you want to, of course."

When I was at last able to speak, I explained to her that my father was trying to force me to marry Georges Bourbonneux.

"He wants me to consent now," I said. "Because that Madame Charpentier is, I'm convinced, going to be our new stepmother. She likes Eloise and to a lesser extent Colette but not me and I don't like her either."

Blanche nodded, giving a wry smile. "I know you don't, it's not hard to tell."

"She thinks I'm too outspoken. She's a hypocrite in my opinion. On the surface she does everything considered correct but I believe that she's cruel underneath."

"It's not really my place to say this," Blanche remarked, "but I don't like that lady either. She's sharp tongued when she speaks to me or the maids like as if she's the mistress here already. Your papa pays me good wages, I admit, and perhaps it's not my place to say this but ..."

She hesitated.

"Tell me what you meant to say, Blanche. It'll go no further, I promise."

"You'd be wasted on that gentleman. There's things I could tell you about him. I won't say now what they are."

I understood what Blanche meant so I hid a smile. All the same, I felt grateful to her for her sympathy towards my predicament.

Shrugging my shoulders, I asked. "What can I do about it, though? Papa is so determined to have his way."

Blanche looked as if she were deep in thought. Then she smiled. "I'm maybe wrong to suggest this but I've got an idea." She sighed, "Oh well, if I'm damned, I'm damned, so be it!"

I was intrigued. "What is it?"

"There's not time to tell you now because I've got to see to the children. I'll explain it to you tomorrow. When we go for our walk in the Champs Elysees, say that you'd like to come, too. It's doubtful your papa will object. I'll find a suitable time to tell you then. For now, I'll send your maid up to help you wash and dress for this evening."

Blanche walked to the door, she carried herself regally although she was plump. "Don't worry, we'll find a way out of this," she said, over her shoulder as she closed the door behind her, leaving me in an agony of suspense.

8

CHAPTER THREE

My maid helped me wash away all traces of my tears before I dressed for the evening. She looked curious but didn't question me for which I was both relieved and grateful.

Taking a deep breath, I went downstairs to meet our visitors at the appropriate time. My red chiffon dress had not been purchased from the House of Worth yet it was certainly elegant so it gave me a certain amount of confidence.

Georges was waiting for me. He was well-dressed, he gave me what I could see he believed to be a charming smile as he took my hand. It was an effort on my part not to snatch it away. Then he kissed it, holding on to it for longer than I believed was strictly necessary.

Madame Charpentier bestowed a frosty smile upon me, I forced myself to smile back.

Blanche led the children in then left the room without looking at me. Eloise's hair had been put up for the occasion making her look older than her fourteen years. Her midnight black hair contrasted with her white dress.

At the age of ten, Colette was excited that she was partaking in an adult gathering. She was also wearing a white dress and already beginning to show that she would be taller than me in years to come. She ran a hand through her long brown hair. "It's exciting tonight, isn't it, Isabelle?" she said.

"Yes, it is," I agreed, feeling hypocritical but not wanting to spoil my sister's pleasure.

After our dinner that I didn't enjoy although it was well cooked, my father asked me to play the piano. I was a competent but by no means brilliant pianist.

I chose two pieces by Schubert, during the second one, Eloise sang beautifully.

Madame Charpentier remarked in a stage whisper to Georges. "My own daughter is a better pianist, such a shame she can't be with us tonight because of her indisposition."

"Isabelle plays the piano divinely," Georges stated in a loud voice.

"I'm learning to play," Eloise said. "My teacher says my progress is excellent. My singing teacher is also pleased with me."

"I like a lot of music," Colette remarked. "The first tune Isabelle played was nicer than the second one."

"I'm pleased to hear you showing an interest in such matters *ma petite*," Papa said. "But it's now well past your bedtime. You'd better retire now too, Eloise."

Eloise pouted but didn't argue as Blanche arrived to escort the two younger girls out of the room. They were both tired although trying not to show it.

After they had gone, a sudden impulse took hold of me. "I'd like to dance now; I know the steps of some ballets."

Madame Charpentier looked scandalized, Papa mildly irritated and Georges faintly amused.

"I hardly think this is the right time or place, Isabelle," Papa said, firmly.

Madame Charpentier spoke up next. "My daughter wouldn't dream of performing this way. We all know what ballet girls are."

"Not all of them," I snapped, earning a disapproving look from my father. "And Madame, I doubt your daughter has the necessary talent to dance in public."

I saw Papa's eyebrows lift as tiny daggers were jumping out of the corners of Madame Charpentier's eyes. Georges stifled a laugh behind his handkerchief.

"Let's have a game of dominoes," my father suggested. To my own surprise I managed to win although I knew this did not please either Madame Charpentier or Georges.

Eventually, Georges' carriage arrived. I was relieved to see him go after he had made an elaborate farewell.

Throughout the whole of the next day, I wondered if Papa would reprimand me for my ill manners. But he said nothing about it, much to my relief.

CHAPTER FOUR

I decided to accompany Blanche and my sisters on their Sunday afternoon stroll. It was a fine day. Sam Lewis, our English groom drove us to the Tuileries gardens. It was common knowledge that years before he and Blanche had had an "understanding" although this relationship had never fully developed, they had remained on friendly terms with each other.

As we alighted from our carriage, Blanche smiled warmly at Lewis. "Pick us up at five o'clock," she said. He nodded, whistling a popular tune as he walked away.

"Can I have a ride on the merry-go-round?" Colette asked.

Blanche nodded. "Yes, if you like."

I saw her glance at Eloise who looked wistful.

"Would you like to have a ride too?" I asked her.

She looked down at the ground, wistfully. "I'm too old now, really."

"You'll be able to look after Colette if you do," I said, understanding how she felt.

"Don't need looking after!" Colette protested indignantly.

"It's a good idea of Isabelle's," Blanche said, approvingly.

Eloise grabbed Colette's hand quickly and started running with her. I thought Colette would protest, however she did not.

"Let's have a coffee," I suggested to Blanche. She agreed, willingly. We sat down on a metal bench in the sight of but not fortunately, the hearing of the children on the merry-go-round

After taking a few sips of her drink, Blanche took a deep breath before saying "Your papa and Madame are going to the *Comedie Francaise* in a couple of nights' time, aren't they?"

"Yes," I confirmed, wondering where this conversation would lead.

"It would probably be the best time to carry out my plan if you're willing because you'll have to think long and hard about it."

I listened, intrigued. "Why?"

"I'm coming to that. Are you positive you don't want to marry that man?"

"Of course," I answered, a trifle impatiently."

"Well, I've got a sister who's a dressmaker. She's a widow who lives in the Marais district. If you can bring yourself to do this, you could leave home to stay with her."

I was startled. "But would she really want this?"

Blanche nodded. "Yes, she'd like your company." She sighed. "However, if you do go ahead with this, you might miss your home comforts, neither would you own fine clothes as you do now."

I was vehement. "I'd rather do almost anything other than marry Georges."

"Well, as you long as you stay determined, Mademoiselle, you'll need to pack your bags. Then go to the stables after your Papa and Madame have left for the theatre. Sam Lewis will be ready; he'll wait for you with a horse already saddled. But you'll have to bribe him."

"I'll do that."

"Please think hard about what you're planning to do, if you do change your mind, be sure to let me know and we can forget the whole thing."

Blanche was looking concerned and although I understood this, I was still determined not to back down.

"No, my mind's made up." I gave Blanche a quick kiss on the cheek. "But what about my sisters? Tell me quickly because they'll be back with us soon."

"I'll perhaps take them to see a conjuror at the café-concert, they'll enjoy that."

The girls returned to us shortly followed by Lewis who drove us to the Opera Square. We went back home amidst the double-decker trams that ran along the boulevards.

Papa was pleased to see us after we arrived home. For a few minutes I felt guilty about the pain I knew I would be causing him and my sisters. But then I had a mental picture of Georges looking self -satisfied.

It was hard to sleep that night. Early the next morning I packed some clothes and jewellery into a large bag, hiding it in my wardrobe, going back to bed and weeping for a long time at the thought of leaving my dear family behind and the pain it would cause them. I knew I would miss them.

When my maid appeared later, I pretended I was ill so she brought all my meals to me on a tray. I had little appetite anyway and did not eat very much, remaining in bed for two days.

On the second day, I composed a note to my family.

Dearest Papa, Eloise and Colette,
I can truthfully, as God is my witness, say that I love you all.
All the same, I hate the idea of having to marry Georges
Bourbonneux so I am leaving you instead of staying here. It's
breaking my heart to do so yet there is no alternative. I have
somewhere else to go although I cannot tell you where it is or
why I am going there. You will probably hate me for what I am
doing. I have to, though. You will always be in my heart. And
I'll pray for you.
Goodbye Papa, Eloise and Colette.
Sending my love to you.
Isabelle

I folded the note up and put it in a drawer, intending to place it under my pillow just before I made my departure.

At the appropriate late hour, my knees were shaking and my heart was in my mouth. I knew I would miss my family and tried hard to dismiss my guilty feelings about abandoning them.

Giving myself a mental shake, I made my quiet way to the stables, carrying my bag and a small torch. Fortunately, I was not discovered.

Our groom was waiting for me with two horses saddled. I handed him the sum of money before he assisted me to mount the horse and ride off into the night. Impatient to reach our destination, I didn't turn around.

CHAPTER FIVE

My new home was definitely a contrast to the one I had previously known. I knew the Marais district close to the Bastille, had once been picturesque, unfortunately, it was now a slum area. The rotting houses had cracked foundations with small windows like portholes called *tabatieres*. There was scant furniture in most of the houses and they became frigidly cold from the draughts through the old thin walls.

Marias was the centre of the dress making and needle trades. I carefully watched Susanne Binoche, Blanche's younger sister at her work, trying not to mind the pungent smell of the paraffin lamp.

"You're very good at what you do, Susanne," I told her.

She smiled, pleased by the compliment. "You've been watching me closely, that's a good thing. I'm grateful to you for the jewellery sales you've made."

"I'm glad you've been able to benefit from them as well as me. I'm really hoping to get a job soon."

"You'll probably be able to if you try hard enough."

I helped Susanne as much as I could with household tasks, in some instances she had to show me what to do, this must have delayed her with her own work but she didn't complain. It was embarrassing for me the first time I asked her but she had smiled and said, "Ah yes, Isabelle, I know you had servants before. Don't worry though, you'll soon get more used to things like this."

After three weeks in my new home, I did obtain work as a salesgirl in a department store. This store was not one of the showier emporiums, the kind I had requested my father to let me train in as a *demoiselle de maison*. This shop's clientele was mainly drawn from the middle classes. Only a few of the clothes there came from the great houses of fashion. I loved the feel of their fine materials. Mostly, they were simple and practical gowns for ordinary wear. They were also designed for a great variety of activities including work, sport and holidays.

There was an embroidery table in the back room where the *petite-mains* sewed and chattered in the back room. Two older *vendeuses* were always clad in black silk. They stood rigidly almost like soldiers on parade. They were haughty with the *petite-mains* and disapproved of my attempts at friendliness with them. The *petite-mains* weren't unpleasant with me but I always had the feeling that they saw me more as an outsider than as one of them.

A tall, graceful model called Rose was amiable with me although she didn't speak to me all that much. I envied her the sole use of a dressing room called *La Cabine*. One day she said to me, "I'm lucky that I'm sometimes given clothes after I've showing them."

Sometimes in our limited free time, a couple of friends and I danced in the changing rooms.

"You're really good at this, Isabelle," one of them complimented me one day while the others nodded in agreement.

I was delighted by this compliment; it gave me a warm glow.

Occasionally, these friends at the shop and I attended a *café-concert*. There was no entrance fee but the public were required to sit down and order refreshment immediately. I usually ate an ice cream or drank cocoa while some of the other customers munched chestnuts. We sat amongst the crowds who came and went.

Dancing made me forget my cares. After a while however, due to the long hours at work and the basic worry that my circumstances would never change, I was becoming pale and fatigued. And the colder autumn weather would be arriving in the not- too-distant future.

During the daytime I saw workmen in the streets wearing baggy velvetine rousers and cotton smocks. The *garcons patissiers* wore white linen jackets and trousers. They carried trays of cakes on their heads. Occasionally, I treated Susanne to a cake.

"This cake was delicious, Isabelle," she said, the first time I did so. "Don't make a habit of it though, it will waste your money."

I noticed that working class women of the district only wore hats on Sundays and holidays, unlike the women I had associated with formerly. They would only venture into the streets with gloves, veils and monumental hats with decorations of flowers, birds and similar ornaments on them. The *gendarmes* still wore the cocked hats of Napoleon's time. Now and again, a barrel organ grinder playing a popular tune and accompanied by his monkey would pass by.

All of these sights would have intrigued me were it not for the fact that I could not entirely help feeling a little depressed by my surroundings. Then I would mentally chide myself because Susanne was even tempered and we liked each other.

I became friendly with the two other sales girls; we were all around the same age. We worked from seven in the morning until nine at night. As well as selling the dresses, we had to deliver them to the customers.

When our manager went out to his lunch, my two friends and I would dance in the fitting rooms, the other girls commented on my aptitude for dancing. I have to admit I found it diverting to be admired by an appreciative, albeit tiny audience.

When I danced, I managed to forget my cares. Due to my long hours at work and the basic worry, no matter that I tried to push it to the back of my mind that my circumstances would never change, I was becoming pale and fatigued.

Occasionally, in the little spare time we had, we would attend a café-concert with one or other of my friends. There was no entrance fee but the public were requested to sit down and immediately order refreshment. I usually ate an ice-cream or drank cocoa while some of the customers munched chestnuts. We sat amongst the crowds who came and went, some of the working men keeping their hats on. Some also smoked or drank beer. We watched short plays and acrobats as well as listening to the small orchestra that accompanied the singers and dancers.

These entertainments were cheaper, more convenient versions of the dramas and operas I had attended when I lived at home. But I still enjoyed them.

At the rear of the platform, 'the dressing scene' I was fascinated by the half circle of women called *dames du bouquet*. They had brightly enamelled complexions, elaborate hairstyles and wore sumptuous gowns, certainly not manufactured by the shop we worked in. These women were called *bouquet ladies* because of their traditional willingness to accept, with consequences, whatever flowers admiring spectators might care to send up over the footlights. "I used to know one of these women," one of my salesgirl friends whispered to me, one day. "She used to be a farm girl."

"How did she become one of these?" I asked, intrigued. "Got lucky, meeting a rich man, did she?"

"Afraid I can't tell you about that."

Although still curious, I smiled and didn't press her to do so.

The *cafe-concerts* were varied, some were dingy. I never wanted to stay long at them. The pleasanter ones were the outdoor cafes in the Champs Elysees set among the trees and shrubbery. They were shut in by vine covered trellis walls under chains of flickering yellow gas lamps with alternating tremulous glows and wavering shadows.

The people who attended were an interesting mixture. There were bureaucrats and businessmen of the Boulevard de Strasbourg, labourers from Belleville and the bohemians of Montmartre and the Latin Quarter.

In some of my wilder moments I wondered if I would ever dare to become a *bouquet lady*. It would possibly be a way of changing my present circumstances for something more lucrative. But this was not an idea I would ever have dared voice to anyone.

CHAPTER SIX

One day, now we were into early autumn, the manager of my workplace asked me to deliver a ball gown to a certain address on a rainy day. When I realized from looking at the slip of paper the address was written on, I was horrified to realise it was that of Madame Charpentier.

Calling on what I hoped was the reasonable acting ability I possessed by pretending to faint.

"Look," one of my friends called out. "Isabelle has passed out."

She made me hope the manager would send me home. My supervisor came over to me with a glass of water in her hand. Smelling salts were also pushed under my nose.

When I "regained consciousness," the manager approached me.

"How long have you been unwell, Mademoiselle Lefevre?"

"It just came over me this morning, Monsieur. But I still feel shaky."

He looked displeased as I became bolder. "May I be allowed to go home?"

He shrugged his shoulders. "Suppose so, do you realize you'll forfeit a day's pay?"

"Yes," I replied in a resigned tone, thinking he was being mean, considering the comfortable profits the store made. It was prudent, however, to keep this opinion to myself.

Susanne looked up from her sewing, surprised to see me home so early. Taking her into my confidence, I explained what had happened. "Hope you don't get given that address again," she said.

"To be honest with you, Susanne, I'm sick and tired of the shop. I'd like to find something totally different."

She frowned. "Is that wise? What else could you do? I can't imagine you becoming a *grisette* though you can of course sew. Neither can I see you going into service except as a lady's maid. But for that as well as being a governess or companion would mean you needed references. I'm not exactly the most suitable person to give you them, am I?"

I didn't answer her question merely saying, "I'm not sure myself what else I could do. But I'll try to rack my brain."

Susanne frowned again before she hesitated. Then she said, "Well, I've been working on a new design for hats that I invented myself."

I knew by now that Susanne was a good designer who sometimes had inspired ideas. She had made two dresses for me to wear in the store because I was keeping a few of my better clothes in case I ever needed to sell them for cash although I hoped this wouldn't happen, I was prepared for the possibility.

"I'm going to take a gamble by knocking on doors to see if they'll sell," Susanne said next. "I'll be going out in a few minutes time. Do you want to come with me?"

"Yes, but I hope nobody from the store will see me, I'm sure to be dismissed if they do."

"If you do see anyone from there, pretend you've had a miraculous recovery."

We looked at each other and laughed, some of the earlier tension I had felt eased slightly.

Susanne took me to a small shop tucked away in a side street. A young girl stood behind the counter. She had been lounging but stood up straight when we entered. She was thin and almost emaciated looking but had thick brown hair.

Susanne showed her the newly designed hats. "May I leave one behind?"

"Leave more than one. Three might be better to show my boss when he gets back. Can't promise he'll take them; you never know with him."

"Thank you, what's your name?" Susanne asked.

"Marguerite Lamont. I know you ain't seen me before. I was an orphan, used to live in an attic doing embroidery. The owner of the shop next door offered me a job behind the counter. I really liked it there but …" Marguerite's eyes were downcast. "He tried it on with me a few times."

A cynical thought entered my head. Sounds like Georges Bourbonneux but I kept this opinion to myself. I felt sorry for the girl.

Susanne looked a little shocked at her frankness.

An idea suddenly occurred to me. Was it a little wild? Maybe, however, I was still going to attempt it.

I asked Susanne to give me a pen and piece of paper as she had written down some names, she had suggested for a few of her hats. She looked bemused but did so.

"If he gets too much for you, Marguerite, this store has a vacancy for a sales assistant. If you're interested you should apply soon. Please don't mention my name to the manager if you do. Just say a friend recommended you for the post."

She looked interested; Susanne looked disapproving. Recklessly, I felt uncaring.

From that day onwards, Marguerite became a close friend of mine.

As we left the shop, Susanne's face was like thunder. "Isabelle, have you completely taken leave of your senses? You've probably thrown your job away for nothing."

"Might not have done. If she thinks I've done her a favour, she might be able to return it by persuading the owner of that shop to buy all of your hats."

"He may not want anything to do with her when she tells him she's leaving."

"If she does, she might not let him know until he's bought your hats," I suggested, airily

"That's neither here nor there. How do you think you're going to live, young lady? On fresh air or dreams, perhaps. Do they pay the rent?"

"No but I'm sure I'll find something that will."

I realized the confidence in my voice was misleading, there was a little anxiety on my part about this.

Susanne snorted then checked herself as we were in the street. She only spoke to me when it was absolutely necessary for the rest of the day. I tried not to let it bother me but fortunately, on the following day her attitude had mellowed to a certain extent, much to my relief.

Fortunately, the shop owner did like Susanne's hats and bought them all with one exception. Her good humour was restored by this for which I was grateful.

Marguerite called upon us, delighted to inform us that she had obtained my old job in the store. By now, I had mixed feelings about this news.

One evening, I persuaded Marguerite to come with me on a visit to the gas lit pleasure gardens of the Closerie des Lilas at the corner of the Boulevard Montparnasse.

Marguerite looked paler than ever. I had regained some of the colour in my own cheeks since leaving the store but I was now reduced to one set of fine clothing that I was now wearing in honour of this excursion. I had sold most of my better gowns, giving half the profits to Susanne who had begun to utter dire warnings against our forthcoming fate of sliding downwards on the slippery descent to real poverty. This, she prophesied would happen if I didn't find work soon. Outwardly I laughed off her warnings although I was beginning to worry a little myself.

Marguerite and I passed an itinerant chestnut seller and a few beggars. She threw a coin to the latter. When I had lived at home, I hadn't given much thought to the poor. Now, I wished I had not been so selfish. Nowadays I felt more sympathy towards them although I certainly didn't wish to join their ranks. There was also an uncomfortable feeling that in my present position I could do nothing to help their wretched existence.

The orchestra at the garden was playing polkas, their liveliness cheered me. We watched the dancers making hundreds of movements, a fascinating sight. "I love watching this, the people dancing," Marguerite said.

"I'd love to join them," I agreed, wistfully.

"The girls at work told me what a good dancer you was."

"Nice of them," I smiled, happily.

"In that case, Mademoiselle, will you let me have the honour of this dance?" a deep masculine voice asked as the orchestra struck up another tune.

I whirled around to observe a young man, flamboyantly dressed in a black velvet jacket covering a red shirt and yellow waistcoat and scarf His long legs were encased in high boots, he was naturally tall but the boots made him appear taller. For some reason unknown to myself because I wasn't usually shy or coy, I cast my eyes down to the ground and replied demurely. "Yes, I'd love to, Monsieur only I've never been taught the polka steps."

"I'll have to teach you then; it will be my pleasure."

He smiled at me, displaying even white teeth. Then he took my hand, leading me forward.

"Excuse me," I said to Marguerite who looked intrigued.

It felt entirely natural to be in this unknown man's arms, we were soon laughing over some of the polka steps although I didn't find them especially difficult to learn

"The girls in the shop your friend mentioned were right," he said. "You can dance very well."

My face coloured up, much to my private annoyance. "Thank you," I said, simply, deliberately withholding further explanation about the store.

"We haven't been properly introduced but please tell me your name?"

"Isabelle Lefevre, will you now let me know what you're called?"

"Leon Prideaux. I study art and live in Montmartre." So, he was one of those bohemians. That probably accounted for his clothing. Well, it was interesting to talk to one of them rather than merely observing them from a distance.

"May I ask where you live?"

"Marais," I answered, quickly. From the startled look that appeared on his face I could tell he was surprised. However, he made a valiant attempt to once more assume a bland expression. I didn't want him to find out too much about me on our first acquaintance so I excused myself by saying. "It's been lovely dancing with you Monsieur but I must rejoin my companion. I don't want her to be left alone all night and we really must go home before it's too late."

"May I escort you home?"

"It's kind of you to offer though I believe she'd prefer us to be alone."

He looked crestfallen making me feel a little flattered then he said, "As you wish, Mademoiselle Lefevre. I'm not allowed to come with you in body though I shall do so in spirit.

So please accept this money for the hire of a cab so that you both arrive home safely."

He pressed some coins into my hand. "I can't possibly accept this," I said, shaking my head slightly.

"Yes, you can, it's a small price to pay for the pleasure you've given me this evening. Will you repay me by coming here alone and dancing only with me?"

"Certainly, Monsieur Prideaux," I replied, demurely.

Rejoining Marguerite who clearly thought the whole incident had been an exciting adventure, I was relieved when I arrived home safely also that Monsieur Prideaux hadn't seen the house where I was now living.

I plucked up my courage to go alone on the following night to the Closerie de Lilas. To my great disappointment Leon wasn't there. I gazed idly at the nearby Hotel Luxembourg wondering if he might be drinking there and would afterwards stroll into the gardens.

This proved to be an idle fancy. Nevertheless, I had plenty of gentlemen partners willing to dance the polka with me. I didn't remain with any of them for very long as the partner I really wanted was absent.

When I arrived home, Susanne complained, "It's unnatural for a young woman like you to go out alone at night and wander the streets. Nothing good comes of this sort of thing."

"I'm careful," I said, earning another disapproving look from her although she made no further comment. I didn't wish to feel restricted by her or anybody else. Hadn't I rebelled against my father? However, I made no further comment.

As I climbed wearily into bed, I wondered about trying to become a dressmaker's assistant. I had decided I really must try to find a position soon to add to our reserves and placate Susanne. She had been good to me after all, in spite of her grumbles and I felt grateful to her.

CHAPTER SEVEN

Occasionally, I persuaded Marguerite to go with me to a *bal musette*. We sometimes listened to the amateur singers, drinking a glass of wine, our glasses glistening from the lamplight that shone on them. I always enjoyed this activity.

We would, if the weather permitted, stroll a little way along the riverside. The main attraction for us both was dancing to the accompaniment of the small orchestra, especially the waltzes and polkas played by the accordion.

Our favourite was the *Moulin de la Galette* in Montmartre, that favourite haunt of artists. We did, however, take care to avoid the local thugs in their striped sweaters who waltzed between the crowds committing their petty crimes. Beyond the wooden barrier that separated the tables from the dance floor, local girls improvised their own versions of the quadrille or can-can.

This dance, some people including Susanne considered shocking because it involved a great deal of whirling around with a daring lift of skirts to show flounced petticoats. I wasn't shocked by it although I had once blushed at a *café-chantant* Marguerite had once attended.

The crowd there had been rowdy but good natured as they shouted, whistled, laughed and joined in the choruses of the songs. When the dancer appeared, I heard men shouting, "Drawers off, higher, that's it, let's have a better look." The poor girl looked upset.

"Can we leave, Marguerite?" I asked.

"Suppose so," she answered, sulkily. She was not her usual talkative self on our return journey. Much to my relief, she appeared to have forgiven me the next time I suggested an outing.

As I watched the girls at the Moulin de la Galette going through their paces, I couldn't help wondering if any them knew, as I did that the can-can was based originally on an ancient fertility dance then a sixteenth century dance called the *Traore* performed by peasant women in Brittany.

After a while I gained the courage to join these girls. Marguerite knew a few of them although she preferred to watch them rather than join in like me. I let my hair fall forward over my face as I kicked my legs high, experiencing an inward amusement if I could see Madame Charpentier's face and hear her remarks if she could see me now. It would be a good base for an illustration, I thought.

A smallish, middle aged gentleman began to talk to Marguerite quite frequently but he always disappeared when I rejoined her. Perhaps he desired Marguerite, I didn't know, anyway it was no concern of mine. On one occasion he didn't leave my friend's side when I came back and I was amazed when he spoke to me.

"Excuse me, Mademoiselle," he said. "I should like to make your acquaintance as I have been admiring your performance tonight, not for the first time I might add."

I couldn't help feeling pleased by the compliment.

"How would you like to perform this dance professionally?"

I stared at him, stunned into silence, not quite believing my ears, wondering if I would presently awake from a dream.

Somehow, I did find my voice. "I'd very much like to perform professionally, Monsieur. But I can't see how it's possible. I don't even know where I should enquire about this sort of employment?"

He beamed. "Then look no further, Mademoiselle. "I own a *café-concert* in the Champs Elysees. If you don't believe me, here's my proof."

This strange little man showed me his business card with his name, Henri Devereux and his address printed on it in bold black print and in larger, bolder letters the address of his *café-concert*.

"If you come to my premises tomorrow, I'll arrange a contract for you."

"Thank you, Monsieur, I'll do that, what time should I arrive?"

25

"About noon. You'll see that I own a fine establishment with a lovely dance floor, a well-stocked bar, a booth for a fortune teller or a belly dancer."

An expression of concern crossed my face as I heard Marguerite sigh.

"Don't worry," Devereux consoled me. "I'm not expecting you to become a belly dancer. I just want you to perform in my place in the same high-spirited way you do here. Most of my clients come from the Moulin Rouge after eleven o'clock at night. Tell me, Mademoiselle, have you heard of Monsieur Zidler?"

I nodded. "Of course, who hasn't?"

"Quite."

I knew that Zidler was an impresario who had originally come from a humble background. It seemed that no-one knew how he had made his money. His entertainment career had started with circuses and now he owned the Moulin Rouge no less.

"I wouldn't go quite so far as to say I'm a companion of his," Monsieur Devereux said, modestly. "But I do know him quite well. Forgive me if you find this question impertinent but have you visited the Moulin Rouge yourself?"

"No, I haven't had that pleasure,"

"Nor me," Marguerite added, wistfully.

"I'll take you there tomorrow evening after we've discussed your contract."

I was thrilled but knew I had to be careful. "Thank you very much, Monsieur," I said, pointing at Marguerite. "But I shouldn't like to go there without Marguerite here."

She looked happy yet incredulous.

"I know she would also love to visit the Moulin Rouge."

Henri Devereux swallowed then replied. "That's no problem, I look forward to having the pleasure of escorting you two young ladies tomorrow evening. I must go now as I'm a busy man. Looking forward to seeing you tomorrow, Mademoiselle."

He started to walk away then turned, saying as an afterthought

"Bring your friend with you if you like. But she might have a lot of waiting around to do."

"Won't mind that, Monsieur," Marguerite stated.

We returned home, both of us in an excited frame of mind. "Just think," Marguerite said.

"Maybe you'll be famous one day, Isabelle."

I laughed. "He's not definitely promised me the job yet, Marguerite."

"Come on, he has as good as."

"I'd love you to come with me tomorrow but will you be able to get away from the shop?"

"I'll find a way, don't worry. I'll probably pretend to be sick. Tomorrow's going to be a fairytale day for us, I can sense it."

Her face was almost radiant with excited anticipation then it fell.

"But what the hell am *I* going to wear? Ain't got no fine clothes."

"I'll help Susanne make a dress for you," I announced confidently. "I'll provide the material for it. You won't have to pay me for it straightaway, you can pay me back a bit at a time if you like. If this Monsieur Devereux *is* genuine about his promise of a job for me, you can have it as a present from me."

She kissed my cheek and thanked me so profusely that I was almost embarrassed. We strolled to our respective homes, arm-in-arm, singing a popular song at the tops of our voices. Some passers-by in the street turned around to look at us with disapproving glances but we were too happy to care.

"Name of a name!" Susanne protested when I had explained Monsieur Devereux's request. "You used to be a well brought up young lady, Isabelle. Now you're turning into a … a" She scowled. "I'm sure you know what I mean!"

"Understand what you want to call me, Susanne but you can't bring yourself to use the word, 'prostitute.' Well, I'm not *that* as you very well know!"

"Not quite maybe." She put her hand on her brow. "But you'll still be flaunting yourself, not sure I can bear it!"

"You probably will when I start bringing more money into the house for us."

27

I hadn't meant to be cruel but annoyance made me so. "We'd both appreciate a few more home comforts. I don't what else I could do to make a living apart from dancing."

"There's dancing and there's well, showing all you've got and leading men on."

"I wouldn't do that and Monsieur Devereux I know, wants a restrained sort of dancing."

I wasn't entirely sure this was true but I wasn't going to tell Susanne that. "His place is a respectable one that families go to."

Another doubtful thing in my secret opinion.

"And Marguerite is thrilled, it would be a real shame to disappoint *her*. She was so excited, I promised we'd make her a dress, she knows how beautifully you can sew. We might even be able to get orders for you from the lady customers."

Susanne hesitated, frowning then her brow cleared as my last suggestion penetrated her thoughts. The idea had seemed to cross her mind in a more favourable light.

"But Isabelle, have you thought… well, about gentlemen philanderers?"

Her slightly old-fashioned expression amused me although I managed to keep my face straight. "Promise to be on my guard against them," I said.

"Always be on your guard." Susanne added, darkly.

"Could we start to make Marguerite's dress now?" I asked, glad to change the subject. "I'll fetch the material I had in mind."

"Yes, go and fetch it before I have second thoughts," Susanne said as I hurried away, breathing a huge sigh of relief.

CHAPTER EIGHT

Before going to my appointment, I slipped into the Cathedral of Notre Dame in the early morning. It was turning out to be a dry but dull, not particularly warm day. Light was venturing through the three exquisite rose windows made of the original old glass. I looked around the Cathedral then prayed about my new position.

I didn't particularly believe in divine miracles, nor was I especially devout although I still had my basic faith. When I lived with my family, on most Sundays we attended mass but this had lapsed since I had moved into Susanne's house. She went to mass regularly without me accompanying her. She never complained about this.

Religious feelings apart, the cathedral gave a sense of peacefulness.

Marguerite was waiting for me at our arranged meeting place. She seemed no less excited and was thrilled when I showed her the pink striped dress Susanne and I had sat up almost all night to make for her.

"It's beautiful, Isabelle," she enthused. "I thought you'd make me something nice but this is better than what I expected."

I smiled. "You're welcome, I'm glad you like it."

She shook her head. "No, I love it."

We realised when we reached our destination that Monsieur Devereux had not been telling lies about the elegance of his establishment. We gazed around in both interest and wonder at the gilt and mirrored interior.

He was courteous enough to only keep me waiting for a few minutes. "I'd like to speak to you privately in my study, Mademoiselle Lefevre," he said.

Marguerite looked a little suspicious as she sat down on a sofa in the foyer. Looking at her, I quickly put my finger on my

lip to urge her to keep quiet when I was a little behind
Devereux. Then I swiftly removed it when he turned round.

"I'm probably walking too fast for you," he said. I'll slow
down a bit."

"Thank you."

Marguerite had reminded me of Susanne earlier. To my
disappointment, my rising early had not prevented her from
doing the same thing. She had been up and about only a few
minutes after me. She had sighed a few times, shaken her head
and studied me carefully as we drank our coffee. So, I
deliberately chatted cheerfully about any everyday thing that
came to mind. As I left the house, relieved to leave her behind,
she had shaken her greying head one last time. At least she
hadn't tried to detain me.

Monsieur Devereux said to me. "One of my dancers left
because she was … " he coughed. "In the family way to put it
delicately." He paused before he let me know what my salary
would be. I gasped as it was much more than I had earned at the
shop. He showed me the written contract detailing my hours.
They were long but compensated for by my wages.

"If you sign this contract," he said. "You'll be bound to me
for six months. Is that acceptable to you?"

"Yes, Monsieur."

After I had signed the contract, Devereux shook my hand
and thanked me.

As I went back to rejoin Marguerite, Monsieur Devereux a
few steps behind me, I had a clear view of my reflection in one
of the mirrors. A petite young woman with shining dark hair, a
light in her big dark eyes and a happy smile on her wide mouth.
My reflection pleased me apart from the too high colour in my
cheeks.

When we were reunited with Marguerite, Monsieur
Devereux said. "I insist upon taking you two young ladies out
to dinner this evening. Come back here at six o'clock and we'll
go to the Moulin Rouge."

"Can't wait till tonight," Marguerite said, as we parted
company.

"Nor me," I agreed. "But let's meet each other first and get
an omnibus to Monsieur Devereux's place."

"Good idea."

When we reached the café-concert, we took our seats in Monsieur Devereux's elegant carriage. I could see from Marguerite's expression that she considered she had never before known such luxury

After eating a delicious meal as well as drinking wine in the superb restaurant Devereux took us to, his coachman drove us through Montmartre, past the many windmills to the Moulin Rouge.

I knew that the *bal du Moulin Rouge* had been opened by Zidler the previous year. It was basically a dance hall with supplementary attractions, the main one being the can-can. We saw strolling crowds in the romantic garden, pausing between dances to watch conjurors, balancing acts, ventriloquists and dancers. The audience was cosmopolitan, speaking many different languages.

Neither did we miss the prostitutes lurking in the garden while they waited for their clients. Marguerite was fascinated by the enormous stucco elephant at one end of the garden. "Look," she said. "It opens up." The elephant had a rectangular opening in the flank, revealing a small stage.

"That's for the specialty acts," Devereux explained.

As if the garden itself were not intriguing enough, there were 'genuinely nude' *poses plastiques* and waxworks in the foyer. I was relieved Susanne wasn't with us. Marguerite didn't seem at all embarrassed. Monsieur Devereux as he was familiar with the place, took everything for granted.

I had never seen such an immense dance floor. Monsieur Devereux noticed my reaction.

He said, "Impressive, isn't it?"

I nodded in agreement.

"Pay particular attention to the way the girls dance the can-can, Mademoiselle Lefevre," he said.

"Yes, Monsieur, I shall."

"Good."

I concentrated hard on the can-can dancers. I saw that the dance involved a lot of high kicking, a turning of energetic cartwheels displaying billows of lace frills plus the gleam of flashing black silk legs.

I noticed that the girl who appeared to be the main attraction had a male partner who wore a greasy stove-pipe hat, a frock coat and skin tight trousers. At the finish of her act, she held her leg over her head, spinning round and round, she spread yards of black lace into a huge umbrella. Then she kicked off her partner's hat, descending into splits. This seemed to me to be quite a feat.

She turned her back to the audience and bowed, flipping her skirts over her head to show a scarlet heart on her black silk panties.

I glanced out of the corner of my eye to Monsieur Devereux. He didn't seem completely impassive but neither did he seem overly impressed by what he had just seen.

For the first time I began to have my own doubts about whether my new profession was a suitable one. Had Susanne been right after all? Well, it was too late now for me not to move ahead with my life. However, I still missed my family. And couldn't help wondering if they missed me too. I hardened my heart, deciding they had probably disowned me by now.

CHAPTER NINE

Monsieur Devereux introduced me to his troupe of dancers as a new member. On the whole they were friendly and helpful so I began to relax a little. Although my own style of dancing was to a certain extent improvised, he didn't find fault with it. The work was tiring yet also exhilarating. There was a heady excitement in performing to an audience despite the fact that most of them were small.

I managed to give extra cash to Susanne and obtain orders for patterns for her from the other dancers, pretending they were from clients' wives. Not all that many of our clients took their wives. I never allowed myself to be propositioned by the clients and Susanne accepted the orders gratefully.

I was now managing to put a little money aside for my own private use, a great relief to me. Kind and generous as Susanne had undoubtedly been to me, I had decided that I should like to search for my own apartment.

The six months I spent at the *café-concert* passed pleasantly enough. Devereux didn't speak to me all that often, occasionally smiling at me or giving me a nod of approval.

Monsieur Zidler called at our *café-concert* one evening unexpectedly. He arrived with some of his patrons after hiring a fleet of omnibuses.

"Isabelle," Monsieur Devereux called to me, signaling to me to join him. "Monsieur Zidler would like a word with you."

I was intrigued.

"Would you like to dance at the Moulin Rouge?" Zidler asked me.

Would I "like to?" My astonishment almost made me tongue tied. When I recovered, I was able to say. "I should love to, Monsieur."

Zidler looked me up and down. "Maybe you won't be robust enough."

"I'm as strong as an ox," I exaggerated. He still looked a little doubtful

"I'll find out if that's true once you start working for me."

Devereux looked displeased. "She might be better off staying with me," he said.

"Tell you what I'll do if Monsieur Zidler does decide to have me at the Moulin Rouge … "

"*I've* already decided I shall, Mademoiselle," Zidler announced.

My heart felt as if it were leaping inside me. "Thank you so much," I turned to Devereux, "but I'd like to stay with Monsieur Devereux until he finds a replacement for me."

"I'm grateful to you for that, Isabelle," Devereux remarked. He seemed relieved.

My replacement was found speedily by a strange twist of fate. Devereux had a young mistress. All of his staff were aware of the situation, we often gossiped about it but his wife remained in complete ignorance of the fact for some strange reason. Or perhaps she knew but turned a blind eye.

One day, his wife discovered the lovers in a café, sharing a drink of absinthe.

"Who is this young woman?" Madame Devereux had asked, angrily.

"A new employee of mine so I needed to discuss things with her."

"Not sure that's true. You're probably lying to me."

"Look, I'll take all the family out tonight to our concert and you'll see what a good choice I've made for a new dancer."

Afterwards he rushed his open-mouthed mistress through a hasty rehearsal with me. I taught her a few basic steps. Fortunately, she had a good memory as well as a natural grace.

"Thank you, Isabelle," he said, afterwards. "You'll be happy to take her place, won't you, Amelie?" His question wasn't exactly threatening but it was certainly demanding.

"Yes, Claude," Amelie agreed, sounding almost contented. I considered that Monsieur Devereux must be thanking his lucky stars for his quick thinking in a tricky situation.

Marguerite was thrilled for me that I was going to perform at the Moulin Rouge. She had become engaged to a young man who often accompanied his mother on her shopping trips.

Marguerite had frequently served them or delivered items to their house. The couple often attended our concerts.

After leaving Monsieur Devereux's establishment, I had three weeks at leisure before I began appearing at the Moulin Rouge. I became a live-in pupil at the house of Nini *'Patte-en-Vair* ('foot in the air') as she had been nicknamed.

Susanne had been dubious about this move at first, warning me to be on my guard against 'misfortunes' as she called them.

I tried to reassure her "There's plenty of other girls in the house beside me, Susanne. What's more, I'll be chaperoned."

"Hope you're right but you can come back here if anything does go wrong for you."

"I'm grateful to you for that and other things."

We had embraced. My feelings were mixed, knowing I would miss Susanne's company yet a new, more exciting life for me to take part in was on the horizon.

Nini was a short, thin woman with haggard features. Her foot quivered as she held it high in the *porte d'ames* (shoulder arms.) We learned the arts of the high kick and splits; also how high we could raise our petticoats without being unseemly. The training was strenuous but I enjoyed it even though it often left me feeling tired.

I was on reasonably friendly terms with the other young women although not especially intimate with any one individual. There were two I disliked because they were spiteful, however I tried to avoid contact with these two as much as possible.

While we trained the house was besieged by gentlemen callers, would-be 'protectors' with various propositions, impresarios and curious hangers-on who squeezed past the door into the corridor. It was then that Nini's shrill voice attempted to send them all packing. I had an amused mental image of Susanne's face if she could have seen them. Just as well she could not, I decided.

One cold morning when I felt I was practising my routine more mechanically than usual, having no idea why I was doing so, I met the gaze of a pair of clear, red-brown eyes. A young man was watching me intently, a winning smile on his handsome face.

I experienced a totally inexplicable surge of excitement flow through me as I tried to recall where I had seen him before. He was lounging back slightly against the wall when recognition struck me. It was Leon Prideaux, the artist I had met all those months ago at the Closerie des Lilas. He was more warmly, less flamboyantly dressed than he had been at the pleasure gardens. Nevertheless, his tall figure still stood out from the crowd. He left with a shrug of his broad shoulders when ordered to do so but not before managing to push a visiting card into my hand with a hastily scribbled note on it. "This is my address."

Later that same day, I received a beautiful bouquet of flowers together with a note stating

"Please meet me at the café on the corner, Mademoiselle at six o'clock tonight. I'd love to see you there if I can."

I was not sure if it would be unwise to do as he asked, Susanne's unwelcome warnings ringing in my ears. But my desire to meet him again overcame my doubts as to its wisdom. I hurried to the small cafe

Leon was waiting for me at a wooden table. I approached it hesitantly as he turned around. His arresting smile drew me towards him as he stood up, beckoning me over. "Mademoiselle Lefevre," he said, bowing slightly over my hand. "I'm so pleased you've come, delighted in fact. I was afraid you wouldn't."

"I was curious," I stated, trying not to betray my inner turmoil. My voice sounded flat and devoid of emotion even to my own ears. He smiled again, displaying even white teeth.

"You'll most likely soon be making a career for yourself at the Moulin Rouge."

"Hope so, hope so very much."

"I'm convinced you'll do very well. But I've forgotten my manners, I'm neglecting you. What would you like to drink, a glass of absinthe perhaps?"

"No thank you, Monsieur. I'd prefer a cup of coffee."

"Sensible of you." He signaled to the waiter and ordered coffee for me.

As I sipped my drink, he seemed to be watching me intently, making me more self-conscious than ever. Somehow, I managed not to spill it. He appeared to be reading my thoughts. "You dance very well so I don't know why you're so bashful."

I felt curious. "Why did you want to see me here? If you like my dancing, you could always watch me at Nini's house."

My tone was unintentionally blunt, I regretted this just after I had spoken but Leon didn't seem unduly disturbed by it.

He shrugged his shoulders. "Yes, but there's plenty of other girls there. I was attracted to you and wanted to know the person behind the graceful dancer, especially having recognised you from the gardens where I first met you."

"You never came to the Closerie des Lilas again," I said, more wistfully than I had intended.

He shook his black, curly head so much like an Italian's. "No, I didn't though I meant to. I had an urgent appointment the day after I met you."

I believed him although I was not usually gullible.

"We haven't been acquainted long; I know but would you permit us to call each other by our Christian names. I know yours is Isabelle and you know mine."

"I don't object to being called by my Christian name, Monsieur Leon."

He laughed. "Will you now permit me to escort you to the *Le Chat Noir*, Isabelle? You'll probably enjoy it."

I had no idea what the place called 'The Black Cat' was or would be like; however I was curious enough to find out.

"Yes, I'll be happy to go there with you."

Leon looked pleased as he took my arm and we left the café together. I was also smiling inwardly.

CHAPTER TEN

Do you know how *Le Chat Noir* got its name?" I asked Leon, conversationally trying to imply I was familiar with the establishment.

"Supposed to be because a stray black cat was found on the pavement outside while the cabaret was being decorated."

So, we were attending a cabaret, one mystery had been solved.

"I know the owner slightly," Leon added. "Rudolphe Salis, he used to be an art student like myself. He publishes a journal of the same name. It contains poems by some of his customers. Some of them are better than others of course."

"I'd like to read them some time," I said. Leon smiled.

We entered a long, smoke-filled room, it made me cough a little although I was looking around with interest. It was lit by mock-medieval oil lanterns. There was a small stage at the end of the room where some men recited poems and both men and women sang songs, some more tunefully than others, accompanied by a piano. They also performed short dramatic sketches. Some of the singers, especially the female ones, sang romantic, sentimental ballads. Others sang about everyday life or made social protests. There was also a shadow show.

"Unusual, this," I remarked. "Haven't seen anything like this before."

"Inspired bv a singer named Jules Jouy," Leon informed me. "He decided to have cut-out puppets and silhouettes to accompany his songs."

"Sounds intriguing," I said. Leon nodded. "Bit out of the ordinary, yes."

We watched an animated shadow show with music and a spoken running commentary by a compere.

I noticed that the audience was an interesting mix of society ladies, foreign tourists, bankers, playwrights, journalists, artists and workmen.

Leon seemed to be acquainted with a lot of the artists. "The performers get no wages," he said. "They just get applauded well if they're lucky when they've finished."

I couldn't help feeling sorry for the performers who weren't well received. However, I was still fascinated by the cabaret.

It was late when Leon took me home and I was tired. "I've enjoyed tonight very much, thank you for it," I said, truthfully, omitting the fact I now felt a little weary.

"May I see you again, Isabelle?"

Hesitantly, I replied, "I'd like you to, unfortunately though, I don't have a lot of spare time at the moment."

He smiled. "We'll have to overcome that problem, won't we? I'd love to show you my studio one day. I'd like to paint you dancing at the Moulin Rouge. I'd need to pay a visit both to watch you and make a preliminary sketch."

"You're flattering me, Leon. You could think I'm not very good so you might change your mind."

"No, I wouldn't. Painting's my profession after all so I should know what are the most likely subjects to draw. I'm lucky to be in a position where I can illustrate anything I'm interested in.

"Thank you for your faith in me."

Leon grinned. "I'm certain it will be repaid."

At my front door he said, "I'm sure to find some way of contacting you again." Slightly irritated by his self-assurance I didn't reply, merely nodding to him before I went indoors.

Most of the other girls in the house were interested in our activities as he was well known to some of them and seemed to be popular with them. This fact wasn't altogether comfortable knowledge to me.

"You're lucky to have been taken to the *Le Chat Noir*," a girl remarked. I couldn't help wondering if he had ever taken her anywhere but didn't bother to ask.

The next time I met Leon was a coincidence. I had gone out to do some shopping when I saw him loitering in a side street near the house. He looked pleased when he saw me and came up to speak to me. We exchanged a few pleasantries then he said. "May I take you to supper one evening?"

It was impossible for me to pretend indifference so we made arrangements to meet each other.

After eating the best meal I had tasted for a long time, Leon took me to another cabaret. It was called *Le Mirliton* or The Reedpipe, the name having the additional meaning of doggerel. The owner was Aristide Bruant, a former singer at *Le Chat Noir*. Once again, Leon was acquainted with him slightly.

"Bruant originally worked on the railways," Leon said. "He came to know the zone really well."

I knew the zone was a wasteland of the outer boulevards and fortifications of Paris.

"He got used to the slang of that area," Leon added. "And used it in the songs he wrote himself. One was about a street walker."

Leon glanced at me to see if I were shocked. But I kept my face impassive.

"It became famous, lucky for him," Leon commented.

The décor of *Le Mirliton* was a contrast to that of *Le Chat Noir*. It was sparsely furnished and decorated. People sat on chairs and benches to enjoy genuine working-class humour, wit, and coarseness. There were also, however, well known writers, actors and elegant ladies in the audience. So, they were a mixed bunch, making it interesting for me.

Bruant was outstandingly dressed. I couldn't help wondering if Leon were trying to copy him in any way, then I dismissed the idea as fancy. They were probably both leading a Bohemian sort of life.

Bruant had a strange habit of insulting his audience, this startled me at first but they didn't seem to mind at all. They all sang from eleven o'clock at night until two o'clock in the morning by which time my eyelids were beginning to droop so Leon took me home. We rode in a hired cab through the cold streets.

"What was your opinion of *Le Mirliton*, Isabelle?"

"Certainly, different from *Le Chat Noir*. It was interesting enough."

"I like it there but I wasn't altogether sure you would. Hoped you wouldn't hate it."

"No, I didn't, not at all."

"Good." He smiled. "I'm relieved."

I reflected that he had introduced me gradually to a new adventure. I knew that the name 'cabaret' had originated from a wine cellar or tavern and now I had drunk wine at two of the best-known ones. Formerly, I would never have been able to imagine myself frequenting this sort of place. I couldn't help wondering what other new experiences Leon would introduce me to.

He became my constant companion as I had started all my spare time with him, gradually discovering I didn't care for occasions when I was deprived of his company. Leon escorted me to cafes, suppers and even, occasionally to the Opera where I was afraid, I might see my family. To my relief, I was spared from this fate.

Much as loved being with Leon, there were a few occasions when he seemed to be abstracted. Remarks I made didn't seem to register with him and his eyes looked a little glazed.

A few of my fellow dancers hinted that our association wouldn't last. I deliberately ignored them, hoping it was only jealousy encouraging them to make these remarks.

CHAPTER ELEVEN

Leon had shown me some of the sketches he had made of me while I was performing at the Moulin Rouge. They were good but I found it hard to see a resemblance to the young woman depicted in the drawings and myself.

"May I take you to my studio so that I'll be able to paint you properly?" he asked me. To begin with I was hesitant to agree but after a while I gave in.

On the appointed day for me to pose for him it was by now spring and the chestnut trees were in blossom. I wore my best red silk gown and put a matching artificial rose in my dark hair. For some reason I didn't fully comprehend, nervousness threatened to overwhelm me. However, I somehow managed to overcome this unwelcome apprehension.

Leon's studio was much larger than I had anticipated, it was also more luxurious. The predominant colour was red so I felt that it was a fortunate coincidence that I blended in with the surroundings. There was a gilt model throne in the centre of the room and two smaller gilt chairs. I was surprised to see fencing equipment lying around as well as canvases and paints. I knew by now that Leon was not an impoverished Bohemian but I hadn't imagined him owning an opulent studio.

"Take a seat, Isabelle."

Feeling a little apprehensive, I sat down on a large cushion in a gilt chair.

Waving my hand around all the various items, I asked. "How have you been able to ...?" breaking off in case the word afford sounded rude.

Leon smiled, not appearing to be offended. "My father's a lawyer, he had many successful cases. I was born in Lyons, I'm not really a Parisian though I do feel like one now. My father insisted I should study law when I went to the university although I privately believed I was born with a paintbrush in my hand."

"Not hard to believe."

"Don't blame you for smiling. Anyway, I started to draw not long after I could walk. I cut my classes whenever I could because I felt desperate to sketch and paint more than anything else in the world. I also failed the Civil Service exam, much to Papa's disgust. He told me I'd never in my lifetime become anything worthwhile."

"I'm sure that's untrue. Expect my father still sees me as disgraceful because I ran away from home."

Leon looked sympathetic, giving me a broad wink. "Glad you're here with me, now."

"How did you become an artist?"

"Papa had a friend, an actor. This man paid me several hundred francs for a poster I designed for the theatre he was appearing in. My old man was delighted so he relented and said I *could* have an art career. The best thing that happened in my life then."

"You told me you lived in the Latin Quarter when you first came to Paris. Did you find that exciting?"

"Yes, it was good on the left bank of the Seine with all the other provincials and foreigners. They all hoped to either write poems or paint masterpieces to bring them fame and fortune." He smiled before saying. "Only a few succeeded of course."

"Still, those were the days, cheap enough to hire studios and find cheap eating places. Streets always noisy and lively. You heard all sorts of languages at every café terrace. I trained at the *Ecole des Beaux Arts*. Had its faults but I liked it."

Leon smiled. "Why am I wasting our time, boring you when I should be working?"

"You're not boring me at all."

He shook his head slightly, amused by my vehemence. "Stand up, Isabelle." Then, he deftly removed my hat, removing the pins in my hair so that it fell loose around my shoulders.

"Please sit on the model throne for me."

I did so, finding it surprisingly comfortable although I was nervous.

"Relax while I gather my materials together. I'll tell you when I'm ready. Try to keep as still as you can my love. Keep your eyes open and don't nod off to sleep."

He painted solidly for two hours, at the end of the session, I was weary. "You've been patient, that's enough for today, I'm pleased with what I've managed to do."

Leon looked at me with a concerned expression. "You're looking pale, *cherie*. I'll fetch you something to bring a bit of colour back to your cheeks."

He left the room, returning with a glass of red wine for me.

As I drank it, he said, "I've got an apartment upstairs, would you like to see it?"

"Not yet, Leon." I didn't want him to make love to me then forget all about me.

He shrugged. "All right."

I finished my wine, put the glass down and stood up. As I rose from the chair, I accidentally kicked the glass, causing it to break, shattering into tiny pieces, my face now naturally turning to the same colour as my dress.

"I'm sorry, will you fetch me a broom?"

"Leave it," Leon said, carelessly. "The maid can sweep it up. You didn't hurt yourself, did you?"

I shook my head. "Not at all."

"I'm relieved about that."

Leon drew me away gently from the shining glass slivers. The next moment I found myself in his arms. He was touching my hair then cupping my face in his hands before we kissed. His fingers hastily unfastened my bodice to stroke my small breasts as he bent his head to my pink nipples.

I ran my fingers through his black hair as he undressed me completely and gently lowered me to the floor. I felt his hand move between my legs then moving higher. Leon took off his own clothes rapidly and we explored each other's bodies tenderly.

There was a little pain after we had fully made love but after Leon whispered "Now you're truly mine, Isabelle, I want to live with you permanently" and carried me up to his flat, I felt that it been worthwhile.

Shortly afterwards I did move in with Leon.

CHAPTER TWELVE

My imagination had never included Leon living in poverty in an attic room yet the luxurious décor of his flat was a little ostentatious for my taste. All the same, I would have been prepared to live with him anywhere. It was also pleasant to now be able to use the services of a cook, a maid, and a groom.

Modelling permanently for Leon in the daytime then dancing at night at the Moulin Rouge began to tire me out.

"Become my full-l time model, darling," he said. "You're not the only one I use but you're my main and favourite one."

"But I trained hard for my dancing career, Leon," I protested.

"Frankly, Isabelle, the Moulin Rouge proprietors are always looking for new attractions."

Reluctantly, this fact was conceded by me although his words had disappointed me.

"My profession as an artist was launched when I managed to have a painting of a young girl sold after it was exhibited at the Salon in the Palace of Industry. It was thrilling for me."

"It must have been."

"Engraved reproductions of this picture were made and I'm happy to say they sold well. Lucky me. It led to me getting commissions from theatres and music halls. They wanted posters with explosive colours and striking designs."

"Isn't the day of the Salon the same when the best fashion houses show their newest styles?"

"Excuse me being blunt. You haven't got all that many clothes, have you?"

"Not really because I've needed money for expenses. I've put a few francs by in case I ever need them desperately."

Leon must have seen my embarrassed expression. "Didn't mean my remark to hurt you. We'll go out tomorrow so that you can have a lot of new clothes. So many we'll probably need a new wardrobe. I know the colours that will suit you."

"Like that idea, I'm already looking forward to it."

"Good."

It was enjoyable to visit more exclusive stores than the one I had worked in. Leon bought me gloves from Jouvin's on the Place de l'Opera, hats and fans from the Magasins de Louvre, that vast department store with its many branched gasoliers where we were served by sales ladies wearing stiff whalebone collars. He also bought me dresses, petticoats, corsets, ribbon trimmed garters, lace chemises and stockings.

I might have felt embarrassed by another man buying me such intimate garments but with Leon I didn't mind in the least.

"I'm overwhelmed by all this," I said. "Thank you so much."

He smiled. "Glad you're happy about it."

"I'm not just happy, I'm delighted."

"Good."

Leon had bought some cheap contraceptives he had seen in a newspaper advertisement. He often whispered to me that my body was soft and warm to his touch. I reflected that Susanne would have been horrified if she knew this. The thought made me smile. I visited her occasionally, not actually lying to her but letting her believe that I still lived at Nini's house.

Leon had a wide circle of acquaintances, fellow artists, actors, poets and entertainers of all kinds, students and working people.

"I'm going to take you to my favourite cabaret," he said to me one evening. "It's not *Le Chat Noir* or *Le Mirliton.*"

"What is it, then?"

"*Le Soleil d'Or* (Sun of Gold.) "It's in the Latin Quarter. It's a café-cum-cabaret. It was started up by a poet I know who started a new magazine. I've done some illustrations for him he paid me well for which I was naturally grateful."

As well as visiting Le Soleil d'Or we went on one Saturday to Les Soirees as they were called. These events were held every alternate Saturday. We made our way to the basement café, passing through the ground floor, past a few of the locals playing cards. Then we descended a narrow flight of steps behind the bar to the basement.

Downstairs in a large smoke-filled room with decorated walls, we drank glasses of wine and listened to songs and poems. They were sung or recited on a rough stage to the accompaniment of a tinny piano. We paid no admission fee but visitors had to sign a book. Sometimes a celebrity appeared causing a great deal of excitement.

As I was small, I had to crane my neck to see them. Leon laughed at the sight. "You're a tiny doll of a girl, I'll have to lift you up so that you can see over other people's heads."

"I'm not as little as all that," I protested.

Leon grinned, as he glanced quickly up and down my figure. "Perhaps not."

We were also invited to theatre suppers and receptions.

My favourite daytime outing was going to Barbizon, a lovely village south of Paris in the Forest of Fontainebleau. We strolled by the river, arm-in-arm. Leon sketched many of the trees and flowers. Sometimes he met some of his artist friends there with whom he exchanged reminiscences of their student days.

One morning after Leon had been painting me dancing, he paused, his eyes were resting on a tapestry on the wall. This occupied one of the few spaces not taken up by one of his pictures.

He cleared his throat. "Why don't you pose for me in the nude, cherie?"

I frowned, shaking my head.

"Oh, come on, I've seen you naked several times."

"Yes, but that was just for you. It wouldn't feel right for other people."

He moved towards me, slipping his arm around my shoulders, winding a strand of my hair around the fingers of his other hand. "Please, Isabelle, we could make a lot of money this way."

You mean you could," I retorted. "We're not poor, surely one of your other models could do this for you and welcome some extra francs."

"Probably they would but you're my favourite model. If I paint you naked, it could be an even bigger success than last time."

47

I knew he was referring to a painting of me lying in bed, wearing a lacy nightgown, still drowsy, with my long, loose hair in disarray. He had sold this picture for a large fee and prints of it had been much in demand.

"You know my answer to your second question, I'll think about your first one."

He shrugged his shoulders. "I'll just have to wait patiently then, won't I?"

As we were dancing at the Café Anglais that evening, having drunk a fair amount of wine, I was in a mellow mood although I had managed to remain sober. I whispered in his ear that I had decided to agree to his request. "I'll do what you asked me to," I said.

Leon nodded, obviously pleased. "Thank you, I'm so glad."

"It's on one condition, though," I teased.

He gave a slight bow took my hand and kissed it. "Name your favour, Mademoiselle."

"None of your other models are to be present at the same time."

"Think I could make that arrangement."

I burst into almost loud laughter, startling him.

"It wasn't that funny, what I said."

"I know it wasn't, love. I couldn't help imagining poor Susanne's face if she could have overheard our conversation."

CHAPTER THIRTEEN

I had been dancing the can-can and posing for Leon since early in the morning. Feeling in need of some fresh air and exercise to liven me up a little, I said, "Do you mind if we finish for now, Leon and go riding in the Bois de Boulogne?"

He nodded. "When I've finished this final brush stroke of mine."

We were watched by curious passers-by and various coaches as we rode along the beaten earth avenue towards the Bois.

My eyes were surely deceiving me with what I saw in the street as I gave a start. These people were surely not ... yet I knew my eyes weren't really deceiving me. My horse tried to bolt. I had to exercise all my strength and concentration to bring the animal under control. Behind me, Leon chased after the horse, trying to catch it but by now it had calmed down.

"That's lucky," I breathed.

"That was a shock, I know," Leon said. "You're safe now, though, thank God! You're as white as a sheet and shaking like a leaf. We'd better go back home."

I pointed to the street; Leon followed the direction of my finger to the group. "You see, those people there, they are ...." My voice faltered.

"What I see a middle- aged man and woman. And there's two girls, suppose they're the daughters. The elder one's very beautiful."

He paused. "Something about her is familiar. Can't place what it is." Leon turned back to look at them. They were now turning into a side street. "What's so extraordinary about those people?"

Taking a deep breath, I explained. "They're my father, my stepmother, and my sisters. Please take me home now."

"You've received an understandable shock, Isabelle but they've gone now. Why don't we continue with our ride?"

I shook my head. "No, I really *must* return home. Can't stay here another minute."

"Very well," Leon said, in a resigned tone.

In the flat I began to shake and cry. Leon handed me a glass of wine. "Drink it down, *cherie,* it will do you good."

As he wiped my tears away. I was sure I must look a real sight. He didn't seem to mind.

Leon swept me up into his arms and carried me to bed. He helped me undress then quickly discarded his own clothes. He lay beside me, taking me into his arms but made no attempt to make love to me, merely soothing me to sleep. I had some strange dreams on that afternoon.

When I awoke after a long rest, Leon was no longer beside me, neither was he anywhere in the flat. The servants didn't know where he had gone either.

My head was throbbing so I asked our maid to make me some tea before I went back to bed and slept more peacefully. In the early hours of the morning, I saw Leon enter our bedroom. Did I imagine it or were his eyes glazed slightly? Maybe it was just my fantasy.

He took off his plum-coloured coat without bothering to summon the new valet he had hired.

Leon lay down beside me. "Where have you been?" I asked him, drowsily.

"Out on business, lots of details to sort out, it was tedious."

Was it my imagination that I could smell a different perfume to the one I used on his skin? I really hoped he didn't have some sort of relationship with another young woman. I didn't want to ask him about this so I merely said, "Suppose you're tired now."

"Yes, very much so, love. Need my sleep."

The next moment I could hear his deep rhythmic breaths just before I relaxed into sleep again myself.

CHAPTER FOURTEEN

"You ought to visit your family, Isabelle," Leon said, on a rainy morning a couple of days after we had seen them in the Bois.

I was amazed. "You know the circumstances of my leaving home, Leon. How can you expect them to welcome me?"

"Didn't say I think they'll welcome you with open arms. However, I'm sure they'll forgive you if you tell them you're sorry you ran away."

"Already told them that in my note. Don't want to seem to be begging to return to them."

"You have missed them, though. Told me so yourself."

"I know but I don't want to appear to be throwing myself on their mercy because I'm incapable of managing my own affairs without them."

"I'm sure they'd never believe that."

"You don't know my father. Anyway, why are you so anxious for me to call on them?"

The horrible suspicion had crossed my mind that he wished to bring some other female back to our apartment. I tried hard to dismiss it.

"I'm sure they'd be pleased to see you. It would do you good to have some different company."

"We've got lots of friends and acquaintances. Admittedly, I met most of them through you but I now feel they're my friends too."

"Ah yes but friends and acquaintances aren't quite the same thing as your own family"

"You're a fine one to talk. You who never visits his father."

"We live in different cities. What you could do if you're unsure that yours will receive you, is write to him or your old nurse. She can read, can't she?"

I nodded. "Maybe I'll send her a letter, I'll think about it." Turning on my heel, I left the room.

During that week, we had other discussions in a similar vein. There was no reply to the note I had sent to Blanche and it took me some time to decide what to do. Leon kept urging me to make an unexpected call. I still had my doubts as to this course of action. Finally, Leon and I agreed on a compromise.

"I'll accompany you to your Papa's house and wait to see if you're well received. If I can see that you are, I'll come back to our flat on my own."

When we reached my family's door, my heart was racing at a furious pace. A manservant answered the door, a new one I didn't recognise.

"One moment, Mademoiselle, I'll see what your father says."

He came back, as stiff in manner he announced. "Your father will see you for a short while only."

My heart sank as Leon winked at me before strolling away. For half a minute I contemplated running after him, clutching his sleeve, begging him to take me home. However, believing this would be cowardly on my part, I took a deep breath and entered my father's house.

Papa's face wasn't wreathed in smiles when he saw me, his expression was almost severe. My sisters looked as if they would like to speak to me but were scared to do so.

My father spoke first, breaking the strained silence between us. "I trust you are well, Isabelle."

"Yes, I am."

He studied me, critically. "Well, at least you're better dressed than I would have expected."

I flushed both with disappointment and irritation. I was wearing a primrose-coloured brocade dress with a matching cape and a cream hat, knowing they all suited me.

Eloise had been discreetly studying my clothes. My father then sent the younger girls out of the room, they seemed disappointed and I felt sorry for them.

I was startled when the woman Papa summoned wasn't Blanche. He asked her to make us some coffee.

"Where's Blanche, is it her afternoon off?"

My father shook his head. "No, she's retired. She's gone to live in the country."

"Wish I'd known. I'd like to write to her. Can you tell me her address?"

"Suppose I could, I'll give it to you later."

"Where's my stepmother?"

"She's decided to stay in her bedroom. Said it was because she needed to rest. I knew better. Louise wished to keep out of your way."

I gave an unladylike shrug of my shoulders. "She never liked me anyway."

My father's next sentence shocked me. "Doubt that you know that Eloise is now going to marry Georges Bourbonneux."

"Surely she's too young."

"Georges is prepared to wait two or three years for a substantial dowry. They'll get engaged at the appropriate time."

I thought I would try to appeal to his better nature. "Papa, can't you see what a waste this is of a lovely young girl? I'm horrified by this news."

My father's mask of cold self-control slipped as he became angry. "Who do you believe you are, Mademoiselle Lefevre? You who were too haughty to accept Georges, now you dare lecture *me*!"

Papa walked over to a small table where he picked up a magazine. Opening it, he showed me a nude painting of myself. Gasping as I looked down at the floor, I felt my cheeks burn with embarrassment.

"Yes, you can blush, Isabelle, you've got good cause to. You've brought disgrace on myself and the family. The proprietor of this magazine happens to know both myself and that artist fellow you live with."

Catching my surprised gaze, Papa said. "Yes, I *do* know all about that. I'm prepared to forgive you even if I don't forget what you've done. There's not much hope now of a good marriage for you. My wife will accept you if you give up that artist and come back home. We might be able to find you a position as a governess in another town from the connections I have at my work."

Feeling my face colour, I began to protest. "I don't want this at all even if I appreciate you having good intentions towards me, Papa. I'm don't intend deserting my 'artist-fellow' as you sneeringly call him. He's good to me and we love each other. Leon will never do such a thing!"

My father's face turned a puce colour. "Show some sense, girl! That sort never *marry* their mistresses."

The maid entered with the coffee; I gulped mine down quickly although it tasted bitter in my mouth.

"It's no use continuing to argue with you, Papa," I said, as I put my cup down. "We're obviously not going to agree on this subject. May I occasionally be allowed to visit you? I'll be grateful for this."

My father shrugged. "Perhaps. Let us know in advance so that we can possibly arrange a few discreet visits from you. I'll think about it. Bit don't assume too much, too early."

"Thank you, Papa. You'll be relieved to know I'm now leaving."

He neither confirmed nor denied this, merely stating, "I'll arrange for you to be driven home."

"You don't need to; I prefer to hire a fiacre."

"As you wish," he said, coldly before ordering the maid to show me to the front door as if I were a stranger. I walked out with my head held high. Once in the street, I finally lost control and shed a few tears. They flowed freely before I wiped them away with a lace edged handkerchief that Leon had given me. I closed my eyes in relief when the fiacre left the district.

As I entered our apartment, I noticed a sweetish smell. In the living room I saw Leon reclining in a chair, his feet resting on a white fur rug. He was still with his eyes closed. On a nearby table a small ceramic angel stood on the top. Leon had recently purchased this from a female pupil of an atelier as the art schools were called. The ateliers were really intended only for men, women were debarred from formal classes.

But Leon had explained to me. "I know the Principal, he agreed to give classes to this young woman for reasons of his own. They were never explained to me."

"I'm not entirely sure that I like it."

"I bought it because I knew she was having a harder time than the men."

"A fair reason," I conceded.

A pipe also lay on this table, nearby was a packet containing a substance. There was no doubt in my mind that this was opium. Some of the Moulin Rouge visitors had used it. So, Leon had wished me to be out of the way while he took a drug! I was annoyed by this. Did he also know what opium could do to people? Apparently not, this also angered me.

"Leon!" I said, sharply. There was no response after I repeated his name more loudly. I gave his foot a slight kick, making him awake with a start.

"How was your visit?" he asked, after he had become less dazed and more aware of me and our surroundings.

"Not too hopeful but I don't want to talk about that yet." I picked up the pipe, staring at it for a few moments.

"You've been smoking opium, haven't you?"

Leon looked sheepish. "Suppose you had to find out, eventually."

"You're a fool! Don't you know this stuff can kill? Has in fact, killed people?"

"Don't worry," he said, complacently as if drug-taking were the most natural thing in the world. "I won't become addicted like some fellows do. I've got more sense because I only take a little."

I wrung my hands in exasperation. "That's what they've all probably said, you idiot!"

"Maybe but *I* know what I'm doing."

"Wish I could believe that. When did you first start smoking opium?"

"When I was a student in the Latin Quarter."

"Expect some dimwit there introduced you to it. Always wondered why in some of your paintings the colours are so much brighter and the outlines bolder. Even in some pictures of me, my body seems unnaturally elongated and my eyes are huge."

"You do have big dark eyes and I know very well what you look like. Anyway, don't know what you're complaining about with your criticism of my art." He waved his hand to encompass the room. "It makes a good enough living for us, don't you think?"

Leon was particularly sensitive about criticism of his artistic ability but I was too upset to care.

"Oh, I hate today! Firstly, my father was impossible, now you are. I've had enough!"

"Don't be so hard, darling." There was a pleading note in his voice that I tried to ignore. "This pipe just helps me relax now and again. Did you know you look beautiful when your dark eyes are flashing?"

He closed his eyes again. I ran out of the front door, slamming it behind me. I went to a café Leon did not very often frequent. Ignoring the disapproving stares condemning a young woman's presence on her own in a place like this, I ordered a glass of absinthe, drinking it quickly even though I didn't really care for the taste.

It was pouring down with rain when I hired a fiacre to take me to Susanne's place.

CHAPTER FIFTEEN

Susanne had as usual, been sewing when I called. A pile of garments was strewn about the room. She was surprised to see me there.

"This is a pleasant surprise, Isabelle," she said. "Not having seen or heard from you for a long time. Wondered if you'd left Paris."

I felt a little ashamed of my neglect. "Sorry I didn't call earlier only I've been busy with one thing and another."

"Can believe it. Are you still at the Moulin?"

"Yes, I am. It's hard work," I lied.

"Got a night off, have you?"

I nodded in what I hoped was a convincing agreement.

"Don't overtire yourself, will you?"

"Of course not."

Susanne must have noticed my strained expression because she then asked. "There's nothing else worrying you isn't there, Isabelle? You look a bit pale."

I shook my head. "No, honestly, I've no other concerns. Look, I bought this cake on the way over. Hope you'll share it with me."

She was all smiles. "It's an unexpected pleasure. I'll make coffee to wash it down with."

"Thank you. Could you do me another favour afterwards? Let me help you with some of your decorative work on the hats?"

Susanne's face was a picture. "Whatever do you want to do that for, on your night off? Wouldn't it be better for you to have a well-earned rest?"

"Please, Susanne, I need something to do badly. I'll like doing it especially as it I'll also be helping you."

She still looked doubtful but said. "Well, if you're sure. It would be useful."

"Can you give me Blanche's address?"

"I can but how did you find out she's retired?"

"Visited my family this afternoon. My father told me."

Susanne sighed. "Ah, that explains a lot. Good you made contact but was your papa not as sympathetic as you hoped?"

"Please, Susanne, I'd prefer not to discuss our conversation."

My tone was sharper than I had intended it to be.

She gave me a knowing look. "Understandable, I'll go and cut our pieces of cake and make the coffee now. Then we can start on a pile."

She pointed to the piles of fabric that would be used for the hat manufacture. "I'll give you Blanche's address afterwards."

"Thank you."

Susanne went to her kitchen, leaving me feeling ashamed of the way I had spoken to her

She returned with two cups of coffee and two slices of cake on plates. She handed me a piece of paper with Blanche's address written on it. Blanche now appeared to be living in a small village near Angouleme.

When we were ready, we started working on a large pile of hats. Susanne chatted about new customers she had gained. I was grateful for the chance to become immersed in something creative.

I became so immersed in my self-appointed task that the hour grew late.

"Stay here overnight, Isabelle," Susanne suggested.

"Thank you for asking me but I really should go home because I have an early morning rehearsal and wouldn't want to disturb you at an unearthly hour."

"I'm sure you wouldn't."

"I'm going to hire a fiacre," I said, firmly.

Susanne shrugged her shoulders. All right, I can see you're determined."

"I'll come and see you again another time."

"Hope so, I'll be glad of your company and will look forward to it."

Leon had been waiting for me before I reached home. His drowsy, complacent mood of the afternoon had vanished. He was in a bad temper. "Where the hell have you been? I've been looking everywhere for you."

"What do you mean by 'everywhere'?"

"At the Moulin and in a couple of the cabarets."

"You know I don't go to those places on my own."

I decided a little mystery would do him no harm. "Went to see a dear old friend."

He frowned. "A friend indeed! Don't you mean a lover?"

I was secretly flattered he was jealous of me but had no intention of letting him see this.

After a slight pause, I said, "No such luck! I went to see Susanne. Helped her with her hats. It's only fair to return favours to people who've been kind to you."

"Returning good deeds Isabelle is admirable, I agree. At this time of night though, it's ridiculous. *And* foolish not to mention dangerous."

"Don't fuss so, Leon. I've not come to any harm. Did anyone ever tell you; you don't look as handsome as usual when you're frowning?"

Slightly startled, Leon began to laugh. It broke the tension between us. He sat down pulling me on to his lap, stroking my hair as I told him of my father's words. Leon had the grace to laugh at Papa's description of him as "that artist-fellow."

"He must be a patient man, that Georges, not like me, eh? Firstly, you run out on him, now he's having to wait at least another two years for your sister."

"The dowry seems to be worth waiting for. Knowing Eloise, she'll probably urge Papa to bring the marriage forward so that she can be the centre of attraction."

I sighed. "Oh, Leon, it seems such a waste to me of a lovely young girl."

He caressed the back of my head. "Your papa most likely thinks you're wasted on me in his heart of hearts."

"Doubt it."

We remained in a companionable silence for a little while then he said. "You know the other night when I came back late?"

Apprehensive of what might confession might be coming next, I merely nodded.

"I'd seen a horrible sight, well to me it was."

"Was it an accident?"

"No, it was outside La Roquette."

"The prison, was it an execution?" I guessed.

"Yes, the criminal was stripped to the waist with his head held in the lunette under the knife of the guillotine. Maybe he deserved his death but I've no taste for this sort of thing. A large crowd watching, could only dislike them for wanting to see blood spilt."

"That's what the old Bastille crowd must have been like. Know how you must have felt. Lots of people like to see things like this but I feel the same way as you. Understand it's questionable for murderers and suchlike to live but I hate the executions being in public. Know some folk disagree with me on this."

"Grim subject for me to bring up with a pretty lady, wasn't it? Should be talking to you about love."

"Don't flatter me so, Monsieur," I answered with mock coyness.

Leon made love to me passionately that night. I nestled contentedly in his arms before falling asleep. But my sleep was troubled with strange dreams in which unnaturally bright colours flashed before me then disappeared. Then Leon was drowning and however much I tried, I was unable to save him. I awoke, trembling. "Bad dream," I said.

"Have a better one now," he remarked as he soothed me back to a more peaceful sleep.

On one particularly fine early spring day, Leon and I went to the formally picturesque garden of the Jardin du Luxembourg where we sat for a while, enjoying the sunshine.

"I'd like to buy you a bouquet from the Flower Market," Leon said.

This pleased me because I knew the flowers there were brought from the Mediterranean. Some were particularly beautiful. We strolled arm-in-arm through the market, past the housewives with their market baskets hung over their arms. Leon bought me a bouquet from a thin, blonde girl. She smiled warmly at him when he handed her the money for it.

"Thank you so much, Monsieur," she said, enthusiastically. She was not especially pretty but the smile transformed her pale face into something approaching radiance.

To my irritation we were then approached by Pierre Moreau who had been a fellow student of Leon's. He was a stocky young man with red hair. I knew that Leon liked him although they weren't close friends. I couldn't share Leon's enthusiasm for Moreau, having an instinctive distrust of him. He had never been unpleasant to me so for Leon's sake, I behaved courteously towards him.

Hanging on to Moreau's arm was a gaudily dressed young woman with a voluptuous figure and untidy hair of an unnaturally bright red-gold colour. She hastily took an object out of her reticule, throwing it down on to the ground. Looking down, I saw the butt of what was sometimes known as a *cigarillo* lying near my feet. Leon drew me aside discreetly.

"This is Celeste," Moreau said. He nodded to the flower seller. "And that's Jeannette, Jeannette Cordier."

"Glad you got rid of your *cibiche*, Celeste. It was crushed, wasn't it?" He winked at her

Even Leon who was rarely shocked raised his eyebrows a little at this remark. I knew that the prostitutes sometimes approached likely looking clients to ask them for a cigarette. Was this girl a *lorette*, I wondered.

There was an uncomfortable silence for a moment before Moreau broke it by saying. "It's lucky we've all met today by coincidence."

This was not how I felt although I tried not to show it.

"You two must come to my studio tomorrow," Moreau said.

"Kind of you to invite us," I stated. "Leon can come, I'm afraid I can't because I have a long-standing arrangement with an old friend I've not seen for a long time. Can't let her down."

Leon gave me a sharp look.

"What a pity," Moreau said, not looking at all sorry I wouldn't be present.

Celeste talked incessantly in the street slang, not all of which I could understand. In contrast, Jeannette seemed shy. However, she and Moreau seemed to converse with each other in a kind of code known only to themselves.

"Isabelle's flowers will wilt in the sun if we don't take them home soon," Leon said, appearing to sense that I was in a hurry to leave the market. I was grateful.

"Of course, au revoir, see you tomorrow," Moreau remarked, as Leon led me away gently.

"Who's your long-lost friend then?" Leon asked me, smiling. To my relief he seemed to be amused rather than annoyed by my lie.

"Oh, maybe it's Susanne or perhaps it's Marguerite. Haven't seen her for a long time and would really like to see her again. You don't mind me not going to Moreau's studio, do you?"

"No, love, it could be boring for you anyway if we start reminiscing about our student days."

"Thought you'd probably be more relaxed if you're just in each other's company."

Leon nodded in agreement; I was still unsure that he believed me. But I didn't want to hurt him by belittling a friend of his.

CHAPTER SIXTEEN

After that meeting, Leon began to see Moreau more frequently. For some reason this made me vaguely uneasy but I said nothing, merely trying to avoid the man myself as much as I could.

Leon brought home a painting of our meeting at the market that Moreau had drawn. An accurate likeness of the four of us with some of the other customers in the background. Leon enthused about it.

"I'm afraid I've little liking for this picture," I told Leon. He looked disappointed.

"Can see it's well drawn; don't really know why I haven't taken to it."

Leon's expression became a little lighter. Recently, I had become concerned that he had begun smoking opium a little more frequently although not in my presence. There would merely be a lingering presence of the sweetish smell when I returned from an afternoon visit to a friend or a shopping expedition.

As we ate our croissants and drank our coffee one late spring morning, I studied his face. He was in an amiable mood, having risen early to set up his equipment in readiness for a couple of his other models' visits.

"Why are you looking at me so closely?" he asked. "Haven't turned green, have I?"

Forcing myself to laugh, I said. "Not exactly but you've been smoking opium more often, haven't you?"

He didn't try to deny it. "Know I have, I'm aware of how much I can take without it doing me too much harm."

"Hope you're right for both our sakes though I won't pretend I don't have my doubts about it."

I stood up before wandering over to one of his paintings of me regarding it silently for a few seconds before pointing at my image and saying. "When you've been smoking it can look like a different person from me in some of your pictures."

"Do you find it unflattering?"

"Not exactly, not sure how to explain it properly. The best way to describe it is that my clothes have much more vivid colours. Furniture and even outside street glimpses seem exaggerated in proportions. Not a great resemblance to myself, my poor face has a lot of hollows and my body's out of line."

Leon frowned. "If you approve of it or not, Isabelle, my art does earn our livelihood."

Oh dear, I thought, realising I had disturbed his former amiability by daring to make comments about his treasured talent.

"Sorry I spoke, maybe I'd better go back to bed."

"You haven't been up long. You looked lovely and peaceful in your sleep earlier. Don't go back to bed yet because I want to make some sketches of you doing the splits in the quadrille. Need an early start, got a very early appointment at lunch time. You can go back to bed then if you want to."

Pleased his good humour was restored, I threw a small cushion at him in a playful way. He pretended to chase me round the sofa. "I'll punish you when I catch you," he grinned.

When he did catch me, however, he kissed me. The white dressing gown I was wearing fell open, exposing my breasts. Leon bent down and kissed them.

After he had left for his appointment, I was searching for a lace scarf I had mislaid. I found it a newspaper Leon had left carelessly on an occasional table in the lounge. I picked it up, browsing through it.

The paper seemed to be an anarchistic one. It was written in a racy slang, inciting people to rebel against the Government or steal food if they were hungry. There were some witty cartoons scattered throughout the pages, I laughed at some of them.

I put the paper back on the table hastily when I heard Leon's key turning in the lock. He entered and we exchanged our usual greetings and welcoming kiss.

"Do you know anything about this paper, Leon?" I asked, as I picked it up in what I hoped was a casual manner.

He glanced idly at it. "Oh, that, yes, its owner's an ex-clerk who lost his job after trying to form a trade union. Moreau was drawing some cartoons for him on a freelance basis. He introduced us. But the owner was looking for some different illustrations so he asked for a sample of my work. Gave him a quick sample by making a rough sketch. He liked it, fortunately so now I draw cartoons for him now and again."

"Thought it looked a bit like your work. Oh love, be careful, suppose the police decide they don't like this paper and try to close it down. You could be prosecuted; I couldn't stand that!"

Leon slipped his arm around my shoulders, giving me a tiny squeeze.

"You worry too much about me, darling. Don't use my own name, prefer to stay anonymous."

"All the same, do you honestly believe it's wise? Its views are revolutionary. That can be dangerous."

He shrugged. "Well, I don't always fully agree with all the paper's sentiments myself. But the owner's set up a commune in one of the eastern districts to help the needy and unemployed. Also provides free schooling for their children. Admire him for doing something practical for those he speaks up for in his paper. It's not just lip service."

I sighed. "Suppose you're right about that."

"Moreau often helps at this commune. Told me he used not to be that concerned about the poor but after one of his relatives fell on hard times, became ill and died, he felt guilty that he hadn't done more to help them. So, he now tries to make amends for his neglect by doing what he can for the needy."

Leon showed me another newspaper he had bought, turning to a particular page. "Read that article, it'll give you an idea," he said.

The account gave details of how a large crowd had gathered in the streets of the small mining town, Fourmies. It described how the police and troops were called in but the sub-prefect and the troops' commanding officer had lost their heads. Orders had been given to fire on the demonstrators. Ten people had been killed including two children in their teens. And forty other demonstrators had been wounded.

A local party of twenty anarchists from the northern Paris suburbs went to Clichy, parading through the streets behind a woman carrying a red flag when the police had pursued them. A scuffle ensued with several shots being fired both by the police and the marchers, some of whom had revolvers. Three men were arrested after the struggle and taken to the police station. They were so badly beaten up that they needed medical treatment before going to court where the judge had given them severe penalties.

I put the paper down. "Agree all that was terrible, Leon but revolutionary views can become dangerous. Look at what happened in the Terror. You need to be cautious of who you're getting involved with."

He sighed. "You don't need to worry quite so much. Promise I won't take too many risks, you don't need to fuss. Now, I've got some good news for us. I've managed to sell a few more cartoons to a magazine owner today. Will you advise me on what we should get for some new furnishings?"

Leon smiled at me, although his smile still had the power to make me feel weak inside, I was filled with an unwelcome dread of what the future might hold for us both. I forced myself to shake this feeling off.

I returned his smile. "Yes, of course, I'm delighted that we can do this."

We bought heavy velvet curtains to be put away until the next winter and a large, decorated mirror. I really liked them both.

"You'll be able to admire yourself in this much more than you can in smaller mirrors," Leon grinned. "It won't dare to show you a bad reflection of yourself and you'll be able to practice pirouettes to your heart's content."

"I'll enjoy that,"

"Seriously, don't overdo it and hurt yourself."

"Don't worry, I know my limits about going too far."

"Glad to hear it."

We had also bought some pretty ornaments, one of which I had decided to give to Susanne, hoping she'd find it a pleasant change to own a possession that wasn't a necessity.

It had been a good day for me but that night the dream in which Leon was drowning recurred. I awoke in a sweat as Leon slept on, peacefully. I was tempted to touch his face but resisted the impulse in case I woke him up.

I looked at Leon's face, handsome and peaceful in repose and prayed that no undue harm would come to him. I was filled with love for him but anxious that the opium he took might have a damaging effect. It took a long while for sleep to return to me.

CHAPTER SEVENTEEN

Leon took me to the *Lapin Agile* Cabaret. To my dismay Moreau was there with the red-haired girl, Celeste on his arm. They came over to speak to us, she was garishly dressed and her speech was more abrasive than ever.

I tried not to show Leon how disappointed I was. "I have a headache," I pleaded.

"I'll take you home early then so that you can rest. Hopefully, you'll get rid of it."

Moreau looked at me with a momentary flicker of undisguised dislike in his eyes. It was a relief to leave the cabaret.

Later that same week Leon had gone out. Not expecting him home until late, I was reading a book. Looking up from the current page, amazement swept over me as I saw Leon standing in front of me with Jeannette, the blonde flower seller we had met at the market. What on earth had he brought her home for?

"Didn't expect you back so soon, Leon. And what is … ?"

I indicated Jeannette who stood with her blue eyes downcast. This, for some inexplicable reason, irritated me.

He flushed but replied quickly. "My business today was over exceptionally quickly. As I passed the flower market, I wondered whether you might find the services of a lady's maid useful. I'll be finishing some of my work in the studio so I'll leave you two young ladies to become acquainted with each other."

Leon avoided my eyes as he hurried out of the room. Jeannette and I both stared at his departing back. I sent for our other maid, Therese, to take Jeannette to the kitchen and give her something to eat and drink.

When Therese returned, I said to her, "Monsieur Leon wishes Jeannette to become my personal maid."

Therese didn't look pleased. "I'd rather have you," I said. "But as it's Monsieur Leon's wish, I've agreed to it."

Then I marched to Leon's studio to confront him. He was putting finishing touches to one of his paintings in an almost feverish haste. Standing rigidly still, I took a deep breath before speaking in a forced calm tone. "Why did you mean by employing that girl as my lady's maid?"

He blinked. "We can afford a lady's maid. Thought you might like a personal servant of your very own."

"That's not answering my question, is it? Why *that* girl? What was your reason for bringing her here?"

Leon shrugged. "She's had a rough life one way or another, even living rough for some time. Thought she deserved something better."

"I see or then again, maybe not."

"She'd suffer, get too cold in that market in winter."

He took me into his arms, I forced myself not to respond.

Leon's tone became pleading. "Please give her a chance, Isabelle. At least take her on a month's trial."

I sighed. "Very well, if you insist but she *must* leave after a month if I'm not happy with her."

"That's more like you. Will you now do me another favour?"

"What's that?" I asked, resigned.

"Smile and give me a kiss. A bit later this year, I'd like you to marry me. Do you accept my offer?"

I grinned. "Well, now, I'll have to think about it, won't I?" My tone was deliberately teasing.

"Looking forward to knowing what your decision is."

We indulged in a fond embrace.

Jeannette settled into our household quickly. She always showed willingness to perform tasks well and was quiet and unobtrusive. She became a little less pale and put on some weight although she was still slim. Jeannette was never lazy or insolent yet there was something about her that made me wary of her. I tried to tell myself mentally that my attitude was irrational but it persisted.

Deciding to question Jeannette about her supposedly rough past, I asked her what she had done before selling flowers.

"After my parents died, I was brought up in an orphanage. Hated it until a man rescued me from it. He was a gardener, a lot older than me. He married me after a while though I wasn't really expecting him to. I was grateful at first. But then he began to drink a lot, he'd come home and beat me so I ran away. Nowhere to go and no money. Tried to find shelter in the park but it was freezing cold. Monsieur Moreau found me there, gave me hot food and shelter. Knowing my husband had taught me quite a lot about flowers and plants he arranged for me to have a stall in the market. He took none of my profits away from me. So, I kept my money not that it was a great deal, it certainly helped me."

"So, you owe a lot to Monsieur Moreau," I said, dryly.

"Certainly do, Madame. He learned me how to speak proper and didn't even expect to sleep with me. Now he's been kind enough to introduce me to you and Monsieur Leon."

There was an almost burning light in the girl's eyes, it alarmed me. "I want you to visit the draper's, to buy me a white handkerchief," I said, before handing her a coin. I didn't really need another one but I wished her to be out of the house for a short while. Had her tale been true or false? I wondered, believing Moreau must wish to use her for some purpose of his own if he truly did not desire her physically.

Despite Leon's words to the contrary, I was not convinced that Moreau was the kind of man who acted purely from generous motives. Then I wondered if it was unfair of me to harbour uncharitable thoughts about him. Maybe I had misjudged him or had he performed an isolated act of kindness? After all, most of us were surely capable of a kind act at least once in our lives.

I went into Leon's studio that evening and was amazed to see that Leon was absent but Jeannette was there. She was washing paintbrushes and a palette, tasks I had meant to undertake myself. She looked startled when she saw me but began to stretch a canvas.

"Leave that, Jeannette, I'll do it. What are you doing in here, anyway? Thought you were ironing my white blouse."

"I've already ironed it, Madame. Monsieur has asked me to model for him."

My eyebrows raised at this piece of information.

"So, you've been doing things that I and his other models do." I indicated the paint brushes. "But I had no idea *you've* been asked to model for him."

She looked at the floor. "He asked me yesterday, Madame."

"Really, seem to remember you telling us you'd once tried modelling for another artist but didn't like it."

Her eyes became very blue and wide. "No, I didn't but Monsieur has been so good to me. Felt I couldn't really refuse."

My own eyebrows raised higher as she added quickly. "You've also been good to me."

This sounded almost like an afterthought.

I tried hard to control my rising anger. I wished Leon had told me he would be using Jeannette as one of his models. He didn't really need another one, having plenty already. She was not particularly pretty in my opinion either.

Leon entered shortly afterwards. "I'm going to visit Susanne, Leon," I said. "Au revoir."

He looked surprised but made no comment, merely nodding.

"Believe Jeannette has promised to model for you."

He looked a little startled before saying "Painting another picture of the flower market would be good, I think."

"If that's what you truly believe."

I could see Jeannette, out of the corner of my eye, watching me carefully with a narrowed gaze, almost like a cat's.

"Unfortunately, as I don't at present have my lady's maid services, I'll have to fetch my own hat and coat. I'm going to see Susanne," I snapped before I left the studio, inwardly fuming.

Outside, the weather was close so I felt uncomfortably hot. However, Susanne was pleased to see me, we had an amiable chat and she was delighted with the ornament I gave her as a gift. The hours passed agreeably until it was time for me to go home.

I entered the drawing room, regretting my earlier bad temper. But the sight meeting my eyes rooted me to the spot in frozen horror. Jeannette was lying on the floor with her clothing disturbed. Her face was filmed with sweat and she was panting in an almost animal like way.

Leon was spreading her thin legs apart. His own clothing loosened; he was about to thrust into her.

CHAPTER EIGHTEEN

After my initial shock, I darted nimbly towards Jeannette and slapped her hard across the face on both cheeks. I had never in my life struck a servant but I was unable to restrain myself this time. She flinched before pulling her clothes together.

Leon stood up, looking sick with shame as well he might in my opinion. "You'd better pack your bags and go, Jeannette," he said.

"There's no need for the little hussy to go," I stated, fighting back tears with a bitter taste in my mouth. "You obviously prefer her company to mine so I'll go instead and leave the two of you together."

"Isabelle, that's not true," Leon protested. I've behaved abominably but I *can* explain it, honestly, I can."

"Don't bother," I snapped, turning my back so that he wouldn't see my tears. "And don't, whatever else you do, try to touch me this time, it won't work."

I saw Jeannette hurry out of the room after giving us both a defiant look. She gave Leon another look, it was full of contempt.

"You won't believe me I know, Isabelle but all I felt for Jeannette at first was genuine pity. It is the truth that later on, I was…"

"Tempted? Oh, for the love of God, Leon, spare me your apologies and weak excuses because I don't wish to hear them. I'm leaving."

I ran upstairs and quickly packed a couple of my bags, pausing now and again to wipe my eyes. From the window I saw Jeannette hurrying down the street, a shabby bag in her hand.

When I came downstairs, Leon pressed some coins into my hand. I deliberately let them fall to the floor. "Where will you go?" he asked.

"Don't know. Anyway, it's none of your business."

"Suppose not but at least let me pay for your fiacre."

I shook my head. "No, I've some money of my own left."

For the second time that day, I hurried into the street.

I ordered the driver of the hired fiacre to take me to a small, discreet hotel. The horrible man leered at me in a knowing sort of way but did as I asked. It was only when I was safely inside the small room I'd hired, that I relaxed my self-control. My emotions had their full rein and I cried until I believed there were no tears left within me. That night, I had a dreadful nightmare that Leon was being executed by the guillotine. I awoke screaming, hating the fact I had no-one to confide in.

The week at the hotel passed extremely quietly, the concierge having been bribed to allow me a lot of privacy. My meals were brought to me on a tray although I had little appetite. I missed Leon terribly, slept badly and tried to immerse myself in a novel. But the pages became a blur. I tried to sew but pricked my finger. The haunting memories of Leon refused to disappear. I attempted to go out in the daytime but tears always threatened as I remembered past excursions with Leon. I had no wish to cry in public.

At the end of two weeks on a hot day, the concierge announced I had a visitor.

"But I particularly asked you to turn people away, didn't I?"

"Yes, Mademoiselle. Only this young man's been most persistent.

Ssys he absolutely *must* see you, it's so important for him to do this."

I sighed. "Very well then, bring him in."

Leon arrived, carrying a suitcase.

"I've brought you the rest of your clothes, Isabelle, the ones you left behind. Thought you might need them." He put the case on the floor. "I'll understand if you still can't forgive me for what I stupidly did."

"How did you know where to find me?"

He looked shame faced. "Underhanded, perhaps, however what I did was bribe my groom to follow your fiacre at a discreet distance. Knew I had to allow you a little time before seeing you again. Expected you'd still be angry with me."

I gave him a watery smile. "Should have been but I've missed you so even if that were stupid of me."

My resolves to have nothing further to do with him, never speak to him again had melted away like snow. I fell into his arms laughing and crying at the same time.

He began to tentatively stroke my hair. "I treated you badly. However, I swear to you it was only on the one occasion with Jeannette. She was arranging some flowers in a vase; I was looking at her bare arms. The day was hot and well, I'm a red-blooded man. Poor excuse from me I know. Felt ashamed afterwards, it's you who I really love, Isabelle. I've been such a fool."

I smiled. shakily. "Yes, I suppose you have, Leon. "Do you think you could be foolish enough to take me back home with you?"

He grinned. "I certainly could but let's lie down here together for a little while before I do."

While we were lying together Leon said. "You probably don't want to hear what happened on that notorious day. It will sound as if I'm making weak excuses for myself."

"Go on, tell me."

"I'd been painting Jeannette. She was still as a statue and followed all my instructions to the letter. When we'd finished, she said she wanted to arrange some flowers in a vase. I watched her carefully as I wanted to make a quick sketch of her doing this. She spilt some of the water and hurried to get a cloth to wipe it up. As she bent down, she loosened the buttons at her neck and rolled up her sleeves. I saw the rosy flesh on her arms."

"Think I know what's coming next," I said, dryly. "But carry on telling me."

"I told her she could have the rest of the day off but she said she'd nowhere to go, no family to call upon or friends to enjoy herself with. Our flat was her home now where she was comfortable and happy with us. I couldn't help feeling sorry for her so I told her to find bread, cheese and wine and wrap them up. We went to the riverside to eat our picnic then I hired a boat for an hour."

"When we came home, Jeannette flung her arms round my neck and kissed me on the cheek. She began to thank me so gratefully that I acted against my better nature."

"She put on an act that she was shy," I protested. "In my opinion, she's a little tart. She's a good actress though, should be at the Comedie-Francaise."

"But I felt guilty about the way I turned her out when a lot of what happened was my fault."

"You weren't blameless, Leon but I can see she probably provoked you."

He shrugged. "Maybe, to an extent. I didn't want to think of her living rough again so I gave Moreau some cash to make sure she at least has a roof over her head until she finds another position."

"She'll manage that, her sort always does. As long as she's no longer under our roof, that's all *I* care about." Realising my tone had become grim, I began to laugh. "Oh, Leon you spendthrift. You've bribed your groom, probably the concierge and now Moreau on Jeannette's behalf. Perhaps you should be considering a dowry from my father though he most likely would refuse it."

"No, I shouldn't, love. I'll tell you what I would like though. I'd love a child, a handsome boy, or a little dark-haired doll of a girl like her mother. I wouldn't have to be careful with..." He hesitated before speaking again. "I'll turn over a new leaf and give up the opium. It's not suitable for a family man."

I threw my arms around his neck. "One of the wisest decisions you've ever made, I'm sure. But let's take one thing at a time. Take me home, I'd like to be in our own comfortable bed not this cramped one."

"Your wish is my command, Mademoiselle." As he stood up, looking down at me, I saw the beautiful love light in his eyes as he bent down to pick up my suitcase.

"Oh, another thing, Leon," I'd now like to have Therese as my lady's maid."

"Yes, of course you can. Therese was telling me her aunt's now a widow and she's fallen on hard times so will you be agreeable to her aunt becoming our general maid?"

"Yes, I've no objection to that." I imagined Therese's aunt would be middle aged.

"Good."

Leon offered me his arm as I rose. It was such a relief to be leaving the hotel where I had been so unhappy.

CHAPTER NINETEEN

Our life settled back into its old pattern, except that Leon was more tender and affectionate towards me than formerly. Yet strangely, he was also more possessive. At one time this would have annoyed me, now I didn't mind so much.

Moreau's manservant arrived early one day. Leon and I were still in bed. He hurried downstairs. "You stay in bed, Isabelle," he said. "No need for you to get up yet."

But I wrapped my white dressing gown around me and descended the stairs. I heard the man say to Leon. "I've brought a message from Monsieur Moreau to say that he urgently needs to see you, Monsieur Prideaux."

"Can't you give me more details?"

"I'm afraid I cannot, Monsieur."

"In that case, I'll come with you to see your master."

For some unaccountable reason, this alarmed me. I clutched at Leon's sleeve.

"Please don't be too long."

Leon looked irritated. "I'll come back as soon as possible. Go back to bed, Isabelle. You could catch a cold, standing around half dressed like that."

Moreau's manservant looked away discreetly.

"Suppose you're right," I said, reluctantly and went back upstairs.

Later, I glanced at the clock, realising it was later than I usually rose. I dressed hurriedly and went downstairs as Leon entered the apartment safe and sound, to my immense relief.

"Maybe you don't wish to tell me but why did Moreau want to see you?"

"His man took me to a working man's club where I met Moreau. Couldn't really see why it was so urgent to be there so early. Moreau's borrowed some cash off me to set up another commune. Couldn't help wondering if he'd had some sort of trouble with a woman or something else like that with the police."

I frowned. "Perhaps he has and really, this commune's just an excuse."

"Don't think so, darling. He seems to have developed a strong sense of sympathy for the needy that I've never known him have before."

"Do you know what this commune's for?"

"Supposed to help poor old people, children of unmarried mothers, the mothers themselves, that sort of thing."

"Admirable cause, hope it works if this is true."

"Said he couldn't afford to finance it himself, though. In return for my favour, he introduced me to Paul Rennette another magazine proprietor who publishes pamphlets and writes songs. I'm going to decorate Moreau's commune and when Rennette's had a look at it, I might be able to draw some cartoons for his magazine."

"What sort of songs and pamphlets?" I asked, a little suspiciously.

"They're about workers and others who might not be doing very well."

I thought this reply was a little vague, guessing that some of the songs might be encouraging workers to rebel against their masters and the pamphlets might be incendiary. However, I kept my suspicions to myself.

"You most likely believe it's no concern of mine, love," I said, "Only I can't help feeling these people you seem to be getting involved with aren't completely desirable."

"Please, Isabelle, don't speak to me as if I'm still a schoolboy. I do know how to take care of myself and you, for that matter."

"I know you can, it's just that I can't help worrying about this."

Leon put his arm around my shoulders. "Try not to be so anxious, promise me."

I nodded although I wasn't completely reassured.

"You haven't even told your Papa we're going to be married yet, have you?"

I shook my head, deciding we really should inform him soon although I was apprehensive about his reaction.

"Do you want to go and see your family today?" Leon asked.

"No, not just yet. I want to ... Good God, what's that?!"

I was looking out of the window to where a small, noisy crowd had gathered in the street, waving banners.

Leon followed my gaze. "That lot will hardly change the Government in spite of all their shouting." Then, he looked at them more closely. "God in Heaven! There's Rennette at their head and there's ..."

His voice trailed off as I followed the direction of his pointing finger to Rennette, a small middle-aged man. Behind him was Jeannette, waving her banner high in the air.

The marchers moved off but I felt shaken to my core. "I must sit down now," I said,

"Yes, you're turned pale, I'll send for a glass of wine for you."

Leon seemed to be making a valiant attempt not to show his own alarm.

"No, thank you, I'd prefer a *café-crème*. Let's drink one together.

"Good idea." Leon rang for Therese's aunt.

We spent a quiet afternoon, Leon sketching while I read the novel I had taken to the small hotel. But we were both still disturbed.

That evening, there was a loud knock on our door. I couldn't help swearing under my breath as Moreau was admitted. He seemed agitated. I stared at him, coldly and Leon didn't look all that pleased to see him, either.

"Leon, you must help me, it's urgent," he said. "You have to do me this favour."

Leon scowled. "What's wrong, for God's sake?"

"I've just seen Rennette being arrested. He was hanging around the streets for a long time after the march."

Moreau took a large brown paper parcel from the bag he was carrying. "These are illustrations he very much needs to be delivered. Please take them to this address for me. The man there will keep them for him. I can't go myself because I need to go to the police station. I know one of the high-ranking officers there."

"I must persuade him to release Rennette straightaway or it'll be too late to stop him being locked away."

"Don't see why ...." Leon started to protest but Moreau interrupted him.

"He needs these pictures delivered because the chap you'll be taking them to will pay a high price for them. The buyer can't wait as he's going abroad tomorrow."

"Why me, though?" Leon asked, perplexed. "Couldn't you have sent your servant?"

"Don't completely trust my servant. He'd probably only pretend to have delivered the drawings after throwing them away. This man will also be able to help you."

Leon's dark eyebrows raised a fraction. "In what way?"

"Can't really explain now, don't have the time. Please do this favour for Rennette, Leon. After all, he's helped you in the past."

Leon shrugged. "Suppose he has."

Thoroughly alarmed now, some sixth sense telling me Leon would be in danger if he complied with this request. I clutched at his sleeve. "Don't go, Leon, please don't for my sake."

Moreau looked at me with a cold loathing he could not hide not that I cared about his opinion of me.

Leon took me in his arms and kissed me gently. "Stop worrying, sweetheart. I am going but I shan't be long, I promise. Try to understand that I do want to return a favour. I'm sorry Rennette's been arrested."

Feeling like crying and screaming because Leon looked so determined, I somehow managed to suppress these emotions. "I'm sorry about that, too but it wasn't your fault. Please don't be too long away."

"No, of course not, I've already promised you. See you soon, au revoir."

"Thank you, Leon," Moreau said. "I've no time to lose." He grabbed his coat and rushed out of the door. Leon followed him immediately.

A little later, I looked out of the window. Moreau was running in one direction, Leon was strolling in the opposite way, looking as if he were whistling. The evening was warm and pleasant.

Leon disappeared from my sight but then I saw the same group of marchers with their flags that we had seen earlier that day. Jeannette was no longer with them. They must have been lucky and managed to escape from the police I thought.

Suddenly, without warning, I heard the most deafening ear-piercing roar I had ever heard in my entire life.

CHAPTER TWENTY

I considered sending one of our manservants out to search for Leon but then decided against it, as they might be placing themselves in danger. I paced up and down, in an agony of self-reproach. Why had I not tried harder to persuade him to stay indoors? Tears flooded my eyes. Eventually, Therese coaxed and persuaded me to go to bed. But sleep was impossible.

Early the next morning I rose, glancing at the bed. In the place where I was accustomed to Leon's familiar body lying beside me, there was now an empty space.

I forced myself to keep busy, washing paintbrushes and stretching canvases vigorously in the vain hope Leon would soon return to end this nightmare of waiting and praying.

Therese said, "Your breakfast's ready now, Madame." I took one bite of a croissant and one sip of coffee but my appetite had deserted me completely.

Picking up the newspaper, I read the report of a bomb that had killed three people. Instinctively, I knew that Leon had been one of the victims. The screaming in my ears sounded harsh even to my own ears. But I found it impossible to stop.

Alarmed by the noise, Therese asked one of the men working for us to bring a doctor to see me. When he arrived, the doctor gave me a sedative.

The rest of that week passed in a kind of blur. I had a vague awareness of eating, drinking, and sleeping. Most of the rest of the time was spent staring out of the window, my mind numb to anything I saw or heard.

A kind, anonymous man sent me a letter, enclosing Leon's diary. The letter writer informed me that he had found it in a working man's club. Now I understood Jeannette's reticence about her past and her private affairs. That shyness had been a consummate act. I thought she must have been an active member of an anarchist organisation and also most likely so was Moreau. My former dislike of them now turned into a bitter hatred.

Otherwise, I had no feelings about anything at all. I ate sparingly, drank, washed, and slept mechanically, took little interest in my appearance, couldn't bring myself to set foot in the studio and was indifferent to the state of the flat. Therese's aunt kept it clean and tidy so I was grateful for this.

Leon's father paid me a visit. He was not quite as tall as his son but wore his years well and was distinguished looking. I could see where he had inherited his good looks. He knew of his son's death but I never found out who had told him, probably the police I guessed later. His manner towards me was gentle and considerate but I sensed that deep down, he disapproved of me. Perhaps he thought I wouldn't have been a suitable wife for his son. Acceptable as a mistress maybe but not to marry.

Taking a deep breath, I said "I don't wish to continue living here, Monsieur Prideaux. It holds too many painful memories. But you're the next of kin anyway so it's probably legally your apartment."

His eyes lit up. "I'll help you find somewhere else to live and give you a financial settlement."

"That's kind of you, thank you. But I'm a bit worried about the servants. Can't afford to keep them but I don't want them to have a hard time if I dismiss them."

Monsieur Prideaux looked thoughtful. I see, how many of them are there?"

"Four altogether."

"Ah, well, that shouldn't prove too difficult. If you give them their notice, I'll help arrange other employment for them. All you'll have to do is write good references for them. I'll see to the rest of it."

I smiled, wryly. "I'm grateful to you for this."

"We've both been dealt a bitter blow, Mademoiselle Lefevre. It's the least I can do."

"All the same you didn't have to do this for me."

He hesitated. "Don't think me hard. The pain of my son's death affects me deeply as I can tell it has also done for you. But you are a young woman with, hopefully, many years ahead of you so you must for your own sake, try to forget this tragedy. You should start to live your own life to the full again. Try to forget all that's happened and …"

"How *can* I forget?"

"You must make the effort; I know it will take time but your grief shouldn't make you ill. Why not go abroad for a while?"

"Can't afford to go abroad." I looked down at the carpet, to a tiny extent, his words had shaken me out of my lethargy.

"Maybe an unwise suggestion on my part. But I don't like to see you looking ill, my dear. My poor son must have been appreciative of your looks when he met you. I must leave now; I'll call again tomorrow to collect your servants' references. Au revoir."

Monsieur Prideaux gave me a quick kiss on the cheek. I sent for his hat and coat and showed him out of the door. He seemed relieved to be leaving.

Now, I had the unpleasant task of giving notice to the servants. I gathered them all together, they didn't look happy but they didn't plead to be kept on either.

I forced myself to write glowing references for them all, knowing they were a little over-complimentary for the groom and valet who didn't really deserve the lavish praise I bestowed on them. But when they found new jobs hopefully, their new employers would form their own opinions about them.

My wardrobe was examined next, deciding which clothes and jewellery, I would keep and those I would sell.

Grief and bitterness had not entirely evaporated within me as autumn arrived. I still missed Leon dreadfully. However, I began once more to take pains with my appearance and decided to visit my family again.

CHAPTER TWENTY-ONE

Papa unbent from his rigid manner enough to say "I'm sorry the artist has been killed, Isabelle.

Still calling him 'the artist,' can't be bothered to call him by his name, I thought, cynically. But I just nodded. "We would have married; I was looking forward to inviting you all to the wedding."

My father couldn't disguise a sceptical look.

"Really?" Madame Charpentier said, raising her eyebrows. She had condescended to be present in my company because I had experienced a personal tragedy.

"I'm to be married earlier than expected, aren't I, Papa?" Eloise announced. I thought this was a little tactless but made an allowance in case it was just youthful thoughtlessness.

Papa nodded, Colette said. "I'm looking forward to the wedding because I'm going to be a bridesmaid. Can't wait to try on my dress."

"There's plenty of time to discuss those sorts of arrangements," Madame Charpentier said. "What we need to discuss now is poor Isabelle. What will happen to her now, that…?"

She didn't complete the sentence, merely waved her hand in the air with a smug expression on her face.

"Monsieur Prideaux, Leon's father, has promised to help find me another flat," I stated, quickly. I'm going to see it tomorrow."

"May I come with you?" Papa asked, much to my amazement.

The apartment Leon's father had found me was nowhere near as luxurious as the one I had shared with Leon. It was, however, comfortable, and much to my relief, Papa approved of it.

I couldn't help being sceptical. It was probably a weight off his mind that I didn't want to move back into his house.

But he made an offer. "This flat's going to need decorating, I'll help you with that."

"Thank you, Papa."

"You may return to us if you find you're in need. While you're here, I'll arrange for decorators to come over here."

"That's generous of you, Papa. But I'd like to supervise the decorators myself."

Papa shrugged his shoulders. "As you wish but if you're ever in any sort of trouble, you can contact me."

"I'm grateful for that advice," I said, noticing Papa's relief at my decision with a tiny amount of bitterness.

"I've decided to visit Blanche for a while again if I can. I've written to ask her if she'll receive me."

"A good idea," Papa approved. "The rest should benefit you."

"Hope so."

Some weeks later, I found myself looking around the Charente countryside at the low-lying hills, the vast skies and the fields bordered by poplars and crossed by a river, taking a last, lingering look at the countryside before returning to Paris.

Blanche lived in a grey house, smaller than most of the others in the area. I had poured my whole story into her sympathetic ears. "I'm sorry about what happened to your young man. But we can't change it and life for others must go on."

"I know. I don't think either Papa or Madame Charpentier believed he would really have married me."

Blanche showed no surprise. "Perhaps not but you believed him and you know that he died loving you so I'm sure he wouldn't want you to be unhappy."

"Still miss him a lot so I can't help feeling sad,"

Blanche gave me a sympathetic look. "Understandable but time does heal all wounds, Mademoiselle Isabelle."

"Suppose so. Please don't keep calling me, 'Mademoiselle Isabelle.' Let it be just 'Isabelle.'"

"It's an old habit of mine, hard to get out of, Mademoiselle."
We both laughed as the atmosphere lightened.

Blanche and I lived quietly, eating simple meals, embroidering, reading, and taking strolls. Occasionally we travelled to Angouleme and went shopping there. Blanche liked to have news of her sister and was pleased that I had kept in touch with Susanne.

I wrote two letters, one to Papa and one to the proprietor of the Folies Bergere. My month's stay with Blanche refreshed me both in body and soul and I knew I would always feel grateful to her for this.

"Please accept some money from me while I'm here," I had said to Blanche one day.

She had shaken her head. "No, I don't want it."

"But it's unfair not to give you something."

We argued for a little while but Blanche finally reluctantly took a small sum from me.

Blanche was genuinely sorry when the day I left arrived. But I had not wished to force myself on her for too long and was by now, ready to go home although I knew I would miss her.

The Folies-Bergere was situated in quite a close position to my new flat. My experience at the Moulin Rouge must have stood me in good stead because I was lucky enough to be engaged there as a dancer, as one of the corps.

CHAPTER TWENTY-TWO

The first time I walked through the open garden of the Folies-Bergere, I trembled with nerves. Nevertheless, it was diverting to see the spectacular juggler and the prodigious magician who performed tricks I would never have dreamt of.

Indoors, variety shows took place again with conjurers and jugglers, also clowns, acrobats, singers and dancers. The sumptuous foyer had staircases that swept up to the dress circle. The swinging doors in the foyer led to the stalls which were reached by passing through the promenade where the 'ladies of the town' plied their trade. The audiences were cosmopolitan and it was possible to hear almost every language in the world. The first rows were always reserved for regular patrons. These seats provided the closest and best view in the house for the shows that began promptly at 8 p.m. every evening.

The promenoir was a vast circular area at the back of the stalls. The stalls were modestly priced as long as the patrons were prepared to stand. The spectators crowded up to the barriers that separated them from the stalls, leaving a large empty space at the back. This was the *'promenoir'* ladies' traditional pitch where they presented cards, valid for two weeks. Every two weeks the general manager held a parade to decide who would be the fortunate ones who could renew the cards. They walked in pairs along the hall's semi-circular promenade. Most of them were powdered and rouged, their eyes drowned in a blur of pale blue, their lips brightly reddened and their bosoms projected forwards over their tightly laced waists. One who was not quite so heavily made up as the others reminded me of the model who had been employed in the same shop as myself. This girl was one of the lucky ones who had her card renewed.

All this bustle and activity suited me, my sadness at losing Leon had by no means vanished yet but activity had certainly appealed to me. I became used to the routine of working regularly again. I was polite to the other girls although I made no special friends. The reserve on my part seemed to puzzle them.

One of them said to me one day, "Why do you never accept invitations from any of the patrons? Some of them like you well enough and you could do well out of them if you tried."

"Prefer to live quietly," I insisted. She gave me a puzzled, disapproving look but made no further comment.

I lived quietly in my new flat with one servant girl, Marie, an absolute 'treasure.'

"What was your family like?" I asked her when she first began working for me.

"They was poor, Madame."

I nodded, not making further enquiries about them. Marie was discreet and seemed to understand my moods. She seemed to know instinctively when I felt like talking or when I wished to be quiet. I found her neither over familiar or too shy. I never heard her complain about anything for which I was grateful.

Having thrown myself into my work with a determined vengeance I was gratified when a critic singled me out from the other dancers from the corps in the article he wrote about me, praising my performance. He had, apparently, found out what my name was.

I showed his remarks in the newspaper to Marie. She looked pleased but also a little embarrassed. "I can't read some of the big words," she said.

"I'll read it out to you, Marie. Then I'll know myself that I didn't dream all those nice things he said about me." Marie looked relieved and I couldn't help feeling mildly amused.

For a long while after Leon's death, I had been unable to look at newspapers. Now, I began to read them again. There was an account of how a man named Ravachol who had placed a bomb in a judge's block of flats in the Rue de Clichy. Fortunately, there was only one slight casualty. He had rented a room in a house where the owner's wife had been friendly with the Clichy anarchists. I couldn't help wondering if Moreau and other anarchists of his acquaintance, had known him.

Ravachol had set off a second bomb, this time however, two people were killed. Then he bombed two restaurants. When Ravachol was finally executed he refused to see a priest and sang. This extraordinary behaviour had made him a hero in a lot of people's eyes but certainly not in mine.

I would never have approved of the anarchists' actions but since Leon's death, I had begun to hate them passionately.

No matter how tired I was at night, I never seemed to fall asleep straightaway. It was a lonely time when I lay in bed, remembering how I had run my fingers through Leon's hair, meeting the warm gaze of his eyes and the way his strong hands had tenderly explored my body.

One fine morning I strolled down Haussman's Grands Boulevards where I saw a procession. The gold fringed flag coloured red, white and blue was borne by an ensign. The colonel was white-haired under his gold-braided kepi and his drawn sword flashed in the sunlight.

Although he was clearly upright with a proud look about him, I fancied his hawk-like eyes were looking at me intently but I dismissed the thought as mere whimsy. He was not unprepossessing for a man of his age.

The colonel passed on, followed by two majors on horseback. In turn they were followed by a captain, then the *piou-pious*, the general nickname for the infantry. The latter were little men in long, dark blue tunics with red epaulettes, baggy red trousers and white spats and rifles.

CHAPTER TWENTY-THREE

At the Folies Bergere, one of my admirers had been particularly determined to meet me. He had showered me with bouquets of flowers, chocolates and bon-bons. They had all been delivered to me, together with complimentary notes always signed 'Colonel Saugez.' At first, I returned many of his gifts but this only made him send me more extravagant ones.

Not wishing to put on too much weight, I usually gave the sweets to Marie who accepted them gratefully. She usually took them home to share with her brothers and sisters. "They'll love these, Madame," she said.

I had smiled. "Hope they will."

I made discreet enquiries of my own to find out this mysterious Colonel's identity. It was amazing to discover he was the very same man that I had seen in the procession on the Boulevards Haussman. Finally, I gave in and capitulated much to the other dancers' surprise to allow him to take me to supper. Leon was still a painful memory but I didn't wish to live like a nun forever.

The meal was a good one in an expensive restaurant where all the correct little touches were added.

"I've admired you for a long time, Isabelle," the Colonel said. "I've loved watching you dance."

"Thank you."

"No need to thank me, I meant what I said."

"I'm grateful for that."

"My wife's dutiful enough but she's generally cold towards me."

I tried not to look at him with cynicism, knowing how common this sort of statement was from married men who were indulging in extra marital affairs.

He then told me some tales of his life in the Army, notably the valiant part he had played during the Siege. I was sure he was exaggerating although some of his stories corresponded with events my father had told me about during the Franco-Prussian war.

"You've had a short life so far please tell me all about it. I'm very interested."

I gave him a brief outline but I was on my guard. I was reticent because I didn't wish to disclose too many details about myself.

Colonel Saugez took me home, leaving me at my door, he didn't ask to be invited in, much to my relief although he did try to arrange another rendezvous to which I reluctantly agreed.

The Colonel took me for another couple of meals in good restaurants. His manner was still courteous but at the end of the second evening, he said. "Will you do me a favour, Isabelle? I'll be grateful for it."

With a touch of apprehension, I asked. "What is it?"

"My wife runs a salon on some Sundays. Successful writers, painters, musicians, society wits and dandies, businessmen, journalists, et al meet there. Could you give them a watered-down version of the can-can for them next Sunday? They'd enjoy that tremendously, I'm sure."

I hesitated for a few minutes then said. "Very well, then."

A carriage was sent to fetch me on the following Sunday. The Colonel and his wife lived in the fashionable district of the Faubourg St Germain. I was curious to see their house and to meet their guests although also a little nervous.

When I did arrive at the large house, I was ushered into a spacious drawing room that had ornaments of black marble fauns scattered throughout the room. Several people stood in little groups. I looked around them with interest to see if I could recognise anyone famous.

With a start of surprise, I became aware of a young man who had been an acquaintance of Leon's. He nodded to me in acknowledgement although I had only known him slightly. His name was Victor Flauret; an elegant and articulate man of medium height, neither handsome nor ugly. Yet he certainly seemed to have the gift of being able to charm a lot of the ladies.

The Colonel came forward and said, "Ah, Mademoiselle Lefevre, it gives me great pleasure that you have been able to come here today to entertain us."

He introduced me to his wife, Jeanne she seemed a lot younger than him. Jeanne Saugez was elegant. She was not a classical beauty but was attractive. She shook my hand. "Welcome, Mademoiselle Lefevere," she said. "Thank you for joining us, today and for agreeing to entertain us."

I swallowed, nervously. Hope you won't be disappointed with what you see, I thought but kept it to myself.

Colonel Saugez had hired a small orchestra to accompany me. I felt more self –conscious than I did in the theatre because I didn't have the company of the other dancers. Normally, I could forget almost everything when I danced but this day could have been different.

I took a deep breath and began to dance. I let my hair fall forward over my face the way Leon had liked and concentrated on trying to give a reasonably modest performance.

At the end I made a demure curtsey, looked up and smiled, trying to look composed although I was apprehensive about my audience's reaction. They all, however, applauded enthusiastically. I was grateful for this.

Madame Saugez hurried forward. "Thank you so much, my dear." She looked around the room. "I'm afraid my husband can be forgetful sometimes. Have you been introduced to everybody here?"

"No, I'm afraid not, Madame."

"You must allow me to do so." She linked her arm in mine, leading me around the room. "We have such a pleasant time here," she said. "It's my favourite day of the week, Sunday."

As well as a lot of workers I thought although keeping this to myself.

I glanced at Colonel Saugez who was engrossed in conversation with a rich businessman.

The last person I was formally introduced to was Victor Flauret. Madame Saugez had just begun to speak when he interrupted her. "I know Isabelle, already, unfortunately we have both recently suffered a great loss. So sorry to hear about Leon, my dear but Mon Dieu, life must go on for the rest of us."

For a horrible moment, tears threatened me but then Flauret smiled at me in a quite engaging way. "She did very well, don't you think so, Jeanne?"

He picked up my hand and kissed it as Madame Saugez said. "Yes, she did."

A knowing look passed between them that made me wonder if they were possibly lovers. Suddenly, I wished desperately to be out of this house. But I didn't want to be rude so I forced myself to stay a little longer. Eventually, I said to Madame Saugez, "Thank you for your hospitality, Madame but I'm a little tired and should like to go home now."

She sent for my hat and coat before speaking briefly to her husband. He came up to me. "I'll escort you to your home," he said.

"Kind of you but there's no need."

"Yes, there is," he said, firmly.

"Don't you have your own carriage, Mademoiselle?" he asked once we were outside in the warm spring air.

I shook my head. "Not now, I'm afraid."

"Never mind, we can walk to your apartment. It will be a pleasant change for me as I do so much riding."

We walked back together, neither of us saying much. The Colonel held himself in a very erect way with his white hair blowing in the slight breeze. When we were nearly at my door he said. "Jeanne enjoys her Sunday afternoon salons so much. Of course, I'm happy that she does but in all honesty I'm sometimes a little bored by them. Would you like to join me at the race meetings at Longchamps next Sunday, Isabelle? We could travel there in my carriage; Jeanne won't need it then."

Why not? I thought, wearily, it would make up for the loneliness I sometimes felt.

"Yes, I'd like to go there with you."

Observing a gleam in his grey eyes I decided my acceptance had excited him. At my door he left once more without having been asked to go. But I knew perfectly well that this state of affairs would not last much longer.

CHAPTER TWENTY-FOUR

My conscience troubled me; I was also indecisive. If I formed an association with the Colonel, I knew I would be well provided for because he had money and I had had enough of keeping careful accounts of every sou I spent. On the other hand, I knew I could hardly expect my family or Susanne to understand the necessity of this liaison.

I would have to be deceitful, explaining that my visits to them were now rare due to fatigue and hope they would believe me. I would have to put on an act, I still had too much pride to run to my father for money.

There was also an element of self-loathing, a most unwelcome emotion. I would certainly never love him but maybe I could begin to respect him. He was old, yes but presentable. His wife couldn't care for him that much I decided as I had the impression, she found her own amusement elsewhere. In fact, I thought, almost wickedly, it might well suit her own purpose if I divert her husband's attention. Then, I started to hate myself for thinking like this.

The day Colonel Saugez and I attended the races, it was a beautiful sunny day. The Colonel won quite a large sum of money. "You must have brought me luck, Isabelle," he beamed. "I'll buy us some champagne to celebrate."

I smiled and thanked him.

After the day at Longchamps, he often took me out for days in the country. We also went to suppers and receptions where there would be a gleam of rich materials and a glitter of crystal and jewellery in the candlelight.

Occasionally, I danced at his wife's salons although I didn't like to go there too often. Victor Flauret was always present. I was unsure if the Colonel suspected they were lovers or was he possibly too vain to realise the true situation between them?

The Colonel told me in detail about his military campaigns. I didn't doubt that he had probably shown courage during some of them but he talked for such a long time about them that I couldn't help growing bored by them.

The first time that he was intimate with me was after one of Louise's salons. We were in my darkened bedroom. At first, we were fully clothed then he slowly undressed me. With great difficulty, I had to repress a shudder so I closed my eyes tightly, mentally concentrating on remembering Leon's features.

"You'll have to forgive me, Isabelle," he said. "I'm afraid I'm not as young as I was so there are unfortunately, certain things I am incapable of so I would very much appreciate it, if you could do something for me."

"What's that, Christian?" I asked, apprehensively. He'd told me to call him by his first name but when I spoke to other people about him, I always referred to him as "The Colonel."

He turned on to his front. "Can you scratch my back for me?"

I was relieved it had not been a worse request so I complied and he thanked me afterwards. "I can't still maintain the vigour of most young men."

"Do understand."

He ran his hands over my body, exploring it but full physical contact wasn't made, much to my relief.

Later, I did manage to tolerate his embraces without becoming too concerned about them. I managed to close my eyes, conjuring up memories of Leon. There were, however, other strange practices the Colonel asked me to take part in. I agreed although I didn't like them very much.

Out of gratitude, Colonel Saugez provided me with a newer, larger house in a quiet street that I furnished to my own satisfaction. Marie was thrilled by it also the fact that she was now my personal maid as he had provided me with a few more servants. Now and again, he bought me gowns and jewellery. This was agreeable and I was grateful but he didn't take me out so often.

"I'd like to see an Offenbach operetta," I said, one evening.

Saugez didn't reply, merely saying, "Would you like to leave the Folies?"

"Not yet, no."

He looked disappointed but didn't press the point.

I visited my family and Papa frowned. "You're looking prosperous the way you're dressed, Isabelle."

Madame Charpentier gave an audible sniff so I looked over her head.

"I've received a salary increase."

"Lucky you," my stepmother said, with a hint of sarcasm in her voice. I ignored her comment.

I left as early as I could without seeming rude, wishing that just for once, we could all be more relaxed with each other. Would that day ever arrive? I hoped so, deep down.

I also paid an afternoon call to Susanne. "I've changed my address," I said, handing her the slip of paper I had written it down on.

"You seem to have gone up in the world," she said.

I nodded. "I'm getting better paid."

Susanne looked slightly sceptical but made no further comment.

The next evening the Colonel called upon me, he said, "I've something special planned for you, an event you're sure to enjoy."

"What is it?"

"I know an amateur photographer; you know him too. I thought you might like to perform a tableau for him. Are you agreeable?"

"Well," I replied, hesitantly. "I'll think about it."

Saugez nodded as if I had already consented to this so I couldn't help feeling a little resentful.

After he had left, I gave the matter some consideration, finally deciding it would be a diversion from my usual routine. When the appointed day arrived, I noticed the studio had been rigged up as a boudoir. To my amazement, I saw that the photographer was Leon's friend, Victor Flauret. He seemed a little surprised to see me with the Colonel but soon regained his composure.

"We'd like you to recline in bed, Isabelle," Saugez said, "Smile up at me while Victor takes the photographs. You'd better take your outdoor clothes off."

I was relieved he hadn't asked me to take them all off. "What's going to happen with the photographs?" I asked, curiously.

"They'll be used in postcards and albums."

Later, I discovered to my embarrassment that these albums and photographs were saucy ones. But fortunately, I was not shown in the most risqué ones.

I made a couple more visits to the studio with the Colonel and each time the sketches gradually became a little more daring. In one, I had to pretend I was suffering from an itch given to me by an insect. Afterwards, I slowly took off my garments until I was left in my shift before climbing into bed. In another sketch entitled "The Bride at Bedtime," I was dressed as the apparently shy, demure bride whose character changed enormously later.

These themes were used for silent films that only gentlemen watched. Colonel Saugez watched some of them with his companions. The unwelcome feeling of despising myself returned. Why was I willing to do this sort of thing? Then, I looked at the emerald bracelet Saugez had bought me shortly afterwards.

When I was alone again, I burst into laughter, nearly on the edge of hysteria. I was picturing Susanne's face if she could have seen one of the films.

CHAPTER TWENTY-FIVE

My life followed a regular pattern of dancing at the Folies and receiving Colonel Saugez. It was almost becoming a monotonous even if admittedly somewhat luxurious existence.

Then an event occurred that very much disturbed both Colonel Saugez and myself. It took place at 4 o'clock in the afternoon in Parliament on the 9th December 1893.

A bomb was thrown from the public galleries exploding in a shower of nails. Several deputies, one of whom was an old acquaintance of the Colonel and some members of the public were found to have been wounded by inch-long nails.

"A terrible thing," I shuddered, when recalling the incident.

"May the animals who did this all rot in hell!" the Colonel added.

The nails were discovered when the smoke cleared, fortunately no-one had been killed.

Auguste Valiant, one of the injured people, confessed to the police in hospital that he had been the individual who had thrown the bomb. It seemed that when he was a baby he had been abandoned by his parents and after growing up, had moved from one ill-paid job to another. He had borrowed money to make the bomb and filled it with iron scraps so that he would not kill anybody. Nevertheless, he was sentenced to death, despite representation from a clever lawyer. This caused much public indignation and demonstrations were held but they were all to no avail.

"In spite of what he did," I said. "He didn't kill anyone so I don't think he should die. Life imprisonment might have been a better sentence."

The Colonel shook his head. "No, he deserves to die. I might watch the execution."

I shuddered with distaste.

"An unpleasant subject I know but a necessary thing. You don't have the stomach for it, do you?"

I made no reply.

When I asked Susanne if I could stay with her for Christmas, she was delighted. To my amazement, my father sent me a note asking me to stay with him and my family.

My reply was:

Dear Papa

I am surprised yet grateful by this invitation of yours to spend Christmas with you all. However, Susanne has already invited me to spend the season with her. I have accepted her invitation and know she will be disappointed if I now turn it down.

But I should like to visit you during the daytime on Christmas Eve and during the New Year. Hope you all enjoy the season.

With love from
Isabelle

Papa replied, saying yes, although they would miss my company over the holiday, they would be pleased to see me on Christmas Eve.

Bet Madame Charpentier won't care if I'm not with them, I thought.

"I won't be able to see you over Christmas for two weeks," I said to the Colonel.

Saugez frowned. "That's disappointing but I'll bear it. Changing the subject ..."

I sighed, knowing what was coming.

"Why don't you take my advice and leave the Folies, Isabelle? It's not now essential for you to be employed."

"I'd suffer from ennui if I left. I could have a rest but I'd regret it later."

"I'll change your mind one day."

"No, you won't," I answered, irritated. The Colonel had a possessive streak. He always hated me talking about Leon. It annoyed me because what sort of rival was a dead man? It hardly made sense to envy the deceased.

I spent a quiet yet happy and peaceful Christmas with Susanne. "I've loved my time here," I said to her afterwards. "Please don't refuse it."

I handed her an envelope. Her mouth fell open after she had opened it and counted the money notes inside it.

"Can't possibly take this much from you, Isabelle," she protested.

"Yes, you can," I stated firmly. "I'll be offended if you don't."

She beamed. "In that case, all I can say is thank you very much."

I took my other gifts, a leather-bound book for Papa, a muff for Madame Charpentier and pretty dresses for my sisters to my father's house.

Everyone was civil to me, even my stepmother. They gave me presents of trinkets and jewellery although I had more than enough of these already, it would have been churlish not to have shown pleasure when I received them.

Madame Charpentier's married daughter and her husband were also visiting. They were quiet and unobtrusive.

In an unguarded moment Papa said. "You seem a little withdrawn, Isabelle. Are you happy with your life now? I couldn't help wondering about this."

I nodded. "Oh yes, Papa, I am," I tried to reassure him almost too eagerly.

He scrutinised my face. "Don't overtire yourself. Let me know if you're ever in need of assistance and I'll do what I can for you."

There was an unwelcome lump in my throat. "Thank you."

When I returned to my own house, I had a much deeper feeling of contentment than I had experienced for many months. Maybe a change of surroundings had once again refreshed me both in mind and body.

I looked around at all my possessions, resolving that in future I would try to be more amenable to the Colonel. He'd been generous to me, after all. It was hardly his fault he was no longer young and handsome. It was true he had some slightly odd tastes but I didn't find them unbearable. It was, I decided, a small enough price to pay for the comforts I received in return.

CHAPTER TWENTY-SIX

Colonel Saugez had sent me a note to inform me of his arrival one winter's afternoon even though there was snow on the ground that could have delayed him. It was not inconvenient for me so I didn't try to put him off.

I dressed with more care than usual in a white velvet dress, trimmed with coffee coloured hand-made lace at the collar and cuffs and tied a ribbon in my hair.

Marie had been assisting me. "You look lovely, Madame," she said.

As the Colonel entered the room, he looked at me approvingly. "My dear," he said. "It's such a pleasure to see you again. I've been so looking forward to seeing you come back."

He gave me a chaste kiss on the cheek.

"It was pleasant for me to see Susanne as well as my family once more. How is your wife, Christian? Well, I hope."

"She is and also in excellent spirits."

"Good, I'm glad to hear it."

"You're looking pretty but a little pale, I fear. Is it the dancing that's caused it, do you think?"

"No, it's certainly not that!" I said, a little too sharply.

"If you're fatigued, you'd feel better in bed, wouldn't you?"

"Didn't say I was tired. Let's have a drink together. I'll ask Marie to bring us a glass of wine each."

From the Colonel's point of view, the drink had the desired effect upon me. I allowed myself to be led into the bedroom where Saugez began to undress me slowly. For a moment I felt a shiver of repulsion stir within me but managed to suppress it. I had begun to almost dislike myself for having an affair with an older, married man who I didn't even especially like but I tried to suppress it, often wondering what would be a satisfactory alternative.

I became aware of the Colonel's hands exploring my body. I closed my eyes feigning sleep that became a reality.

When I awoke a short while later, Saugez offered me another glass of my own wine. Annoyed, I could easily see that he had sent for another bottle.

"How did you get that, Christian?" I asked, pointing to it.

"I sent your maid to fetch some more."

"Don't you think it's a liberty for you to give her orders? She's my servant."

The man looked annoyed. "If it were not for me, my dear Mademoiselle Lefevre, do you honestly believe you could pay her such high wages? Evan an old fool like myself who throws away francs on you, can see she's happy in your service. I merely thought you might like some refreshment after your sleep."

I was a little mollified, knowing his words were true and apologized, for my bad temper.

"Were you tired because you'd been entertaining another lover before I came to see you?"

The hot, angry, colour flooded into my face. "I do *not* behave like your wife," I retorted, immediately regretting what I had said.

He gripped my wrists, hurting me, there was a look of jealous fury in his face. With an effort I stifled a cry of pain as he demanded in a voice of thunder, "Just what do you mean by that?"

"Can't you work it out for yourself?

"I demand to know what you mean." By now, he was shouting loudly.

"Lower your voice for Heaven's sake and let go of my poor wrists. Then I might tell you."

Saugez loosened his hold and spoke in a quieter tone. "Now, will you tell me?"

"No idea whether they're true or not but I have heard rumours concerning your wife and a certain male person. Let's just drop the subject because I might be naming somebody who's completely innocent."

He glowered. "If you keep insisting on obstinately refusing to tell me, I'll be able to find out from another source, I'll make every effort to do so."

"Please, must we quarrel over an impulsive remark I now regret making? You anger me when you talk of me taking lovers. Where would I find the time? As you know, I work long hours. I love dancing as much as you love riding. And sometimes, I need a change from these four walls even though they're filled with luxuries. I'm truly grateful you've provided me with these belongings. But you never seem to take me out nowadays."

The Colonel sighed. "I'll take you to see one of the operettas you like."

"Thank you, I'll look forward to that."

"Isabelle, there is an act you perform well. Do you think you could oblige me now?"

He turned over and I raked my nails down his back, digging them in hard. Revenge felt sweet after the way he had hurt me.

On his next visit Christian Saugez brought me another present. It was a beautiful, flowered hat. I tried it on and looked at myself in the mirror.

"That suits you, Madame," Marie said. I could tell she had admired it.

"Pleased to know that, Marie. When I buy another one later though I don't know when that will be yet, you can have it."

She looked pleased. "Thank you, madame."

CHAPTER TWENTY-SEVEN

When I next visited Victor's studio on a cold day, I was determined this would be the last time because my heart was sinking at the prospect that lay before me. The subject matter was entitled "The Maid Takes a Bath" This didn't surprise me because it was one of the Colonel's favourite themes. What did surprise me was seeing a stranger with Victor.

He was young, tall, and seemed to be dressed in foreign looking clothes. He smiled at me in a pleasant way. I was conscious of a flush spreading through my body. I wasn't particularly embarrassed in front of Flauret and the Colonel as I was used to their gazes by now. My usual feeling of self-loathing, however, intensified in front of a stranger probably also a foreigner.

Then I gave a mental shrug. After all, I had to continue with this unpleasant form of play acting. I had given my word to do so. I looked down at the floor as I hurriedly prepared myself.

When I was ready, both younger men took photographs of me, I found this an ordeal. After the session was over, Flauret introduced the newcomer. "This gentleman is Alan Fergusson from Edinburgh, Isabelle."

Alan was tall and slim with chestnut coloured hair and grey eyes. Not quite a handsome man, I thought he had a pleasant face.

"Pleased to make your acquaintance, Mademoiselle," he said. He had a deep voice, speaking in fluent yet accented French.

He studied my face for a little while. "You know, you're somewhat familiar to me, let me think where I know you from."

Alan Fergusson pondered for a few more minutes, then he asked. "Might I have seen you dancing at the Folies Bergere?"

"Yes, I do work there, Monsieur."

Out of the corner of my eye, I saw Colonel Saugez scowling slightly.

"If that's the case, Mademoiselle," Fergusson added. "Could I ask you to do me a big favour?"

I smiled. "That depends on what it is, Monsieur."

"It's somewhat forward of me when I don't know you very well yet. But I should feel honoured if you would dance for us all now and I could take photographs of you while you're doing so."

My surprise seemed to show on my face because Alan next said. "Maybe you don't want to dance at present. Please forgive my impulsiveness, it's just that I've always enjoyed watching you dance. You're always lively."

I was pleased by this compliment. Glancing quickly at the Colonel, I saw that his scowl had deepened.

Smiling again, I said to Alan. "I shall be delighted to dance for you."

I performed a restrained version of the can-can as if I were once again at Jeanne Saugez's salon. As I began to dance, I felt my earlier depression lifting. Finally, I curtsied, not looking at Saugez. I was thrilled to see that both Victor and his new friend had been thoroughly entertained. They were both applauding enthusiastically.

Alan came forward, beaming. "Thank you so much, Mademoiselle."

"You were very good," Victor said.

"I'm afraid I have an urgent appointment," Saugez snapped. "So, Isabelle and I must go now." Much to my annoyance he ushered me out of the house. I was vaguely aware of Alan running his hand through his hair as we left.

"What's this urgent appointment I know nothing about?" I protested once we were outside

Ignoring my question, the Colonel said, "Didn't like to see you making an exhibition of yourself, particularly in front of a stranger and a foreigner at that!"

"You didn't object to me dancing at your wife's salon in front of strangers."

"That was an entirely different matter. Nobody there took photographs of you and performing to a mixed company wasn't the same as being in a confined room with three males watching you."

"It was your idea for me to be photographed in the first place. I'll certainly not be taking part in another one of these sessions."

"Don't mean to be angry with you, Isabelle, honestly. I just hate the idea of a foreigner looking intently at your body."

I frowned "I see. So, you and Victor Flauret are the only ones allowed to do that, then?"

To my surprise, the Colonel changed the subject. "How would you like to go to the Opera Comique?"

Taken aback, I said, "I don't really think it's to your taste."

He smiled. "It's not really but I can stand it for one evening."

"You might even enjoy it."

Saugez smiled, ruefully. "That's doubtful. I prefer more serious music."

We did both enjoy the operetta. After the first act had finished, the Colonel had a good look around the auditorium to see if he recognised anyone he knew. His gaze seemed to linger for a while in a particular direction. He seemed angry. His face was turning alternately from red to white. He had a coughing fit which alarmed me as I feared he might choke.

I put my hand on his arm. "Are you ill, would you like to leave now?"

"No, we'll stay till the final curtain." I was relieved that his coughing had now ceased but felt too tense to fully appreciate the rest of the performance.

As we rose to leave, I immediately became aware of Saugez's annoyance and discomfort. A few yards ahead of us, Victor Flauret and Louise Saugez were leaving the theatre together, their arms linked and laughing together at some private joke of their own.

CHAPTER TWENTY-EIGHT

Colonel Saugez hurried me into the street. Due to his rushing to get out of the theatre, he was red-faced and out of breath. He was practically dragging me after him.

I half slipped. "You could have helped me," I protested. "I nearly fell over then."

He ignored my remark. Crowds of people were milling around but there was no sign of Jeanne Saugez and her lover. I overheard the Colonel swear under his breath.

"Why are you so anxious to find them?" I asked. "Didn't you really know what was going on behind your back?" I had thought this affair was common knowledge to a lot of people.

He shook his white head. "Never thought Jeanne would stoop to this. My wife has failed me, made me look a fool. Not even with a stranger, with a man who's been a guest at my house. How *could* she? All of this must have been going on under my very nose. She's no better than a whore!"

Saugez's face by now had almost turned purple.

"But how do you think she'd feel if she knew about *us*? I've danced at her salons so I'm not a stranger to her. You visit me at my flat whenever you can and I don't like some of the things you expect me to do. Yet, all you can see is that she's doing wrong. Doubt she imagines all *your* pleasures are completely innocent."

He was offended. "That's another matter entirely. I've provided well for her as I also have for you, I might add and this is the shameful way I've been repaid."

"Your association with me, don't you think that would be equally offensive to *her*?"

Saugez shook his head. "That's different! A man has appetites a woman doesn't share. At least, not a lady, it's a separate thing."

I was annoyed now. "So, what you're implying is that I'm *not* a lady?

"You're a dancer at the Folies-Bergere. Anyway, your background is different from Jeanne's."

Angered by his contemptuous tone, I demanded. "And what is wrong with my background?"

"Jeanne's is different, that's what I meant, Isabelle. Louise appeared suited to me in every way with her refinement and knowledge of social graces. And now she's failed me!"

"You snobbish old fool!" I shouted out loud, unable to hide the contempt I now felt for him.

"How dare you call me such a thing in public?"

"It's true what I said. You're a silly hypocrite who believes money plus all the benefits it brings should buy a woman's loyalty. You've given me gifts and enabled me to live in comfort, I admit. You've often been generous to me. But all you really consider me to be really, is a common prostitute even if not exactly a streetwalker. You believe I'm just around to give you pleasure in repayment for your presents and all the rest."

I paused for breath but my tirade was not quite finished. The Colonel looked stunned.

"Your dear wife," I continued. "Who you believed adorned your home dutifully has proved to be no better than myself. A common dancer from the Folies as you saw me yet I never deceived you at all despite being able to do so."

"But your precious wife *has* been unfaithful to you with an acquaintance of yours. You certainly won't like looking a fool in front of your friends, will you?"

Beside himself with rage, Saugez gave me a sharp slap across the face that brought tears to my eyes.

"How dare you speak about Jeanne like that?" he yelled.

"I was telling you the truth and you didn't like hearing it."

His enraged features were still imprinted on my mind as I turned around, running swiftly into the nearest crowd. Blinking my tears away, running as fast as I possibly could.

A few people stared after me but I didn't care. Eventually, I had to stop as there was a nasty pain in my side. Pausing for a few moments, I found a handkerchief to dab at my eyes. The Colonel was nowhere in sight, much to my relief.

I mentally willed myself to calm down as much as possible, realising that I had been unconsciously running in the direction of Susanne's house.

She was shocked by my dishevelled appearance. She looked me up and down. "Whatever's happened to you, Isabelle?"

"There was a disturbance at the Folies," I lied. "It didn't involve me personally but I was glad to get away from there."

"You're welcome to stay with me overnight rather than going through the streets on your own without an escort."

My relief probably showed on my face. "Thank you, I'd like to do that."

"Right then, we'll have a glass of wine and some soup and bread afterwards."

"What a lovely idea/"

I went to bed early, sleeping more soundly than I had imagined I would.

The following morning, Susanne said. "I did like that hat you wore yesterday, Isabelle." I had been wearing the flowered one but intended to give it to Marie soon.

"Would you mind if I copy the design so that I can try to sell similar ones myself?" Susanne asked.

I shook my head. "Shan't mind at all. In fact, I hope you'll be able to sell a lot of them."

"It will be thanks to you if I do manage that."

I smiled. "You're a dear old friend, Susanne. I'm happy if I've done you a small favour."

"Not as small as all that, Isabelle."

I smiled again

CHAPTER TWENTY-NINE

I reluctantly returned to my house in a calmer frame of mind although knowing that I would soon have to search for a different place to live. I was determined to be optimistic about this but understood that I would probably have to give up most of the luxuries that I had formerly been taking for granted.

I had to let most of my servants go although I did my best to ensure they were placed with other employers. I now only had Marie and a younger girl who helped her with the cooking.

My contemplation of the future was interrupted early one morning when Marie appeared in my bedroom after knocking on the door.

"Madame, sorry to disturb you. But Madame Saugez is downstairs. Says she desperately needs to see you."

I sighed, reluctantly. "Tell her I'll be down soon. Then come back up here and help me get ready."

"Yes, Madame."

When I saw Jeanne Saugez, I could see she was flustered and distraught. She took hold of both of my hands, gripping them tightly. She wasn't weeping but her eyes had tell-tale red rims

She hardly paused for breath. "My dear, you must help me because I'm sure my husband has turned into a madman?"

My tone was cold. "Excuse me, Madame but I have no wish to see your husband again."

Jeanne made a dismissive gesture. "Understand that, honestly, I do. However, you *must* help try to prevent a tragedy. An accident's bound to happen, even worse there could be a death. I would never forgive myself if either of these things happened."

I sighed. "Please, Madame, why are you being so melodramatic? What exactly is happening? I would appreciate you explaining it clearly."

"I knew my husband was with you when he saw me with Victor Flauret. I thought you knew about us but he's not always observant especially where I'm concerned. My husband's pride has been badly wounded by our affair. His pride means a lot to him, you know."

I nodded in contemptuous agreement.

"Victor means everything to me. He's the whole world to me. But my husband has called him out, challenged him to a duel."

I managed to stop myself saying it was the sort of stupid thing the Colonel would do. I knew that duels were now illegal and supposedly old fashioned but many still did take place. Being considered to be a man who avenged his honour would be important to Saugez.

"That *your* pride might have been offended by his affair with me didn't occur to him then?"

I knew I was being slightly malicious and didn't like myself for it.

Jeanne shrugged. "Oh, he's like most men, views our actions in a different light. Come on please, we're wasting time talking. We must hurry to the Bois."

"Just a minute, Madame. What influence do I have over the Colonel to prevent bloodshed? Surely, you're the one who should be pleading on your lover's behalf."

She flushed. "Christian will hardly listen to me when I have hurt his pride so. The two of you may have had your quarrels but I do know he thinks quite a lot of you."

I almost snorted. "Doubt that, now. Didn't realise you and he discussed me in quite so much detail, Madame Saugez."

"Maybe I shouldn't have spoken so freely. However, I'll be in your debt all my days if you do me this favour. Are you going to come with me or not?"

I could see that she had become more agitated. I sighed. "Don't really believe my presence will be all *that* useful. But I wouldn't like to hear of Victor Flauret's death or wounding. As for your dear husband thinking a lot of me, he struck me the other night because he didn't like something I said."

I hesitated for a few minutes before making my decision. "However, I'll come with you even though I doubt I'll be able to do anything useful."

A look of relief passed over her face as she squeezed my hand in gratitude so hard that it hurt. I pulled it free.

"I'm truly sorry my husband hit you," she said. "He must have been beside himself."

"He was, no doubt about it. But come on, we'd better hurry up."

Our carriage raced to the Bois de Boulogne where we dismounted as swiftly as possible although impeded by our long skirts. Then we both picked up our skirts and ran as fast as we could.

I was amazed to see that Alan Fergusson was one of Victor Flauret's seconds. He looked both disgusted and dismayed. He gave a visible start when he recognised me.

The two duellists were on the point of taking aim with their pistols. I ran towards them with the stupid intention of trying to place myself between them. But Jeanne had beaten me to it! She had rushed past me towards them. And had managed to knock both of their arms with a force that I would never have guessed that she possessed. The guns fired harmlessly into the air as the duellists stared up at them in astonishment.

I held my breath in horrified fascination. Jeanne was very pale although I wasn't close enough to hear what she was saying, I knew she was making an impassioned speech.

Feeling sick as blackness surrounded me, I sank to the ground. The next thing I was aware of as I began to recover from my faint was Jeanne holding smelling salts under my nose.

A small crowd had gathered around me, some of whom I had never seen before. A short distance away, the Colonel and Flauret stood. I glanced in their direction, neither of them appeared to be hurt, not even slightly. They were too far away for me to see their expressions but I guessed they were probably both shame-faced. I looked away from them. I was embarrassed, feeling that Jeanne had been brave whilst I had been a coward.

"Are you quite recovered, Mademoiselle?" the doctor who had been present to attend to the would-be duellists asked, as he was helping me to my feet. I knew the colour was returning to my face. "Will you need further treatment, do you think?"

"I'm feeling better now, thank you for your help. I'm grateful for your assistance," I managed to say I although I was still shaken to my core.

The doctor nodded and walked away, relieved. I turned to Jeanne. "I'm afraid my presence was useless. I did nothing to help you, you assisted me instead."

"It was the least I could do after your agreement to come here with me."

"You've been both brave and kind. But I wish to go home now."

Jeanne nodded and walked away, as she passed by, I could see some of the men giving her admiring looks. My cheeks turned crimson with renewed shame at my own timidity.

The rest of the crowd began to drift away.

There was one man, however, who had been watching me, not Jeanne. This was Alan Fergusson who strode up to me. "Are you well?" he asked. "I'm afraid this is no place for a lady. Please allow me to escort you home. I know you'll feel better away from this stupid scene."

Without waiting for an answer, he offered me his arm. I took it, deriving a certain amount of comfort from his gesture.

"I'm so ashamed," I said, having a need to confide in someone even a person I hardly knew and a foreigner. "Madame Saugez was courageous while I was such a coward."

He shook his head. "No, you weren't. Yes, Madame Saugez was brave but she had much more to lose than you. You were kind enough to accompany her. I reluctantly became involved in this ridiculous event myself. I thought the duellists looked like a pair of statues. Enjoyed seeing that."

Alan gave a school boyish grin that I found engaging. He handed me into his carriage after I had told him where I lived.

"It would be a change to talk about something more pleasant that what happened today. Have you ever been to Scotland?"

I shook my head. "No, nor to England."

Alan smiled. "Nor to Wales or Ireland either I expect. Well, perhaps one day. We're not such eager duellists over there."

He grinned and I smiled back.

When we arrived at my house, he didn't ask to come in. However, he said. "Do I have your permission to visit you?"

Feeling weary of the male sex, I tried to evade his question. "I'm afraid I have a lot of private matters to attend to."

Alan looked disappointed so I softened. "You can leave your visiting card at the beginning of next month if you like."

He looked a little more cheerful as he took his leave of me but I doubted that I would hear from him again.

Once I was indoors, I said, "Marie, will you make me a tisane? I'm going to bed afterwards, don't disturb me again until early this evening."

She gave me a questioning look. "Tired, Madame?"

"Very and ..." I shrugged my shoulders. "Oh, never mind."

"I'll make your tisane now," Marie said, instinctively knowing I wasn't in the mood for further questions.

"Thank you."

After I had finished my drink and gone to bed, I fell asleep almost as soon as my head touched the pillow. I had vivid dreams of a strange land full of cities, mountains, and streams that I did not recognise.

CHAPTER THIRTY

For the next few weeks, I lived quietly. I continued to dance at the Folies Bergere but declined all invitations from admirers. I sensed a change was in the air but didn't yet know the direction in which it would take place.

One cold and rainy day, unexpectedly, the Colonel called in the hope of seeing me. "Send him away with a flea in his ear, Marie," I ordered. "Tell him I never ever wish to see him in my life again. After the way he's humiliated me, he's got a nerve!"

She went out to speak to him again but when she came back, she said, "He's gone, Madame."

"Good, I'm glad to hear it."

"But he was in a real rage."

I was alarmed. "He didn't threaten you, did he?"

Marie shook her head. "No, just gave me a filthy look and went away, swearing."

"Good riddance. We don't want his sort, do we?"

"No, Madame, I agree we don't."

I didn't care about the Colonel leaving in a bad temper but neither did I wish him to become a nuisance by repeatedly trying to call upon me. He was the sort of man who might believe I was feigning dislike due to my hurt pride

Much to my surprise, I received a note from Alan Fergusson later that week. It surprised me. It read:

"Dear Mademoiselle Lefevre
Hope you are in good health and have recovered from the unfortunate incident you were forced to witness."

I privately thought this comment was a slight exaggeration but was touched that Alan had enquired after my health.

The note continued: "I've heard from mutual friends that you're still working. I've been very busy myself lately but I do hope to watch one of your performances soon. I'd love to visit you soon with your permission of course. I'll leave a visiting card for you."

A beautifully decorated visiting card of a kind I had never seen before was duly deposited at my house. I took the bull by the horns to send a reply to Alan, inviting him to dine with me. He accepted my invitation with another note, saying he looked forward to seeing me again.

"What brought you to Paris?" I asked Alan on the appointed cool autumn evening, as I put my soup spoon down.

He smiled. "My father's business published little books of small picture cards and when I grew up, he took me into partnership with him. I've been travelling on the Continent but I shall soon have to go home because my poor father died recently. I mean to make the most of the time I have left here."

As we started on the fish course, I expressed my sympathy. "Expect your mother took it badly."

"My mother died years ago." His tone was blunt.

"So did mine. But I still have my father and sisters. So, I'm fortunate in that I suppose."

"I was an only child, my mother died giving birth to me and my father unusually, never remarried."

Not wishing our conversation to become gloomy, I changed the subject. "Is your business flourishing? Hope it is."

"Yes, it is, thank you. A lot of people buy our cards to keep as souvenirs for their scrap albums. We had enormous sales with our postcards of Marie Studholme, the English actress and singer, well known in musical comedy. Naturally, I was delighted by this although I really prefer the beauty spot cards to castles and royalty."

"Did this actress have royal connections?"

Alan laughed. "Only indirectly. She took the leading part in 'A Gaiety Girl,' a story about an aristocrat and a gaiety actress at the Prince of Wales Theatre in London. The Gaiety Theatre was designed on similar lines to your Theatre Lyrique."

"That's interesting."

"My family and I lived at a place called Leith when I was young. It's a seaport. I used to like to watch the arrivals and departures of the merchants' ships. A lot of the merchants used to sit in leather armchairs with decanters of whisky. Our house

was really in Royal Terrace but it was nicknamed 'Whisky Row.'"
He grinned. "We didn't all get drunk all the time, though."

By the time Marie had brought in the chicken, I had eaten enough food and drank enough wine to feel mellow to be relaxed enough to ask Alan. "What made you go to Victor Flauret's studio?"

I was still embarrassed by the fact that I had met him there but was also curious about the reason for his presence.

"I'm particularly interested in new developments in photography. Especially when the subject is pretty young ladies.

I blushed slightly as I looked down at the table.

"But I don't think I'll ever be brave enough to take those kinds of photographs, myself, mind. Victor just raised my curiosity.

"If I may ask, where did you meet him?"

"You don't like him very much, do you?"

I hesitated. "He's not my favourite person."

"Can understand that. I met Victor when I came to France from Germany. I found lodgings in the Latin Quarter and mixed mostly with other foreigners. One of them introduced me to Victor at a café. Victor showed me some of his paintings and told me he was becoming more interested in photography than drawing and painting."

"That's believable," I said, dryly.

"Victor was interested in my father's cards particularly the ones of Marie Studholme. He told me I was free to visit his studio at any time. On my first visit not long after he'd acquired the premises, there were just a few mothers with children and some actors. Then, I saw you not long afterwards. By far the most interesting subject."

He smiled again and I returned it, pleased by the compliment.

"If you don't mind me saying so, please don't take offence. I thought you were like a clockwork doll suddenly injected with life and energy when you danced for us."

"Didn't you like my dancing then?" I asked, a little stiffly.

He shook his head. "On the contrary, I loved it. Sorry if I were too direct. I also thought you had such delicate features that you might turn into a fragile piece of china, afterwards. It was a relief to me that you didn't."

"I'm glad I didn't too," I said, a little dryly.

"No offence meant, honestly. I was persuaded to become Victor's second in that ridiculous duel, much against my will. But I'm sure you don't wish to be reminded of it. It was maybe insensitive of me to mention it."

"No, not really but II must admit I don't want to talk about it now."

"I'm sorry I did. Didn't want to distress you."

"It doesn't matter."

Alan kissed my hand. "Thank you for the delicious dinner, I said."

"You were welcome. May I contact you again before I return to Edinburgh?"

"Yes."

He grinned. "I'm glad, thank you."

Alan had not attempted to take any liberties with me for which I was grateful. But I wondered if he might just be biding his time. He had, after all, seen me in various stages of undress in the studio. The memory made me blush even though I was, by now, hardly a naïve young girl, innocent in the ways of the world. With an effort, I managed to suppress the memory of our first meeting.

I worried that the Colonel might try to take my house away from me but no news came of it, much to my relief.

Alan regularly kept in touch with me. When the weather permitted, we took a picnic to Versailles or drove to a quiet square of trees, sitting quietly on a bench. We went to the Vert Galant; I liked this spot with its green trees and view of the Seine with the Louvre on the right bank.

"It's romantic here," Alan said. encompassing the scene with a wave of his hand. Occasionally, he took me to supper after watching my performance at the Folies. He had still made no attempt to touch me apart from polite kisses on my hand.

I had begun to feel content in his company and was sorry that he would be leaving soon as I knew I would miss him.

CHAPTER THIRTY-ONE

Some British people had seemed arrogant to me. Probably because they had an Empire. They were not unique in this, other European countries had them too but theirs was so large.

Alan Fergusson had patriotic feelings about his homeland. He said to me one day. "I love my country like most of my fellow countrymen. If you met one of us who didn't sing Scotland's praises, he'd be of mixed blood. I like my hometown too, most of the time, anyway."

He had grinned after he'd said this.

One cool evening, I gave in to the impulse to confess the whole story of my former life to him. Alan didn't appear to be shocked.

"Do you still like me now?" I couldn't help asking him, feeling that I would not entirely have blamed him if he did not.

He shook his head. "Of course, I do. Why would you believe I wouldn't?"

"You could have thought I've sometimes behaved a little, well ..." I hesitated. "Scandalously."

Alan shook his head. "No, I didn't, as I see it, it was just your circumstances. It's all in the past now, anyway."

I was grateful for his understanding.

Alan took me to our favourite restaurant one evening after the Folies. It was not the Café Anglais. It was a small, family-run place where the waiters were discreet. I liked its intimacy.

Alan seemed restless, he kept gazing down at the table and tapping his fingers on his wine glass. I wondered if he wished to sleep with me before he returned to his own country but could not quite summon the courage to ask me. He seemed a little distracted, gazing around the room.

Alan cleared his throat. "I've really enjoyed our times together, Isabelle."

I couldn't help wondering if he wished to break off our relationship. Aloud, I said. "So have I, I know I'll miss you when you leave."

118

"Yes, well, maybe you'll not miss me... that is to say ..."

I wondered why Alan was stuttering.

His next words came out in a rush. "What about if we were married and you came back with me to Scotland?"

Astonished and dumbfounded, not quite believing I had heard him aright, I stared at him, unsure if I had been dreaming. Alan's expression was pleading so I snapped myself out of my reverie.

"Are you asking me to ... did you mean you wish me to...?" I was stammering slightly myself, now.

Alan grinned. "Become my wife, yes exactly that. It's a bit sudden I know but I'm tired of being a lonely bachelor. It's time I settled down with a wife and family to care for."

"Are you sure you want to go ahead with this? Considering what you know about me?"

My hand was lying palm down on the table. He laid his own over it. "I've swallowed up your delicate little hand with my own big, ugly one. Look, your past means nothing to me now even though you've been honest about it. It's over and done with. It's your future I'm concerned about as I wish you to share it with me. I do understand that you might want to think it over first, though."

"Yes, I'll certainly consider it," I said, demurely, looking down at the table. Then, I looked up, smiling. "I'll try not to keep you waiting too long before I give you, my answer."

He winked at me. "Thought you might enjoy a rest from being photographed."

I smiled. "It could become a bit tiring." My expression was demure. "I prefer dancing."

Alan laughed and took me home. At my front door he kissed me full on the lips for the first time but didn't attempt to come indoors with me. He walked away, whistling a popular tune.

You sound confident, I thought. I wasn't quite sure that I was in love with Alan but I did like him a lot and knew that I enjoyed his company. If I went abroad to live, I would be a respectable married woman and no-one except him would know of my past. I still loved dancing but I could hardly remain in that occupation for the whole of the rest of my life. If I married

Alan, I reflected, I would no longer have to worry about Colonel Saugez's removing my house from my possession.

"Marie," I said, needing someone to talk to, "Will you make us both a cup of coffee for us both? Need to talk to you."

She looked alarmed. "Do you wish me to leave, Madame?"

I shook my head. "No, it's not that, not exactly. I'll explain when we have our drink."

After explaining Alan's surprise proposal to me, I said. "If I decide to accept his offer, I'll be willing to ask him if you can come with us."

Marie looked a little sad. "It's kind of you, Madame but I really wouldn't want to do that. My family are here and I wouldn't want to leave them."

I nodded. "I accept that, you've been a great help and comfort to me that I've much appreciated and I'll be sorry to lose you. But I'll help you look for a new place and give you a great reference."

"Thank you, Madame, I believe you will marry him and be happy."

On the following day I went to see Susanne.

"I know I've never met this Alan," she said. "However, I have a feeling you ought to wed him. I've felt for a while I'd like to see you settled down although it's none of my business really."

"I'm not offended, Susanne."

"Good, I'll make you a special new hat to go away in."

I laughed. "I'll look forward to seeing it."

The visit I dreaded most was to my family. But Papa looked delighted. I had wondered if he might not have liked me marrying a foreigner.

"Your future husband's a businessman, then," he said.

"Only on a modest scale," I corrected.

"I'll give you a settlement," Papa said. "My promise to you."

I was taken aback. "No, I don't expect that, Papa."

"I insist, you'll upset me if you don't accept it."

120

"Well in that case, thank you very much." I was almost overwhelmed with the gratitude I was feeling towards him.

Madame Charpentier sniffed and said "All things considered, you've ended up doing quite well for yourself, Isabelle."

"Yes, I have," I replied, bestowing my sweetest smile on her. We exchanged glances but mine held the longest until she looked away.

Both of my sisters were thrilled. I half expected Eloise to feel resentful that I would probably be a married woman before she was but she gave no sign of this. I imagined she was most likely imagining how lovely she would look in her new bridesmaid's dress, maybe even eclipsing the bride.

"Sure, it'll be a wonderful day," she said, confidently.

"Hope the sun shines all day," Colette said.

I smiled at her. "Be delightful if it does."

"I'd want it to on my day."

I laughed. "That's a long way off yet, cherie."

After taking a far more affectionate leave of my family than usual, I sent a note to Alan informing him I had decided to accept his generous offer, hoping, and praying he hadn't had second thoughts and changed his mind.

I opened his return letter with trembling fingers. To my huge relief, he said he was delighted by my acceptance of his proposal.

We set our wedding date as early as we possibly could as neither of us wished to marry in a cold winter month.

I helped Marie find a new position as a lady's maid to the daughter of a musician I knew. There were tears from both of us when we finally parted. The younger girl became a kitchen maid for a businessman who I knew slightly. He had many interests in the theatrical world.

Now I had a lot of preparations of my own to make for my forthcoming wedding.

CHAPTER THIRTY-TWO

Our wedding day was a quiet one. Alan looked handsome in a cream-coloured shirt and grey trousers covered by a cream silk waistcoat with a red necktie. Susanne and I had worked furiously for four afternoons, sewing my white satin dress and veil. I carried a bouquet of mixed flowers. My sisters both looked lovely in their lilac bridesmaids' dresses. They were excited.

My father was wearing a smart suit and Madame Charpentier, I had never been able to think of her as anything but this although my sisters had been taught to call her 'Maman,' wore a light pink dress with a matching hat.

The other guests were Madame Charpentier's quiet married daughter and her husband, Susanne, and Marie whose new employer had allowed her to attend.

I had taken Alan to my father's house only once before so that my family would at least be able to see him once before the ceremony.

"How did you think I did?" he had asked me afterwards.

"I'm sure you made a good impression on them all. You were well mannered and respectful. Think even Madame Charpentier liked you."

Alan grinned. "Not your favourite woman, is she?"

"Hardly. Had to force myself to be polite to her."

Alan had deliberately looked as if he were deep in thought. "Don't think you made too bad a job of it." He grinned.

The ceremony seemed to me to pass in almost a dream. Papa had given me an elegant purse. I was amazed when I counted the huge number of notes inside it. Alan also gave me an envelope in which a considerable sum of money was enclosed.

"How did you know about this custom?" I asked, intrigued.

He smiled. "Your papa told me about it. Didn't want to let the family down."

I returned his smile. "I'm grateful to you for that."

At the meal afterwards where my meagre trousseau was displayed, Alan whispered in my ear. "I'd have laughed at the expression of some British matrons' faces, the more strait-laced ones. They'd have been taken aback by your pink stockings I caught a naughty glimpse of." He looked almost like an errant schoolboy so I had to suppress a laugh, smiling instead.

More seriously, Alan said. "I'll buy you some new clothes when we reach London."

"Thank you, I like the new hat Susanne kindly made for me."

"I do, too. it's becoming. I like the little rosebuds on it."

"Do you, really? You're not just saying that to please me?"

"No, of course not."

We boarded our train to Boulogne at the Gard du Nord Railway Station. Papa's expression was a mixture of happiness and sadness at the same time. My sisters cried once more and Madame Charpentier looked relieved. Trust her, I thought privately although naturally keeping this opinion to myself. Her daughter and her husband, Susanne and Marie hadn't come to the station, feeling it was more suitable for only the immediate family to be present.

I kissed them all on the cheek, even giving a quick peck to my stepmother. At last, I had to blink my own tears back as the train began to slide out of the station. I gave a last farewell wave as the little group on the platform became smaller and smaller, finally disappearing altogether. I gave Alan a shaky smile as I sat down and he returned it in a sympathetic way.

He looked at me in a slightly worried way. "Not feeling homesick already, are you?"

I shook my head. "No, of course not."

Alan smiled. "Relieved to hear it."

At Boulogne we saw some interesting sights. There were sailors from warships who wore blue and white striped shirts with plunging necklines with red pom-poms on their berets. There were fisher-women in embroidered aprons and huge fan-shaped white coifs. Railway porters were dressed in faded blue smocks and rakish caps with leather peaks. There were two-horsed station buses and large trawlers and steamers from Russia, Norway, and Germany as well as fishing smacks.

"Lot of foreigners here, aren't there?" Alan said. They'll be taking the place over soon."

I knew he was joking but I also thought there was some truth in his words because Boulogne had become almost like an outpost of Britain.

We watched the boat excursions arriving from that country. I knew they were known locally as the '*Fleau de Dieu*' or 'Scourge of God.' The Britons came ashore for four hours and were delayed at the customs where they were searched for safety matches. They were entitled to one box only, if they possessed more, they were liable to a fine of ten centimes. We watched drunken casualties from the trip being taken back in wheelbarrows.

"Not very good ambassadors for Britain, are they?" Alan asked, his grey eyes twinkling.

Does it make you believe you're going to live with heathens?"

I smiled. "As long as you don't behave like this yourself, I shan't be worried."

He winked at me. "Drunkenness is not one of my vices but I refuse to tell you what they are. You'll have to wait to find out."

Knowing this was only banter, I spoke in the same vein. "Not really sure that I want to, not just yet, anyway."

He smiled and winked at me.

We crossed the Channel by paddle steamer, it wasn't very comfortable but I liked gazing out to sea.

To strangers I would have appeared to have a serene composure but there was an inner turmoil raging within me. I had no regrets apart from wishing my family weren't such a long way away. I couldn't help wondering what Fate had in store for me. Peace and plenty or unhappiness and uncertainty? I mentally chided myself for being foolish perhaps, it was, after all, too late now to turn the clock back.

Alan's face lit up at the first sight of Dover's white cliffs. I started to feel more excited myself as I realised that my new life as a respectable married woman was about to begin. It wasn't just a fantasy of mine.

CHAPTER THIRTY-THREE

From Dover we travelled by another train to London. All these journeys were making us feel a little weary. Nevertheless, I was interested in the highly polished brasses in Charing Cross Station. In Pall Mall we saw brightly lit clubs and the gentlemen in opera hats and cloaks strolling along the pavements. I gazed at the mansions in Piccadilly and Park Lane as well as the runners who valiantly kept up with the carriages.

"Wouldn't like to have their job," Alan said. "Couldn't run as fast as them so I'd lose it almost as soon as I'd started it."

I laughed. "Nor me."

We ate our dinner in a small hotel with mahogany furniture. Having a basic knowledge of English, I tried hard to listen to what the people around us were saying. With some, they spoke too quickly, with others I could just about manage to understand the main gist of their conversation. So, I said to Alan in French. "Will you converse with me in English from now on? I know some of it already but I'd like to improve. But if I get into difficulty with it, I'm sure you'll be good enough to help me."

He grinned. "Certainly, Madame but you wait till you hear some Scots dialect words, it'll seem as if you know three languages altogether."

We stayed at the hotel for two nights. As we were both too tired to make love the first night, we fell asleep in each other's arms. On the second day Alan took me shopping for some new clothes. He also bought a few for himself. "We can both feel elegant now," he said.

"Thank you for this," I remarked, after we had returned to the hotel with our packages. "I'm pleased with what you've given me. Very much so."

"Glad to hear it. Looking forward to seeing you wearing them."

We retired early that evening and were intimate on this evening. Alan was both affectionate and considerate as I had imagined he would be yet not lacking in a certain amount of passion.

The following cloudy morning, we embarked upon yet another train journey. I didn't dislike this form of travel but I couldn't help thinking I should be grateful not to see the inside of another carriage for a while. We spent some time gazing out of the window. Alan explained what some of the places we passed through were like. After I fell asleep for the second time, I awoke to discover him reading a newspaper.

"Some of the news is grim as usual," he said, putting the paper down after I had woken up.

At last, we reached our destination. Alighting at Waverley Station we were almost blown over completely, like straws in a great gust of wind.

"Expect you feel like a kite," Alan said.

"Can you translate the word 'kite' into French?"

Alan laughed and did so. I clutched at my hat that was in great danger of being removed from my head.

"We can take a stroll down Princes Street before we get a coach to my, sorry … it will be our house now."

I smiled in anticipation.

When we arrived in the Princes Street gardens I said, "Watching the people here is like watching a fashion parade."

My remark seemed to please him. Afterwards, we visited the Castle. "This is called the Royal Mile," Alan said. "What we call the New Town and the old are divided and linked by the Princes Street Gardens."

"We'd better get the coach for home, now," Alan said, after we had finished looking around the Castle.

I nodded in agreement. "This has been interesting but I'm ready to do that, see your.. er, I mean … our house."

He laughed. "That's right."

We mounted one of the coaches with their ladder method of boarding. "These sorts of coaches are called 'Four-in-hand,'" Alan said, as he assisted me into the vehicle.

The house was of a medium size, the drawing room consisted of a velvet covered horsehair sofa, two leather armchairs and a cabinet on top of which stood an aspidistra. There was also a sturdy walnut bookcase containing many volumes. There was an oak dining table. I decided that as soon as I had the opportunity, I would try to install a few more feminine touches.

"As you can see, it's not quite a palace perhaps," Alan said, almost apologetically. He smiled. "But welcome, anyway."

I looked around again. "I like it and I'm sure I shall continue to."

He seemed relieved.

Alan's old butler served us stewed trout and Coburg pudding before we went to bed. Our bedroom contained a double bed. The bedspread was attractively embroidered. There was a beech wardrobe and a small table near the bed with a lamp on top. Blue muslin curtains hung at the window.

Alan drew them together quickly before he put out the lamp just before the darkness enveloped us.

CHAPTER THIRTY-FOUR

Alan was concerned about his butler because the man who had been in his father's service for many years was now becoming almost doddery.

"Perhaps we'd do better with just a maid," I suggested.

"Aye but I'm afraid I can only afford one servant. She'd have to be a maid of all work."

"That's acceptable to me. After all, I had no servants at all when I lived with Susanne. I had to fend for myself although she helped me with some things."

"Think I'll give the old butler a pension. Should be enough to let him live in reasonable comfort."

The old man agreed to resign, happily accepting the sum he was offered. We found a young girl called Elspeth Turnbull to employ as our maid.

"She's pleasanter to look at than the old man was," Alan said, unable to suppress a grin. I wasn't offended by his words.

Alan took me to the Royal Park where I saw the lion shape of Arthur's Seat, Edinburgh's highest hill. We also went to the Assembly Rooms in Constitution Street and the Corn Exchange in Baltic Street. Alan took a lot of photographs for his business while we were out and about. I found Leith where we lived the most interesting part of the city although it was not officially part of it. I liked the antique houses and foreign looking streets.

We visited the fishing village of Newhaven where Alan photographed some of the fisher women. They came to Edinburgh to sell the oysters, mussels and other fish that had been caught overnight by their husbands and sons.

Alan wrinkled his nose. "Like them but they can smell a bit."

"Hardly surprising," I agreed.

"Glad you like the fishwives," Alan said to me.

I smiled. "Wouldn't like to be one, myself, though if I'm honest."

One mild day we went on a country excursion to Cramond. Alan photographed the seventeenth century church and the whitewashed houses in the streets. We had a drink in one of the inns that Alan told me was well known. He took another photograph of the minute harbour where the river Almond joined the Firth opposite Cramond Island where it was possible to walk at low tide. From there, we could see the Forth Railway Bridge with its half-moon battery in the castle that fired the daily one o'clock gun.

"They borrowed that idea from Paris," Alan said. "Does it make you feel homesick?"

I shook my head although I did have odd moments of homesickness but it was mainly because of missing my family.

We had a day at the seaside on Portobello Sands when the summer at last arrived. While we were strolling along the pier together, Alan took photographs of the children riding donkeys on the sands.

"We're too old for that," he said, indicating them. "I'd have paid for us to have a ride otherwise."

"I might have fallen off."

"Would have caught you if you had."

"Could we visit the concert hall at the end of this pier?"

"If you'd like to, aye."

I was pleased. We both enjoyed the performance and ate supper in the restaurant afterwards.

"D'ye miss your dancing?" Alan asked, while we were eating.

"No, not really, not now."

He seemed satisfied by my reply. "Thought you might want to go back home after living here for a while and the novelty of a new country had worn off."

I shook my head. "No, my place is here with you now."

Alan smiled, seeming pleased by my comment. He patted my hand. "Good, glad to hear it."

The following day we climbed the Pentland Hills, taking a picnic with us that Elspeth had prepared. Alan took photographs of the plain below us, between the hills and the sea. He also took pictures of the west volcanic rock that the Lothians rose into. This was crisscrossed by a lot of hills and tracks.

"Some of these are old cattle driving roads," Alan said.

I knew there was still a lot of my new country for me to see.

CHAPTER THIRTY-FIVE

An event occurred that changed both of Alan's and my own life although we didn't foresee it at the time. Due to efforts made in Parliament, the General Post Office allowed privately printed postcards of a special size to be produced.

Alan made some arrangements with a printing firm that had been recommended to him. He bought a bicycle and used it to visit various Government Departments, railway companies and industrialists so that he could obtain orders.

"All this exercise should make me very healthy," he said.

"Expect it will, I envy you."

Alan looked anxious. "You're not feeling ill, are you?"

"No, I was only joking."

"Glad to hear it."

At first, he wasn't too successful but after a while he became luckier and his business started to flourish. Eventually, he was able to open a large one-roomed office. As his business grew, his leisure hours decreased.

"It's a pity I can't spend as much time with you as I'd like," Alan said.

"Don't worry about me. I've also got things to do myself."

He kissed me. "I'm pleased you're being understanding."

While Alan was absent from home, I went on shopping expeditions with Elspeth and occasionally alone. I kept my promise to myself that I would add feminine touches to our house by buying patterned cushions, lace table cloths, tray cloths and brass flower vases.

For our bedroom, I bought new pillow slips, an embroidered cloth for the small table, a rug and a few ornaments.

"You haven't minded me buying all these things?" I asked Alan.

He shook his head. "Not at all, if it's made you happy."

"It has, definitely."

"Good, I think Elspeth should be allowed to get a few things for her own bedroom. I'll give her a bit of money for them."

She had been given the old butler's room.

"Thank ye, sir," she said, gratefully after Alan had given her the money for new items. I had a little difficulty at first in understanding Elspeth's accent but I gradually became used to it.

Occasionally, I visited the poor, especially those who were poor or in reduced circumstances, taking broth and fruit to them.

"It makes me sad to see the conditions some of them are living in," I said to Alan.

He nodded. "It is a shame but it ought to make you grateful for your own circumstances."

"I am."

Alan smiled. "As long as you don't suddenly sprout a halo and wings, I'll feel proud of you for what you're doing for those less fortunate."

The manager of a printing firm, whom Alan was acquainted with, invited us to a country house party. He lived at Duddington, set on the loch at the edge of Queen's Park.

"Think we should go to this party, Isa," Alan said.

At first, I had found this diminutive of my name strange but I had now grown accustomed to it.

I nodded. "I'm looking forward to it."

"I'll buy you a new dress for it."

I smiled. "Thank you."

Alan bought me a deep purple velvet dress with leg-of-mutton sleeves in a paler mauve brocade. I knew myself that it would set off my dark hair.

"It suits you, you look beautiful in it," Alan said, after I had tried it. "Of course," he added. "You're bonny enough when you wear other clothes."

I laughed. "Naturally, I am," I said, coyly.

In the evening when the party was being held, after the parlour maid had shown us into the house, Alan introduced ne to Mr Wilson, the owner and his wife, Lucy. "Your husband's a dark horse," Mr Wilson said. "Goes abroad and comes back married to a sweet belle of Paris."

It was flattering to be described like this although I merely smiled at the compliment.

We were offered a glass of champagne and little pastries called 'petites bouchees.' Then, we were introduced to other guests, some of whom Alan already knew but they were all new to me.

Mr Wilson gathered everyone together to show them an album featuring views from postcards, many of the photographs had been taken by Alan.

Afterwards, people chatted in groups and a few of the men present tried to flirt with me in a subtle sort of way. I glanced at Alan to see if he were offended by this but he seemed to be both flattered and mildly amused.

We sat down to a dinner of pheasant gitana as Mr Wilson liked shooting game. This was followed by Savoy cake. Later, we danced to a professional Hungarian orchestra that had been especially engaged for the occasion. Some of the men including Mr Wilson, complimented me upon my grace while dancing.

Alan gave me a discreet wink when no-one else was looking at us. He whispered to me. "I'll keep my promise, I won't let them know about the Moulin Rouge and Folies-Bergere."

I smothered a laugh behind my fan when I imagined what some of the reactions from the respectable matrons who were present if they were informed of my past. Some of them had a typically British disapproval of foreigners. I knew this even though they were all courteous to me, personally.

Before we left, the gentlemen played cards while the ladies watched. Alan won one hand and I could see he was pleased about this. He then decided we should leave and as I was also ready to do so, I didn't argue about it. Our host shook our hands as we left.

"You must visit us again soon," he said.

We thanked him for his hospitality.

"Pease keep in touch with us," Lucy Wilson said.

"What did you think of the Wilsons, Isa, my love?" Alan asked me on our way back home.

I hesitated. "I can see Mr Wilson's useful to you but he does seem to have a high opinion of himself.

"That's only natural. He has reasons enough. This party tonight must have cost him a fortune what with the extra servants he had to hire on top of everything else. And you looked as if you were enjoying yourself."

"I wasn't trying to say I didn't or to sound ungrateful to be invited. Just gave you my honest opinion about the gentleman's character. Anyway, I liked his wife. Thought she was friendly towards me."

"Did you believe the others were unfriendly? I noticed quite a lot of the men seemed to like you."

"Couldn't in all honesty say they weren't sociable. Merely felt some of them didn't like foreigners very much."

Alan grinned. "There's a certain foreigner I like very much indeed."

His comment eased the slight tension between us and we both laughed aloud.

When we were back home, I let my hair down. Alan was watching me. He moved towards me, cupped my face in his hands then slid them down to my shoulders.

"No, not here," I said. "We are married you know. We should go into our bedroom, really."

"Ach. I'm not always an impatient man but seeing the firelight shine on you … well, I don't feel like waiting."

I gave in to his wishes and we both fell asleep, lying on the carpet in front of the fire. We awoke an hour later and went to our bedroom, feeling happy.

CHAPTER THIRTY-SIX

Although it was the beginning of winter, Lucy Wilson kept her promise to keep in touch with me by sending a letter to me. I invited her to visit me for afternoon tea. We spent a lot of time together afterwards engaged in charity work or visiting dress shops. We also went to tea rooms. Alan occasionally played golf on Leith Links with Lucy's husband or they visited a social club and drank whisky.

"There's sometimes a poet at the club, reciting verses," Alan said. "Some are better than others."

"Naturally," I remarked. I felt a little sad because it reminded me of the days when I used to visit cabarets with Leon but my grief over Leon's death had now lessened considerably although I knew I would never completely forget him.

Alan was pleased about my friendship with Lucy. "She's a nice lady," he said. "And it's good for you to have a female companion."

"It is," I agreed. "And I'm glad it's helped your business to get more orders."

Alan now employed three assistants. But our pleasure in this took a fall. The business grew too rapidly, he had obtained more orders than he was able to supply, his reputation began to suffer and he was in financial difficulties. He tried to keep the bad news away from me but I knew from some of Lucy's remarks and from his correspondence. I didn't read his letters but I knew a lot came from officials such as bankers and lawyers. Alan had a worried air about him unlike his former carefree self.

So, I decided after a while, to confront him with my knowledge of his predicament. "Your business has run into difficulties, hasn't it?" I asked, as gently as I could although it was more of a statement than a question.

Alan tried, unsuccessfully, to sound nonchalant. "What makes you think so? Did Lucy say anything to you about it?"

"No, she didn't. But I could tell you were worried about something and when you didn't tell me I made what I now think was a shrewd guess. And you talked in your sleep, I could tell you had bad dreams."

He looked at me, giving a shrug that startled me because it was almost Gallic. "Ach! I may as well confess; I shall have to close the business down. I'll look for work as a bank clerk or in an insurance company, something like that."

I shook my head. "No, I don't think you need to do that, not if you agree to my plan."

Alan was visibly shaken. "*Your* plan! Whatever is it?"

"Just listen to me, please. I've always had a secret dream to own a dress shop and I saw one for sale the other day. It could have an adjoining workshop. I would like to design the clothes myself. Susanne, my dear friend could come over from Paris and work as a seamstress. I'd help her with this and Elspeth could be one of our assistants. We could get ourselves another maid. And then we could ..."

He held up his hand to check my uninterrupted flow of words, shaking his head. "It's well imagined on your part, Isa. But where would we get the money from? The sale of the business wouldn't be enough and I doubt your father would make a loan to me. I wouldn't want to ask him, anyway."

"Neither would I, Alan. I wondered whether to ask Lucy for help. She had a legacy left to her and it was expressly stated in the will that it was for her sole use only. Her husband wasn't very pleased he couldn't touch it. However, there's nothing he can do."

Alan looked thoughtful. "H'm, we'll see," was all he said but I was sure I would be able to persuade him to accept my advice if I gave him enough time and went about it the right way. Then I had an idea about something that would probably appeal to him.

I threw my arms around his neck. "If we found big enough premises, perhaps you could have a room to take family photographs in. Lots of families like to have them, don't they?"

Alan's eyes lit up. "I'll think about that."

I felt that I had triumphed but didn't want to appear more eager than I already was so I said. "Let's not talk about it anymore, today. I'll ask Elspeth to make us some tea."

Alan smiled. "You can have the tea, I'd prefer whisky."

Giving him a mischievous smile, I said. "I've changed my mind; I'll have a glass of wine instead of a cup of tea."

He laughed. "Don't blame you."

I walked over to the cabinet quickly, took out a bottle and glasses, poured the drinks out and brought his over to him. Alan looked grateful as I handed it to him.

CHAPTER THIRTY-SEVEN

Lucy and I continued with our charity visits to hospitals, helping some of the nurses take things to some of the patients, we also chatted to some of them. We also went to orphanages and workhouses; I hated the latter places but tried to help some of the unfortunate inmates in my own small way by listening and talking to them.

Lucy was more God fearing than myself. "It's my Christian duty to be charitable to the poor and unfortunate," she said.

"Alan and I pity them," I remarked.

Initially, I had experienced a certain amount of difficulty in comprehending the local accent although some Scottish dialect words were similar to French words. Lucy was a great help because she knew some French herself and conversed with me in my native tongue occasionally, especially when we were visiting some of the afflicted and she didn't want them to know what we were saying about them.

Alan demurred about approaching Lucy for a loan to buy a dress shop. I didn't try to exert pressure on him to agree to my plan but I hoped and prayed he would eventually accede to my wish. I tried to make things at home as pleasant for him as I could by helping Elspeth cook his favourite meals, ensuring flowers and candles always decorated the table and wearing clothes that I knew suited me.

After a particularly tender night, Alan having received another letter from his banker during the day I again made my suggestion about buying a dress shop and he at last agreed in a weary sort of way. I was secretly delighted but did my best to hide my true feelings from him because I knew he felt it to be a slur on his male pride to borrow money from a woman.

From the sale of his business Alan was able at to finally pay all his creditors. This was at least a temporary relief even if we still faced an uncertain future.

I approached Lucy and explained our circumstances to her as tactfully as I could, also mentioning how much I would adore to open a dress shop.

"Good idea," she said.

"But we don't have the necessary cash at present. We'd need a loan and then we'd have to pay interest on it."

"I'll give you the loan, Isabelle."

I was both amazed and gratified at the same time. After staring at her for a few minutes while her words sank in, I managed to say. "Are you sure about this, Lucy?"

"Of course," she answered, briskly. "I'm never able to resist helping a friend in need."

I was immensely relieved. "Thank you so much. When the shop begins to make profits, we'll repay you with interest, you'll also have a share in all our sales."

Lucy laughed. "Have to say I admire your confidence."

We set about searching for premises. We found a dress shop near Princes Street.

"I know we had that other place in mind, Isabelle," she said. "But let's have a look inside this one. If you look through the window, there's some lovely gowns hanging on the rails."

As we entered, I saw that Lucy had been telling the truth. Inside the shop was more spacious that I had believed at first. I imagined eventually owning a fashion house rivalling those of Paris. It would have crystal chandeliers hanging from the ceiling and silk upholstered chairs for the customers who would receive the best attention in the world.

Abruptly, I jerked myself out of my reverie as I heard Lucy ask the proprietress in a discreet way how much she would be willing to sell her shop for. Lucy made a few comments to me in French that made the proprietress sniff.

"I'm no' altogether unfamiliar with the French language," the woman protested.

"Oh well," Lucy said. "If you're not really interested in selling your property, we're sorry we've wasted your time. Come on, Isabelle, we'd better go."

Lucy began to move towards the door but the proprietress made a detaining gesture with her hand.

"No, please Madam, don't be hasty. I *would* like to discuss your terms in a bit more detail, though. There's a little office at the back, please step this way."

A reasonable price was agreed after a little haggling and I couldn't believe how lucky we had been.

"I could kiss you," I said to Lucy. "Don't worry though, I'm not going to do this in public."

Lucy laughed, looking pleased.

"But what I *can* do," I said. "Is buy us some tea to celebrate."

"I'll enjoy that."

When we were eventually ready to move into our new premises, Alan and I painted the shop ourselves. "I like the situation of this," he said, gazing around and throwing his arms in the direction of the street. The one large room had been converted into two smaller but still spacious ones. Alan was going to use the one for taking customers' family photographs.

I brought paper, pencils and my sewing machine from home and placed them on a desk in the slightly larger room.

One of my observations had been that British servants were not really treated as one of the family as they often were in France. I glanced at Elspeth's slim figure, deciding in was probably appropriate for my purpose, she was tall as well. So, I jumped in with my suggestion to her.

"Would you like to work in our new shop as an assistant and occasionally as a model instead of our maid?"

She stared at me almost open mouthed.

"Well, would you?" I prompted.

For a few minutes Elspeth seemed tongue-tied then she smiled.

"Course I would, mistress."

"I'll miss you round the house of course. Nor sure yet that we'll be able to afford another maid."

"But excuse me, how will ye manage withoot one, mistress?"

"I'll have to do the housework myself. I can cook, you know."

"I do ken that, mistress."

I tried not to grimace. "I've learned other household duties though it's a long time since I've had to perform them myself."

Elspeth shook her head. "Ye'll no need to, mistress because I've a young sister, a lassie of fifteen who'll not need much wages, just her keep and that, like. She's workin' at the weavin' but she doesnae like it o'er much. D'ye think, maybe, Ma'am, she could ..."

"Work as your replacement," I finished Elspeth's sentence for her, reminded of Marie. "What's your sister's name, Elspeth?"

"Jenny."

"Very well, I'll discuss it with my husband and if he agrees as I think he will most likely, you can tell Jenny if she does come here, she's to be a good girl but we can't give her a great wage."

"Oh, thank you, mistress."

"Don't thank me too much. It's not a definite promise yet."

Young Jenny was however, duly installed as our new maid and we were pleased with the girl. She worked hard and was respectful towards us. Elspeth started to work in our shop, proving to be a good employee and went back home to live with her parents.

So, we felt at least for the time being things had worked out satisfactorily.

CHAPTER THIRTY-EIGHT

Alan had decided our new shop should be named after me. "Like a ship," he said, grinning. It was duly christened 'Mademoiselle Isabelle.'

"But I'm no longer single," I had protested.

"Ah but it sounds a bit more youthful and enticing than 'Madame' Don't you think so?"

"Suppose so," I replied, a little reluctantly.

Lucy who owned more clothes than she knew what to do with, donated some of her lesser worn hats that were still, fortunately, in excellent condition. I bought trimmings of feathers, silk flowers and ribbons. I also bought some mourning jet in case any of our customers suddenly needed it if they should have a sudden bereavement. I didn't wish this on them of course, it was just a possibility. I kept the jet in a special box.

Papa had unexpectedly sent me a money gift after I had written to him, informing him of our new venture. I had not told him that Alan's former business had failed, merely stating that we had purchased a new one.

Susanne had also written to me, saying that she would be pleased to make the journey to Edinburgh and was looking forward to her first trip abroad.

"She's such a skilled needlewoman, she'll be a great help to us," I said to Alan.

He smiled. "If anybody should know about that, it's you."

"It will be her first time in a foreign country."

He smiled. "We'll have to help her get used to it, then."

Susanne arrived, delighted to see me again. Fortunately, we had been able to find suitable lodgings for her. The only problem was that she couldn't speak a word of English so I had to accompany her whenever she wanted to go out although she didn't like doing so very often.

"She must feel like a stranger in Babylon," Alan said.

141

We transformed the interior of the shop to our own liking by arranging rails to hang up the clothes and separating it by a partition. One side, we decided, would be for the gentlemen's wear that Alan would be looking after. He was also the general manager; it restored a certain amount of masculine pride in him. Elspeth would sell the ladies' and children's fashions on the opposite side as well as doing a little modelling of the clothes. While she was wearing and displaying the clothes, I would be present, behind the counter. Susanne and I would be in the office at the back where we would both sew and I would also sketch my designs.

I had bought ruffles, lace and embroidery and set to work making morning gowns in striped silk, tea gowns in chiffon and velvet riding habits. I was in my element.

"I love the feel of the materials I work with," I said to Alan.

"Can tell you do and I'm pleased to see it."

I designed a few full busted tea gowns with leg of mutton or balloon sleeves, a high neckline with a wasp waist and bell-shaped skirts in different colours.

We also made evening and ball gowns with elbow length sleeves, a low décolletage and long skirts and trains. I was especially proud of a navy-blue dress and cape we had trimmed with silver braid decoration. There was also an evening gown that I liked so much that I coveted it myself.

It had a dark green velvet bodice, a cream brocade skirt, striped with pink sprays and a white tulle overskirt with flouncing. Another one of my favourites was a pink taffeta dress decorated with green squares that also had a cream lace jabot.

"Make one for yourself too, then," Alan said, knowing how much I had longed for it. "You can keep it for a special occasion. I ought to buy myself a few cycling clothes in case I have to start riding about to places. And I like cycling, it keeps me fit."

Clothes in the past few years I had noticed, had become more varied as they were designed for functions like formal receptions, the theatre, and balls. Some were especially designed for various sports, such as cycling, shooting, and walking.

Alan had decided to advertise the opening of our new shop. "I want to see the customers rolling in like the tide," he said, proudly.

"Don't forget Lucy said she'd give our name to some of our acquaintances."

"Aye, hope she does," Alan said but there was a slight lack of enthusiasm in his tone. So, I decided not to mention her name to him too often.

I showed him a few sketches I had made of my own ideas for some of the gentlemen's clothing.

"I like these," he said. "But I've a few ideas of my own."

"I'll be interested to find out what they are."

"Hope it will be fine feathers making fine birds."

"As long as the birds will come back for more instead of flying away forever."

We both laughed.

"Given enough time, we might be able to employ one or two more assistants."

Alan laughed again. "Don't try to run before we can walk. But we can see later."

We were excited yet apprehensive about the opening of our new shop. However, Lucy kept her promise by bringing some friends of hers to view the dresses before they went on sale to the public. Many of her friends were the wives of prominent businessmen. We thought it would be advantageous to us to gain their custom. They drank the sherry and ate the biscuits we had provided as they watched Elspeth march up and down, modelling some of the dresses I had designed. Lucy had also kindly donated a lot of materials to me as a gift.

"She should now be growing a halo with matching wings," Alan whispered to me as I managed to smother a laugh.

Elspeth had developed a new kind of confidence. She didn't have the same air of professionalism as Rose, the mannequin I had known in Paris but that was hardly a fair expectation. She moved in a dignified way as Alan took photographs of her. "She looks like a female soldier on parade if there were such a thing," he whispered to me. "Doing fine though."

"There has been the odd female soldier in disguise in the past," I said. "They had to disguise themselves."

Alan grinned. "Naturally, must have been difficult sometimes."

The cloudy day when we opened our new shop held us all in an excited yet apprehensive state of mind.

Alan stood behind his counter upon which were displayed the 'Goff' vests and single- breasted waistcoats made of wool and edged with braid. Hanging on the rails were Norfolk jackets and lounge jackets that were popular in the country. There were also frock coats and knee length single breasted overcoats with flapped breast pockets and velvet collars.

I stood with Elspeth behind a counter of scarves, handkerchiefs and discreetly arranged feminine undergarments. Rails of dresses and children's clothes surrounded us.

"The customers will have to fight their way through this forest," Alan said, indicating the garments. Susanne had been given a day off because we had envisaged doing more selling than sewing and she needed a rest.

By the end of the day, unfortunately, our earlier enthusiasm had turned to despondency. Our opening had aroused curiosity and many visitors arrived to look around but they didn't buy much. All that we had sold were a few scarves, a lady's and gentleman's hat plus a few items of children's wear.

"Sair sorry, business has been so bad the day," Elspeth said, despondently.

Alan shook his head. "It's only the first day, folk don't know what to expect yet."

I was tempted to say I hoped he was right but I kept my own misgivings to myself.

Two weeks passed by in the same desultory fashion. Although he remained silent upon the subject, I knew Alan was already considering closing down. I was deeply disappointed.

Then one night, Leon appeared to me in a dream. "I'm now happy where I am," he said. "Don't worry so much, your shop *will* start to prosper. And it will lead on to better things."

I awoke in a disturbed frame of mind. I glanced at Alan, asleep at my side. Then, I began to cry softly into my pillow. Without wishing it, I had awoken Alan.

"What's the matter, Isabelle?" he asked, concerned. "Have you been worrying too much about the shop? Been working too hard, maybe. We could close down, you know."

I shook my head in an emphatic way. "No, not that, not yet anyway. It was just a bad dream I had, that's all."

He smoothed my hair back from my face, took me in his arms and rocked me slightly, trying to comfort me. "Poor lass, never mind, try and go back to sleep now, Isa."

After a short while, I managed to drift into a more peaceful slumber.

CHAPTER THIRTY-NINE

We struggled along with the shop for another week or so. Then one of Lucy's friends, a widow who I knew slightly came in.

"I'd like you to design a new gown for me, Isabelle. I'm attending an important ball in a month's time and I'd like to have it by then. Do you think that's possible?" she asked.

My heart lifted. "Certainly."

"Good, I'll be grateful for this."

Susanne and I between us, designed and made a pink velvet dress trimmed with ribbons, loops, and fringe. The skirt in the front was an elaborate arrangement of vertical folds that ended in a row of pleated pink ruffles. We also made a train for the back.

`The customer was delighted with our handiwork and gave us a handsome sum of money.

"The ball was wonderful," she said, enthusiastically. "And I've recommended some of my acquaintances to come here and see your designs."

I was overwhelmed with gratitude. "Thank you so much."

Female customers started flocking to our shop, much to our delight. As well as requesting dresses for special occasions, they also bought everyday garments. More male customers began to drift in, slowly at first then their numbers started to build up.

Alan said. "Let's give a wee dinner party so that we can thank Lucy for her help."

"Good idea. Jenny and I will be busy, planning and preparing it."

The guests were Lucy and her husband, John Wilson, her friend, the widow who had bought the pink dress and another couple whom John and Lucy knew. They were called Ian and Emily Farmer, for some reason I wasn't completely able to understand, I didn't like them very much. The man was a boot and shoe manufacturer.

I helped Jenny prepare and cook the Macaroni A La Reine with an iced pudding to follow. After our dinner, Lucy, Emily, and I left the table. I had always thought this custom was odd but deferred to it for Alan's sake. Emily talked slightingly in a superior tone of the fashions her friends followed. Lucy neither agreed nor disagreed with her, merely making comments like "Do you think so?" and "Aye, remember her quite well, we met at such and such a place." I deliberately kept quiet.

When we were rejoined by the men, I was relieved. Alan was beaming. "Mr Farmer has contacts with the Army and Navy, he'll probably put some business my way. Isn't that grand?"

"Excellent news, I am pleased." Ian Farmer looked at me as if I shouldn't have said this. I guessed he'd probably thought I should have added the words "for you."

We received an order from the Army for woollen clothing now that the November weather was growing colder. We became so busy that Alan decided we could now employ two more assistants. We didn't work such long hours as I had in Paris but fortunately, we still made profits.

One evening, I sat reading the novel 'Guy Mannering.' I had taken the volume out of Alan's bookcase. He looked at me, thoughtfully. "Seeing you're reading yon book of Sir Walter Scott's has given me an idea. You could see where Scott lived if we go to the Borders. With this order from the Army, we could combine business and pleasure. You could do with a rest. So could I."

"Now it's got going, they'll be sure to manage without us for a wee while. Next summer, we could visit the Highlands."

We boarded the train for Hawick. As I looked out of the carriage window, I noticed the Border Country seemed to consist of rivers, wild rolling hills, lonely moors, ruins of castles and fortified buildings, often roofless.

"They're called peel towers," Alan said. "They were originally built for defence." There were also circles of sheep folds and stone cottages.

We ate our lunch in the dining room of the Lamb and Flag Inn. We heard two men discussing wool sales. There was a picture on the wall of men dressed in the clothes of two centuries ago. They were all wild-eyed and were depicted chasing cattle and lighting fires.

"What were they?" I asked Alan.

He was about to reply when one of the men at the nearby table turned around and said, "They were reivers, ma'am. Mainly cattle but sometimes sheep thieves. They stole beasts on both sides of the Border. Lots of murders, raids and family feuds went on."

The man pronounced the last sentence almost with relish.

"Thank you for telling me," I said.

"Pity we have to buy cloth and wool instead of turning into reivers ourselves," Alan grinned. "Am I not wicked to make that suggestion?"

I smiled and the man at the nearby table turned back and resumed his conversation with his companion.

Hawick had been built along the walled banks of the river Teviot and its tributary, the Slitrig Burn, tucked in a fold of the hills. There was an extensive outlying farming area with an auction market for sheep and cattle. We walked along the narrow High Street flanked in the main by solid plain stone buildings with shops on the ground floor with two or three storeys of housing or offices above them.

The woollen mills were built along the river banks. The manager of one of the larger mills allowed us to look around. Alan made wool purchases and I chatted to some of the women workers.

I had at first felt like a stranger in Edinburgh but there were other foreigners living there. I had also become accustomed to Edinburgh speech. But the Borders accent was different, I had some difficulty with it.

"Did you feel like a stranger in the Tower of Babel?" Alan asked after I had told him about this. "I know what they're saying but I can imagine it being hard for you."

"It was a bit but I'm glad we came here."

He took me to see Scott's mansion of Abbotsford, taking a photograph of me standing in front of it. He also took pictures of the distant Cheviot Hills, the Moorfoot Hills and the wooded Eildon Hills and Ettrick Water and Ettrick Forest.

We stayed overnight at a small inn in Melrose and on the following day Alan photographed me standing near the bank of the river Tweed.

"I'm really pleased with my pictures," he said.

"Most of them are of me," I smiled.

"They are right enough and I'm glad of it."

We also visited the towns of Kelso and Galashiels where Alan bought some woollen hosiery to sell in our shop. The last photograph he took in the Borders region was of me standing by the war memorial with its statue of the mounted reiver.

"You'll have a good collection for your album when we go home," I said.

Alan shook his head. "Not good, beautiful with a lovely lady in it too."

"Thank you, kind sir."

But unfortunately, when we returned home, I caught a nasty chill, it made me feel exhausted and low spirited.

CHAPTER FORTY

I stayed in bed for three days before returning to the shop much recovered. Susanne's hats were sailing like hot cakes. She now had a much better understanding of English. I was pleased when Alan decided to slightly raise her salary. Susanne confided to me that she would like to have a holiday in France. This gave me the idea if Alan were agreeable, of inviting my own family to visit us in the New Year. I was relieved when he agreed, willingly.

Alan also engaged another young maid to help Jenny. She didn't live with us, returning to her parents' house in the evenings.

"Let's go up to the Highlands next week," Alan said. "Seeing as we're just about still in autumn. We could stay there a few days."

"Are you sure you want to do this, Alan?"

"Certainly, hen."

"In that case I'll come with you."

"Good, I'm glad about that."

On our journey I said. "We seem to be following the steps of Queen Victoria. She was known to love the mountains there, wasn't she?"

"Aye, she was. Do you intend to come back to Edinburgh as a queen, a second Queen of Scots?"

I laughed. "No, the first one didn't come to a very good end. I'd rather be a queen of the fashion world."

Alan took a photograph of me standing by a stream that frothed like a fall of white lace at a woman's throat and plunged through craggy rocks. We found a suitable inn and Alan took yet another photograph of me standing near a loch."

"Let me take a picture of you for a change," I suggested.

Alan looked startled but agreed to my request so we changed places.

The rest of our few days away from home passed pleasantly although the weather was a little chilly.

We began to prepare for Christmas both at work and at home. "We could spend our Christmas in London," he said. "It could combine business with pleasure because we could look at the shops in Bond Street. Might give you some ideas for your designs. Not of course that you don't have plenty of thoughts on this already."

I smiled. "Glad you added that sentence."

"I'd like fine to be back at home for the New Year though."

"Could my family visit us then, do you think?"

"Certainly."

The hotel room we stayed in was magnificent. The windows reached to the ceiling and white velvet curtains hung from them. The wallpaper was of a crimson flock pattern and we stepped on to a thick carpet with a blue and white floral pattern. There was a large white wardrobe inlaid with mother-of-pearl, a marble topped table, thickly upholstered chairs with white velvet coverings and lamps with glittering crystal beads.

I gazed around in amazement. "Surely our shop's profits haven't been so good that we can afford all this." I gave an encompassing wave of my hand. Papa had sent me a considerable sum of money as a Christmas present. I had offered it to Alan to put in the bank in case our present run of luck ended but he had adamantly refused.

"No, spend it on yourself, buy whatever you like with it."

Alan winked at me. "While you were ill, I was returning home one evening and found Ian Farmer collapsed in the street. I took him to the hospital where he recovered from his seizure, I'm happy to say.

"Then he came himself to the shop rather than send a servant who might be tempted to be dishonest. He offered me a lot of money; I'm not saying how much but it was immense. I refused to take it at first but he pressed it on Elspeth. He impressed on the lass that he'd be offended if I continued to refuse it. So, you see I've now been able to fully repay Lucy's loan and I wished this to be a surprise for you."

"Oh, Alan, you dark horse, I'm so overwhelmed, I don't know what to say."

"Say nothing then, Isa. Shall we go down to dinner?" He offered me his arm.

We attended the Gaiety Theatre at the eastern end of the Strand near the beautiful church of St Mary-le-Strand.

"You should feel at home in this theatre," Alan said. "It was designed on similar lines to the Theatre Lyrique in Paris."

We watched 'The Circus Girl.' I was impressed by the glamourous scenery and costumes. One scene that I found realistic also making me feel slightly homesick was the one depicting the 'Artists Ball' in Paris. The Circus scene, however, made me laugh aloud. This was because one of the principals had to make his entrance on a white horse. This horse had formerly been employed pulling an omnibus. The stage manager made the animal start by calling out 'Charing Cross,' 'Strand,' 'Bank,' 'Piccadilly Circus,' 'Oxford Circus,' Then, he slammed the green room door, saying "Right behind," as the horse trotted into the ring.

During the interval Alan told me that hundreds of girls applied to join the Gaiety chorus. "They're both middle and working class," he said. "The ones who are lucky enough to get picked become part of 'The Big Eight' as they're called. Most of them are tall, attractive lassies, they often get taken out to supper by their admirers." He grinned. "But you used to get taken out like that, didn't you, Isa?"

I smiled as I nodded in agreement. "Still do by you, sometimes."

"Some of the 'Big Eight' earn fifteen pounds because their admirers buy stalls here for every night of the run. They're mainly meant to be decorative but they sometimes support the principals in a song or they sing a chorus."

"Do you know what the other performers get?"

"The ones in the chorus get two pounds ten shillings."

"You seem to know a lot about them."

"A lass I knew, sister of a friend of mine ran away to become a Gaiety Girl."

Alan was straight-faced but I felt unsure whether to believe this tale. However, I said nothing, I just concentrated on enjoying the show.

That Christmas passed in a whirl of theatre visits, suppers and strolls down Bond Street as well as carriage drives for the purpose of sightseeing. There were so many famous buildings and monuments to gaze at. Susanne had gone on a well-deserved holiday to France and Alan had told the other two assistants to close the shop late on Christmas Eve. We were going to re-open the shop after the New Year.

I was looking forward to my family's visit. We returned to Edinburgh the day after Boxing Day to be in time to meet them.

After they had settled into the hotel we had chosen for them, Papa said. "I'm pleased to see you both looking so well." My stepmother nodded in agreement.

"May I make a suggestion?" Alan said. "Don't have your dinner in the hotel tonight. Come and share ours at our house. Do you agree?"

Papa and my stepmother agreed to do so.

"You must come over to France for my wedding," Eloise said. "It won't be all that long now."

"Can't wait to grow up and be married myself," Colette said, making us all laugh, easing the slight tension we had all up to now felt.

"It will be a little while yet, though," Papa said.

At dinner I gave my family their gifts. A handsome pen for Papa, a fan for my stepmother and gloves for my sisters. My stepmother who I could no longer think of as "Madame Charpentier" was more pleasant to me than I had ever known her to be before.

"Would you all like to see our shop tomorrow although it's officially closed for the now?" Alan asked.

The girls seemed excited by this prospect, I secretly believed they were both probably hoping for a free new dress. I hoped to make this wish of theirs come true.

The next day my stepmother gazed around the rails of dresses almost as fascinated as my sisters. "Isabelle designed most of these," Alan said, proudly. I felt gratified.

"You know, Isabelle," my stepmother said, slowly. "You're really quite talented."

"She always has been," Alan remarked. This pleased me. I also knew I was beginning to warm towards her. Perhaps she wasn't as bad as I had formerly believed.

"Well," I said, hesitantly. "Afraid I'm going to be rude to you all. But I have an urgent appointment."

"What's so urgent?" Alan asked as everyone gave me a puzzled look.

"Forgot to take Lucy's present to her." I picked up one of the elaborately hats from the counter.

"Surely that can wait."

I shook my head, emphatically. "No, I really do wish to go now. Please don't object, Alan. Please take the others to the Castle and I'll see you all later."

Everyone was staring at me with a curious expression.

"Hope you're not going to do this sort of thing every day, Isabelle, Alan said, firmly. You ought to be spending as much time with your family as possible."

It was unlike Alan to lecture me and I couldn't stop myself snapping at him.

"Of course, I shall, it's just this one occasion, that's all."

My father said. "Come on then, let's all go and see this famous Castle while Isabelle goes on her important errand."

I could have both kissed Papa and cried from relief. Alan was still looking annoyed as they all went out of the front door.

When they were safely out of sight, I hurried to my doctor who confirmed my suspicions.

That evening, when we were at last alone, my family having enjoyed their visit to the Castle, I said. "I'll tell you the truth about where I went today."

"I'm intrigued."

"To the doctor's, there's going to be more than just the two of us in the Fergusson family in the future."

He gazed at me for a moment then he said. "Do you mean what I think you mean?"

I nodded. "Yes, I do."

Alan took me in his arms. "Oh, Isabelle, darling. What a beautiful start to our New Year, my own dear, sweet belle of Paris."

He kissed me long and hard before picking me up and carrying me to our bed. There was no longer any doubt in my mind that I loved Alan.

PART TWO: FAMILY LIFE

CHAPTER FORTY-ONE
EDINBURGH, 1903

During the following six years the photographic business Alan had started grew, he gained a good reputation with his customers. He sold his original studio and bought a larger one at the corner of the High Street and North Bridge. It went from strength to strength. He joined the Edinburgh Calotype Club, one of the earliest photographic societies. Their membership was drawn largely from the legal and medical professions, a lawyer friend of his had recommended him to the society.

I began to sell a few dresses I'd designed and made to a local store. It was nowhere near as large as Jensens Department Store but it made a decent profit.

We now had enough money to employ a chauffeur and three maids.

I gave birth to twin girls. After their birth, I had said to Alan, "Expect you're disappointed they're not boys."

He had smiled and shaken his head. "No, they'll be bonny wee lassies just like their mother. Perhaps we'll have a lad later but if we don't, it won't matter."

I was grateful to him for this but I knew instinctively that it was highly unlikely that I would ever have any more children.

"What names would you like them to be called?" he asked. "I'll let you choose."

"Thank you, I'd like them to be called Sylvie and Mirabelle. What do you think about that?"

Alan had smiled again. "Fine with me."

The twins were not identical. Mirabelle was dark haired with dark eyes like me and Sylvie was the possessor of brown hair and green eyes. We both admired their looks as well as hoping they would also have good characters.

I loved them both equally and was gratified that Alan seemed to feel the same way about them. It was a relief to me that neither of us appeared to have a favourite daughter.

Initially, we employed a nursemaid but she proved to be unsuitable, a little careless and unreliable. So, we let her go although Alan paid her, her full salary plus a little extra with a good reference. The next one we had was a lot better but she left to get married when the twins were five. Alan gave her cash for a wedding present.

"Thank ye so much," she said, when she saw the note in the envelope Alan handed to her. "I wasnae expecting this much."

"You deserve it," Alan said. She beamed.

Our girls both had a love of performing and showed signs of talent. Although Mirabelle had a fine singing voice, it was not quite as lovely as Sylvie's. Sylvie was a good dancer, particularly shining in Highland dancing and Irish jigs but Mirabelle's dancing was superior. We had allowed them to have singing and dancing lessons every two weeks.

"They've inherited their love of both singing and dancing from their mother," Alan said, proudly.

I was flattered but at the same time, a little apprehensive. "Do you mind that?"

"No but it shouldn't deprive them of their education in other subjects."

Alan bought a piano. "I want my studio to be modern," he said.

I nodded in agreement as he described the beautiful window displays, he wished to arrange.

"Good ideas," I stated.

He smiled. "Glad you approve."

Alan engaged a private governess for the girls. Her name was Janet Fraser, she lived with her widowed mother. I liked her but noticed that she was trying hard not to frown with disapproval when Alan said. "Miss Fraser, on no account are you to use corporal punishment on my daughters. Do you promise me this?"

"Yes, sir," she said, meekly. But I guessed she probably thought this would be spoiling our girls. However, Alan had offered her a decent salary. This was most likely one of the inducements for her to stay with us in my opinion. However, I kept quiet about it.

My sister, Eloise came to live with us after her husband, Georges, had died after catching a fever. She and Georges had not had children but Eloise was as fond of Mirabelle and Sylvie as they were of her. A great relief to Alan and myself.

Alan had said privately to me. "I go to the kirk because I'm expected to be respectable as a businessman. But when the minister blethers rubbish about hellfire, I pretend there's cotton wool in my ears." He had grinned. "Do you think God will forgive me or will I end up getting too warm?"

I had smiled in return "I've forgiven you even if He won't."

"Do *you* want to go to Mass? I'd never try to dissuade ye."

I shook my head. "No, I'd rather go to your Protestant services."

Alan had looked startled. "Must say I'm surprised but pleased."

Originally, this had slightly shocked Eloise. "Not how we were brought up, Isabelle."

"I know but we're no longer in our parents' old home."

With a slight shake of her head, Eloise had accepted this statement. Alan and I were relieved it had not caused more of an argument.

Mirabelle and Sylvie had lined up their dolls on the window sill of their playroom one rainy Sunday morning in September after they had attended church with us.

"Now, look dollies," Mirabelle was saying. "Ye're no' at school the day so ye watch me and Sylvie do our dancing. "I'll be ballet, Sylvie's Highland. Ye'll be good if ye watch us proper. But first, I'm going tae sing ye two songs. Ye'll like them."

Mirabelle sang 'The Bluebells of Scotland.'

"Lovely, Belle,' Sylvie said. "But let me sing to the dollies now."

Mirabelle pouted but nodded. "Aw right. What d'ye want to sing?"

"Greensleeves."

After Sylvie had finished, Mirabelle said, "No bad, Belle. We'd best start the dancing now, though."

157

I overheard them as I passed their room via the corridor. I managed to suppress my laughter and said to Alan and Eloise. "Come and watch the girls' dancing for their dolls. Think it'll be funny though we'd better not let them see us."

"No, we shouldn't," Alan smiled. "They'd probably be embarrassed."

"Should be good to watch," Eloise agreed. "I'll try my best not to let them hear me laughing."

Us adults secretly watched the twins with amusement and affection.

"That was very good ye seein' us dance for you, dollies, don't ye think?" Sylvie said.

"And Sylvie's songs were no bad too," Mirabelle confirmed.

"Bossy little thing, isn't she?" I whispered to Alan who smiled in return as Eloise nodded in agreement.

We crept away quietly with our hands over our mouths to stop ourselves from laughing. However, once we were in the drawing room, we all burst out laughing.

When we had recovered, Alan said. "Well, at least they have vivid imaginations. No bad thing."

"As long as they don't get too carried away," I cautioned.

"They're too sensible, I think," Eloise said.

The next evening Eloise said to me. "I've had a letter from Colette, she's getting married."

"Oh," I said, surprised. "Who's the lucky young man?"

"He's the son of a restaurant owner, his name's Pierre Bechelet. I'll show you the letter, you can see in it that she's asked me to tell you and Alan. We're all invited and she wants the twins to be bridesmaids."

"That's wonderful, they'll be so excited."

"Colette's said she's made her own choice; she said Papa's pleased by it. He put no pressure on her about who she chose to wed. Unlike …"

Eloise blushed, slightly embarrassed

I smiled wryly. "Unlike me, the black sheep who ran away. I'm pleased for Colette, though. We'll be busy sewing new dresses."

Eloise nodded. "Definitely something to look forward to. It will be nice to go to France again too."

"It will, that."

The twins were filled with glee when they knew they would be going to France. "I'd fair like a yellow dress," Mirabelle said.

"I'd love a blue one," Sylvie remarked.

"Come on now, girls," I said, firmly. "Your Auntie Colette has chosen the colour pink for you and it's her wedding."

Mirabelle frowned slightly but Sylvie said "I like pink, thought you did too, Belle."

"I do but yellow's my favourite colour."

"I'm sure you'll both look lovely whatever colour frocks you're wearing," Alan said as the twins beamed with pleasure.

CHAPTER FORTY-TWO

Eloise had impressed upon the twins that they were to attempt to speak the little French they knew to the other wedding guests, particularly the children and not to worry too much if they couldn't fully understand the replies even if they were laughed at.

"I'll explain them to you," I said. "And don't forget your manners."

"We won't, Mamma, we promise," Sylvie stated. "Won't we, Miri?"

Mirabelle nodded. "Yes, we'll be as polite as we can."

Alan smiled. "I'm sure you'll come home prattling away in French."

Eloise laughed. "That's maybe a bit too ambitious to expect."

"The girls are so thrilled about our journey," I said to Alan when they were in bed that night.

"It's only natural," Alan replied. "They're good lassies on the whole so they should make a good impression and leave one behind when we come back home."

"Hope so," I said. I yawned. "I'm getting sleepy now."

We kissed and cuddled before we both drifted into a peaceful sleep.

The journey to France was a smooth one, the October weather was dry and warm when we arrived safely. We hired a fiacre to take us to our father's house. He welcomed us warmly, so did his wife. It had been agreed upon that Eloise would stay at our father's house while the rest of us went to a hotel.

"It's good to see you all," our father said. "It's been a while now." He kissed everyone on both cheeks and gently shook the children's hands.

"Merci," Mirabelle said.

"Merci beaucoup," Sylvie added.

"Glad they've remembered how to say 'thank you' and 'thank you very much,' Eloise whispered to me.

"I think they've charmed Papa," I answered, as quietly as possible before I turned to my father, saying. "Happy to see you and Madame again, too, Papa,"

"You must dine with us, before you go to your hotel," my father insisted.

"Kind of you, Monsieur," Alan said.

Papa gave a slight shrug. "My pleasure."

I noticed that my father was a little more stooped and his hair was thinner and greyer. In contrast, his wife did not seem to have aged much.

Eloise and I embraced Colette.

"We're so pleased for you," I said.

"Can't say how much," Eloise added.

"I'm thrilled you can all come to my wedding even though you live in a different country now," Colette enthused, quickly wiping a tear from her eye.

I smiled again. "It would have been hard to stop us doing so."

Our stepmother gave a slight nod. "Colette has made a good match. My daughter was lucky that she did the same thing a few months ago."

After our dinner, Alan said. "Thank you for your hospitality. It's much appreciated but we'll take our leave now."

The girls looked disappointed although they were tired. But to my relief, they kept quiet.

"You two have to be up early tomorrow," Alan said, firmly. "You need a good night's sleep."

"And no trying to stay awake, talking to each other," I said, equally firmly. "Your papa and I will be angry if you keep chatting. Do you understand?"

"Aye, mamma," the twins said together. They both looked as if they were in a fever of excitement.

"Our chauffeur will take you to your hotel," my father said.

"Thank you for everything, Monsieur," Alan said, gratefully.

"My pleasure."

I could tell from looking at Alan's face that my father meant what he said. Once again, I was relieved.

"You know a little French from me," I stated.

"And a wee bit more from our governess," Mirabelle said.

"Your mother had a wee bit more to say to you too, I expect, like this," Alan remarked, opening his mouth wide, moving his lips up and down, making us all laugh. He had glanced at me and I could tell he was wondering if his words had caused me offence. But I was mildly amused myself and managed to smile.

When the merriment died down, he said. "So, listen to the rest of what she wanted to say."

"So, be on your best behaviour because you'll be in trouble if you're not. Do you promise?"

"Aye, Mamma," they chorused.

CHAPTER FORTY-THREE

On the morning of the wedding, the twins were excited, each interrupting the other as they discussed the day ahead.

I collected them from their bedroom so that we could all go down to breakfast together. "Remember your manners at the dining room table," I said.

"We will, Mamma," Mirabelle said. "Won't we, Sylvie?"

"Of course," Sylvie confirmed, with such an obvious sense of responsibility that it amused me although I managed, somehow not to show it.

"You'll be towards the back of the procession with the other children," Alan said to the twins after breakfast was over. He grinned. "Don't start stamping your feet about it, it makes a noise."

"The other children might speak a bit too quickly for you to understand everything but remember to smile at them," I added.

"Right, girls, it's time we were all on our way," Alan said.

"Sylvie, Mirabelle, go to your room and put your bridesmaids' dresses on," I ordered. "I'll come up and help you."

Sylvie smiled. "We liked you making them for us, Mamma, didn't we, Belle?"

Her sister nodded.

"You'll all look radiant." Alan enthused. "Including your Mamma."

"Get away, flatterer," I said, although I was pleased by the compliment.

"What does 'radiant' mean?" Sylvie asked.

"Shiny."

The twins beamed.

"What's a 'flatterer'? Mirabelle asked.

"Somebody who praises you a bit too much," I explained.

The procession to the church was led by the bridegroom and his mother. They were followed by the bride's stepmother and bridegroom's father. Next came the witnesses and relatives. Finally, the bride and her father were followed by the bridesmaids.

I thought how beautiful Colette looked and felt proud to be her sibling.

"She's done herself proud," I whispered to Alan.

"And her bridegroom looks handsome too," he replied. He smiled. "And our lassies are almost bursting with pride too, only natural really. They'll remember this day for a long time."

The ceremony was held in a chapel, as the wedding couple proceeded, the children had stretched long white ribbons across the road. Colette cut them.

At the chapel, the bride and bridegroom were seated on two red velvet chairs underneath a silk canopy called a *carre*. When they exited the chapel, small coins were tossed for the children to collect.

The reception was held at the bridegroom's father's restaurant. A piece of toast was dropped into the couple's wine to ensure a healthy life. The newly-wed couple lifted their glasses to 'a toast' and a chorus of cheers. A *croquembouche*, a pyramid of crème filled pastry puffs covered with a caramel glaze was served next

"I love this," Sylvie said.

"So do I" Mirabelle agreed.

The main course of wild boar then the dessert of crème caramel followed.

After the meal, Pierre and Colette came over to speak to Alan, Eloise, and myself.

"I'm pleased you could all come over to see Colette and I wed," Pierre said, looking at his new bride with a lovelight in his eyes. "I'm very glad you all made it today."

"So are we, it's been a pleasure," Alan said.

"You look lovely in your wedding dress, Colette," I added.

"No, she doesn't," Alan corrected me. I was puzzled. "She looks beautiful," he insisted.

Colette turned to the twins. "And you two have been so good, a credit to your parents. Your maman and Papa must be so proud of you."

"What's a 'credit'?" Mirabelle whispered to Sylvie, making us adults smile.

"It's a good thing you've done," Alan explained.

"Here's a little present to you from me," Pierre said to the twins. He handed them some pink and white ribbons for which they remembered to thank him in their best French.

"Ye've got the pink ribbons, Belle," Sylvie said. "I like them best."

"The white yins are bonny too," Mirabelle snapped.

I sensed an argument so I tried to deflect by saying "I'll take care of them for you both and when I give them back to you, I'll make sure you have the same number of each colour."

The girls both scowled.

"Do what your mother's just told you to," Alan said, firmly.

They knew his strict look and obeyed.

"You're going away on your honeymoon now, aren't you?" Alan asked, Colette. "That should be exciting."

She nodded. "Yes, we're spending two weeks in Italy." She turned to the twins again. "We'll be seeing mountains and lakes there."

"Will you be climbing the mountains and swimming in the lakes?" Sylvie asked, wide-eyed.

Pierre and Colette laughed. "No, we'll just be looking at them admiringly," Pierre said.

"Wish we were coming with you," Mirabelle said, wistfully.

"We can't," Sylvie advised.

Alan frowned slightly. "Quite right, you can't. But you may well do so when you're older. However, I'll be taking you around other places in Paris over the next few days. I'm sure you'll be interested in them."

"You'll see some of the places I used to go to," I said. "Wonder if they've changed much."

Alan spent the next few days taking us around Paris.

Eloise had said, "I'd like to spend a few quiet days at home with Papa and my stepmother if you don't mind. Then we can all travel back to Scotland together."

"We've no objections at all," Alan had replied. "You have a well-deserved rest."

Eloise had looked relieved.

CHAPTER FORTY-FOUR

After we returned to Edinburgh Miss Fraser, the twins' governess, was interested to hear them talk about their experiences in France.

I knew that Janet Fraser enjoyed teaching her two young charges. It was not too arduous, she earned a good salary and consumed wholesome food and drink. Alan had impressed upon her when he had offered her the position of governess that although he wished her to be firm with his daughters she was never, under any circumstances, to use corporal punishment on them.

I could see that Janet had wondered about the wisdom of this at first but she needed work because her mother was a widow. However, she found that it was not much of a restriction upon her teaching methods. I believed she considered the girls to be a little spoilt but not impossible to deal with. They tended to be high spirited but I could tell Janet felt that she knew when and how she needed to draw the line. Janet was delighted when both Alan and I said how pleased we were with her.

One morning after I had popped in to the room where the girls' lessons took place to fetch a book, they were seated behind a desk containing pens, pencils, and notebooks. I had heard her say "Write this down, you two. What you did when you were in France. Make it into a story, tell about what you saw, the buildings and the countryside, the people who you met and what happened when you met them. But don't whisper to each other and write down the same things. You will, won't you?"

"Yes, Miss Fraser," they chorused.

Their governess smiled. "Glad to hear it, don't copy each other. I want to hear two different versions."

"What's a 'version'?" Mirabelle whispered to Sylvie.

Her sister frowned, not wishing to say she didn't know what it meant either. "It's sort of a …," she started to say quietly.

Janet Fraser managed to hide her smile and frown instead. "Stop whispering you two. If you don't understand what I say, always ask me to explain, not each other. A version is the way you tell how something happened. Do you know now what it means?"

The girls both nodded, looking a little shame faced.

"It's good you've now learnt a new word. Try to remember it."

"What I'll do," Janet added. "Is ask you to read out your story aloud to me when you've finished it."

"You don't mind if I stay for a while to hear them too, do you?" I asked.

"No, of course not," Mrs Fergusson."

As I sat down, I tried to give the twins an encouraging smile, Janet didn't seem at all embarrassed by my presence.

Mirabelle finished her story first, giving a triumphant look at Sylvie.

"Stand up, Mirabelle and read your story so's we can hear it but don't shout," I said.

Feeling important, Mirabelle read "We went to France, me and my twin sister, Sylvie. We went there for our auntie's wedding. Our auntie is our mamma's sister. She asked for us to be bridesmaids. We wore pretty dresses and ate a lot. Then, after our auntie had got married and gone away, Papa took us round a lot of buildings and we rode in an omnibus."

Janet nodded. "Good, let me have a look at your page,"

Mirabelle handed the paper to Miss Fraser who looked over it quickly. "H'mm, one or two spelling mistakes but I'll tell you how to put it right. You can sit down again, Mirabelle, we'll hear what Sylvie tells us now."

Sylvie stood up, nervously. "We liked meeting our Mamma's Papa and her sister what was getting married. Our mamma helped us put our bridesmaids' dresses on. After the wedding our auntie was going on holiday to a country called Italy what's got mountains and lakes."

Janet Fraser glanced out of the window quickly. I believed that she had noticed that as the weather seemed to be turning colder, she would need to start wearing warmer clothes.

"I've liked listening to your stories, good that they were a bit different," Janet said. "What did you think, Mrs Fergusson?"

"I agree."

Janet continued speaking. "Now, I think we should get on with some reading," Let's start with 'The Babes in the Wood."

"Our Papa's going to take us to see the pantomime of that when it's on at the theatre," Mirabelle said, eagerly.

"He knows the manager of the theatre," Sylvie said, proudly.

"You're lucky, hope you'll both behave yourselves when you're in the theatre and say thank you nicely to your papa afterwards."

"We'll be good," Sylvie promised. "Won't we, Belle?"

"Yes of course," Mirabelle agreed.

"You'd better not let your Papa and I down," I stated, firmly.

Janet smiled. "Sure, you won't. I'm looking forward to you telling me all about that next."

"We'll write it down for you," Sylvie said.

"I'll look forward to that," Janet commented, managing to hide her smile.

CHAPTER FORTY-FIVE

Eloise married again six months after we had returned from France. She wed a lawyer friend of Alan's called John Turner that she had first met at a supper party held at his sister's house. Her second husband was ten years older than her and a widower. Their wedding ceremony was a quiet affair. However, our twins were once again excited to be bridesmaids.

The couple were married in a protestant church and the guests consisted mainly of family but plus a few friends. Eloise wore a cream-coloured jacket and skirt. Despite the simplicity of her outfit, I thought she still looked as beautiful as any other bride I'd seen that year.

We all went to a good restaurant after the ceremony for the wedding breakfast.

"Hope Eloise will be happy this time," I said, quietly to Alan when I could. "She deserves some happiness in her life after what she went through with Georges."

Alan grinned. "Bit grim, wasn't he?"

I couldn't help nodding in agreement.

The newly-weds went to the Channel Islands for a week's short honeymoon before they returned to John's house.

The twins missed Eloise at first but became used to her absence from our house after a while especially as we visited her and her husband quite often.

One evening in early December, Alan met a friend of his called Douglas Phipps at the New Club in Princes Street where they were both members. I had seen this club and been impressed. It had an elegant Italianate façade with an oak panel interior and red leather furnishings. Judges, lawyers, doctors, and bankers as well as other professional men often mixed there.

Douglas came from a theatrical family. He had performed as a comic actor in both Edinburgh and Glasgow before going to

London where he had become a music hall star. He had recently returned to his home city from the metropolis.

"The next thing Douglas is doing," Alan said to me. "Is going to produce the pantomime of 'Babes in the Wood,' At the Royal Lyceum Theatre. He's also going to act a wee part in it." Proud as punch about it."

I smiled. "What part is he playing?"

"The Good Robber.' Didn't know there was such a thing. Hope he won't become one in real life."

"Can't see that happening. Our girls liked that story when I read it to them."

Alan looked hesitant. "He made a suggestion to me; I've given it some thought and am not entirely against the idea."

"Oh, what's that?"

"While we were blethering, he suddenly said. "Your lassies love singing and dancing, don't they?"

"You must have admitted that."

Alan nodded in agreement. "I did, told him it was sometimes a bit hard to stop them sometimes once they've started. He laughed when I told him their dolls like watching them."

"Douglas said he could get them into the 'Babes' in the chorus

"How do you feel about that?"

"I'm willing. But I did say to Douglas that they should only appear on the stage in the afternoons as I don't want the rest of their education to be neglected."

I breathed a mental sigh of relief. Aloud, I said "A wise decision, I think."

"Glad you do, believe they've inherited their talent from you."

I felt flattered by the compliment. "Thank you." It was my turn to grin. "Can imagine how excited they'll be."

"Douglas said they'll be in the opening woodland scene as fairies who can sing and dance. The laddies are all elves and the lassies are fairies. They don't have to speak. They'll be lying on the floor first then spring up like jack in the boxes. Hope they won't slip down again."

"So do I," I said, wryly. "Would they just be in the one scene?"

. "Aye, all the weans in the chorus, the youngest laddies, and lassies are in the opening forest scene. They all do a song and dance together."

"Hope they won't make *too* much of one though," I remarked.

Alan laughed. "Doubt it, however, I have said if they get overtired, they're to leave."

Unable to help a girlish giggle, my reply was "Knowing them, they'll be too excited to be weary." More thoughtfully I added. "Should be an interesting experience for them. Good for them to meet other children who aren't related to them."

The girls were thrilled to be included in the pantomime. As well as Alan and myself, Eloise and John Turner, Janet Fraser, and our maids all went to watch a performance and thoroughly enjoyed it. But Mirabelle said afterwards, "I nearly fell over when I slipped on the stage by the exit door but a nice laddie helped me get up again."

"Be careful in future then, both of you," I warned.

Alan later discovered at his club who the "nice laddie" was. Douglas had remarked to him at the club. "That laddie who helped Mirabelle get up was David Irvine. He's a laird's son, son of the Earl of Roseleans."

"Where's Roseleans?" I had asked.

"It's the earl's country estate near Edinburgh," Alan had informed me. Doug said, "His folks dinna mind him being in the panto but I doubt they'd want him to have a career on the stage. He's the eldest son ye see, his two older brothers died in a riding accident."

"What did you say?" I had asked.

"Agreed with Doug that they probably wouldn't approve of him becoming a performer on a permanent basis especially when he's older. Shame about the two older lads."

"Yes, it was especially if David does decide later on that he *would* like to go on the stage professionally."

"He's musically gifted too, plays the violin."

"Shame if his parents won't encourage this too."

"They might," Alan remarked. "If maybe only privately for their family and friends.

It's early days yet though. We don't know what's going to happen in the future."

"No, we can't," I agreed.

There was to be no performance of the pantomime on Christmas Eve, Christmas Day, or New Year's Eve or 'Old Year's Night' as the Scots called it or New Year's Day. It was due to come to an end two weeks later. I knew the girls would find it an anti-climax when it finally finished. So, I tried to think of other things that I might be able to interest them in when this happened.

CHAPTER FORTY-SIX

On Christmas Day itself, the twins were each given a stocking with an apple, orange, and chocolate inside it. They were also both excited to receive a china doll. Mirabelle called hers 'Susanne' and Sylvie called hers 'Isabella.' They were also given a dolls' house to share. "It's means proper sharing," Alan said. "Taking it in turns to play with it."

"Some hope of that," I said to Alan, afterwards. "They're bound to argue over it, sometimes."

"Hope you're wrong," Alan had said, giving me a cheeky wink.

I was proved right but after one argument I threatened that if I heard another row, the dolls' house would be taken away from them. They did not bicker over it as much afterwards, to both Alan's and my relief.

The girls had given us, their parents, and aunt Eloise handkerchiefs they had embroidered with a tiny flower in the corner as presents.

"Plenty of room for us to blow our noses on," Alan said.

Eloise and I had both smiled.

When it was the day before New Year's Eve Mirabelle said. "This is called Hogmanay, isn't it?"

"I kent that too," Sylvie added.

Alan had nodded. "Aye, that's right. But not quite yet, tomorrow is Old Year's Night or New Year's Eve as they call it in England."

"We're having a party then," I said.

The girls both cheered as their faces lit up.

"We are," Alan said. "But you two must go to bed immediately after twelve o'clock. You can stay in bed a bit longer the next day though."

"And do you promise to behave yourselves while the party's going on?" I asked.

"Aye, mamma," the twins said together.

"Because if you don't, I'm warning you, you won't be able to go to another one."

The party was a great success much to Alan's and my relief. We had invited a few of the cast and their parents to it. David Irvine also came, not with his parents but with a male friend of his called Alexander Patterson. David had been asked to bring his violin along which he had done with obvious pleasure.

Our rooms were candle lit, illuminating the smart clothes of the gentlemen and the bright colours of the ladies' dresses.

Our three maids had been engaged in preparing a buffet and placed plates of sandwiches, biscuits, and cakes on our long table in the dining room. One of their younger brothers had been engaged to serve drinks to our guests. He seemed excited to be doing this. Alan watched him carefully but discreetly at first then decided the young man seemed capable enough.

After a while I said to Eloise "If I accompany you on the piano, will you be kind enough to sing for us?"

She hesitated for a moment, glancing at her husband who gave a discreet nod.

"Yes, Isabelle, I would."

I was pleased as I went over to take my seat at the small piano we kept in the dining room. The larger one was situated in our parlour.

After taking a deep breath, Eloise announced to the company "I'm going to sing a couple of folk songs Isabelle and I learned in our youth in France. The first one's called '*Joli Tambour*' meaning 'Pretty Drummer Boy,' the second is '*Il Etait une bergère,* that means "He was a shepherd."

Her voice rang out clear and sweet and after she had finished, she was applauded enthusiastically. She was smiling but I noticed her blushing slightly. I glanced at John who was looking proudly at her.

I had a quick word with Alan and our daughters after discreetly drawing them into a corner of the room then I said. "And now, our two lassies are going to sing a song together as well as performing a jig and a Highland dance."

The girls looked delighted but nervous. But after they started their act, they overcame their nerves, becoming totally engrossed in what they were doing. Once again afterwards there was vigorous applause and delighted smiles all around the room. Alan and I both felt thrilled for them. They were blushing but obviously happy.

I was privately amused to overhear Sylvie's stage whisper to Mirabelle "We was good, I think."

I noticed that Douglas Phipps had been watching them with a lot of interest. I overheard him say to Alan. "Your lassies were excellent; they've come on a lot since the pantomime."

Looking pleased, Alan then turned to David. "Would you like to play your violin for us now, Davie?"

"Be delighted to, sir."

Alan had smiled. "Don't call me 'sir,' my name's Alan."

David looked impressed by Alan's informality. I thought he looked slightly nervous; like all of us who had tried to entertain our guests.

David was blushing as he began to play Beethoven's 'Moonlight Sonata' but his blushes disappeared after he had played the first few notes. After he had finished, he received the same amount of appreciation that the rest of us had. But I did notice that although he was smiling, he also looked relieved.

After the clocks chimed the midnight hour, we were all waiting with glasses of wine or whisky in our hands although David, Alexander and the girls had been given cordial, Alan shouted "Happy New Year everyone, may it be a 'guid yin'" (exaggerating his accent as he did occasionally) "for us all."

We all drank to that toast but immediately afterwards I said to our daughters. "Right, you two, off to your beds now you've seen the New Year in. And not too much talking before you go to sleep."

They went, only a trifle reluctantly because they were tired. We were allowing them to rise later than usual the following morning.

Our party broke up just over an hour later. After Alan and I were in bed ourselves at last, he said "I've been given several orders for photographs. A lot of the folk who've been here tonight want them, quite a few wished for family ones and the single people just one for themselves."

"I'm delighted for you, well for us both, really," I enthused after we had embraced before falling into a deep sleep.

PART THREE: ADOLESCENCE

CHAPTER FORTY-SEVEN
APRIL 1905

We had all been invited for afternoon tea on a warm day at the country mansion of David's father, Robert Irvine, the Earl of Roseleans, situated nearly eight miles away from Edinburgh.

David had become a frequent visitor to our house after he had bought a couple of photographs from Alan of him playing the violin there on a few occasions after the party. The twins both regarded him as a good friend. But this would be the first time for us to pay a return visit.

Irvine Hall was large and full of elegant furniture and beautiful silver. The earl's estate was not as extensive as a few others that belonged to the aristocracy but it was a decent size. It contained farms and a few coal mines.

David's face lit up with pleasure when he saw the twins. "So nice to see you two again."

"And ye, Davie," they chorused.

"You as well, of course, Mr and Mrs Fergusson."

"Thank you," Alan said.

"How's David getting on with his photography classes?" the earl asked him.

"Very well, he's an eager pupil and learns fast." Alan smiled. "Hasn't got to walk before he can run kind of thing, though. If he could, I probably wouldn't be able to catch him."

The earl gave a stiff smile of approval. "I'm glad the pantomime season's over," he said. next. This remark irritated me but I tried not to show it.

His wife looked surprised. "But Davie enjoyed being in the show so much."

Irvine looked impatient. "Yes, but I think he should be doing more useful things in his spare time."

Poor David looked both embarrassed and slightly angry. I could see he was trying valiantly to keep control of himself.

"Oh, come on, Robert," the countess protested. "He can ride well and takes an interest in our estate and its people. What's more, he's amiable with everybody."

"Agree with you about that but I don't want him to get unsuitable notions of becoming a professional actor."

"But you've never minded him playing his violin."

"That's different, I could just about accept him playing in a professional orchestra. But not acting, he'll earn his keep another way."

Alan noticed the earl scowling slightly and David looking even more embarrassed. So, he said, "All of us in our small family have enjoyed his company when he's visited us after one of his photography lessons with me. And he's taken decent pictures of Edinburgh Castle and its chapel."

The earl frowned. "Yes, a little interest for him. But that chapel's not as intricate as ours."

"No, it's not," Alan agreed.

We had been shown Roseleans Chapel, it was large and had elaborate carvings both in its interior, also on its exterior.

"Actually," the countess said. "Davie's asked me if he can go to Dunoon with the Young Minstrel company that Mr Phipps owns, this summer. So, naturally, I told him he would need your permission."

The earl smiled for a change. "Might surprise you that I'm giving it."

"Our lassies are going there too," Alan said, proudly.

David beamed at them. "I'll enjoy your company while I'm there."

"Thank you," the girls said, together.

"It does no harm for David to mix with people of a different class now and again," Irvine said, in a pompous manner. He frowned. "A little too friendly with some of our miners too, aren't you, David?"

David looked angry. However, we could tell he was deliberately suppressing this feeling.

The countess said quickly. "We've gained some of our wealth from our mines, Robert. And I don't think you should criticise David for that, he does so because he's kind."

I guessed that she was being more outspoken than usual because her husband looked startled.

"Kindness can go too far on occasion. Davie should be cultivating more friendships with his own sort. And, eventually, he'll need to supervise our employees, tenants, and servants."

"A long time ahead, I hope, Robert," his wife said.

I could see that Alan was itching to bristle at the earl's snobbery and ill manners but was making a valiant effort to control himself as he probably didn't want to embarrass David even more.

"And I've heard a rumour, Mr Fergusson," the earl said, glancing at our daughters with a sour frown. "That you allow your girls to appear at your friend's music hall."

"That's right, I do," Alan confirmed.

"But it's usually working-class parents who permit this sort of thing with their family members. Forgive me for saying this but they must be more in need of wage earners for their families."

I could see Alan was struggling for mastery of himself. "I can assure you," he said, coldly. "That my friend runs a respectable place and my wife and I would never allow anything improper to happen to our daughters."

"I can only hope you'll succeed. Could be hard, eventually, though."

I spoke up then although I had been quiet most of the time. "Alan has always succeeded at *everything* he does."

Alan gave me a grateful look.

He stood up. "Thank you for your hospitality," he said, stiffly, to Irvine. "But we should really be getting home now."

"Hope you'll all come again soon," Helen Irvine said. I decided that I liked her much better than her husband.

I don't hope we'll come again soon, even at all, I thought but didn't voice it.

CHAPTER FORTY-EIGHT

We went to the Pantheon music hall for the first show on the Saturday night of the following week.

The prices of the tickets were eightpence for the Gallery, for the Upper Circle one shilling and six pence and half a crown for the Grand Circle and Orchestra Stalls where Alan took us all. Alan had bought a copy of 'The Era,' the publication that advertised music hall acts and vacancies. He had also bought a programme.

"Miss Fraser taught you two about advertising, didn't she?" he asked our daughters who both nodded.

The maids had been given free tickets for the Gallery and allowed to go to the afternoon performance the previous day. They had been thrilled by the show and Alan and I had smiled as we overheard some of their remarks about it.

In the evening as the orchestra played the overture, Sylvie whispered to Mirabelle. "I like this music, don't ye, Belle?" Mirabelle nodded in agreement.

I frowned. "Hush, you're supposed to be listening not talking," I snapped. Suitably abashed, they focused their attention on the stage performances.

After the overture, a Highland pipe band played then a family party of Italian acrobats performed feats of dexterity, they were followed by a male serio-comic singer who made us all laugh.

The next act was a female singer who was a male impersonator, she was followed by a Polish juggler.

"He's got a funny name," Mirabelle whispered to Sylvie after she had looked over Alan's shoulder at his programme. She looked away after she had earned disapproving looks from her father and myself.

A popular male singer who followed the juggler encouraged the audience to join in with the choruses of his songs. The twins were now allowed to join in which they did with gusto. Three sisters who were singers and Highland dancers came on next,

179

they were followed by a Scottish comedian who was beginning to make a name for himself.

The star act was a beautiful female singer, Heather Drew. "I've been friends with both Marie Lloyd and Vesta Tilley," she said. "So, they won't mind me singing songs of theirs."

Alan was unsure if he really believed this but as he told me afterwards, he kept his opinion to himself. We enjoyed her performances of "The Boy I Love, When I Take my Morning Promenade, After the Ball, Jolly Good Luck to the Girl who Likes a Soldier and A Little of What You Fancy Does You Good." Finally, she sang "I'd Like to Live in Paris All the Time." which made me smile as well as feel a little nostalgic for old times. But I managed to shake this emotion off quickly.

As our chauffeur drove us home, the twins were full of non-stop chatter about what they had witnessed. They made varied comments on the performers but didn't criticise any of them

"Love to go there again sometime," Sylvie said, wistfully.

"And me," Mirabelle agreed. "The sooner the better."

"Noticed you both paying attention to what was going on up on stage," I said, feeling proud of them. But I didn't wish them to become over-confident.

"We did, didn't we, Belle?" Sylvie stated.

"Of course," Mirabelle agreed.

"Bear what you've both just said in mind, keep up the good work," Alan advised, giving me a sly wink while the twins weren't looking.

CHAPTER FORTY-NINE

The twins were thrilled about their forthcoming week's stay in Dunoon, 'The Gateway to the Highlands' as it was advertised, with its holiday homes built along the Clyde shores inhabited mainly by Glasgow businessmen. Alan told me its prosperity had been built on the shipping, manufacturing, and tobacco industries.

"The girls can't wait to get to Dunoon, can they?" Alan said to me.

"Yes," I agreed. But I can't help wondering if they'll become homesick while they're there."

"Doubt it, they've got friends of theirs going too. And the organisers will be looking after them."

"Hope they remember their manners."

Alan smiled. "Sure, they will."

"They'd better. I'll be annoyed if they don't."

"Don't think you need to worry."

"Hope you're right."

The girls wrote to us to say they had been settled into accommodation at a comfortable boarding house in Dunoon. And David Irvine had been seated at the same table as they were on their first night. I knew that would have pleased them.

They had seen paddle steamers on the water and had been told they were due to have a ride on one on their last night. They seemed excited about this.

"Hope they'll be careful not to fall overboard," I said.

Alan shook his head. "They won't, for all they get excited sometimes, they're too canny to let that happen to them."

"I'm glad they'll have David's company," I commented. "Even if I don't like his father."

"Oh, Davie's not like his old man," Alan reassured me. "Speaking of him, he owns two shipping companies, one's bigger than the other."

I glanced at the girls' enthusiastic letter again. "They seem to like their organiser."

Alan nodded. "William Kerr, aye. And they like fine that they'll be appearing at the Castle Hotel."

"With its lovely gardens," I added, remembering this phrase in their letter. Alan smiled. "They believe there'll be a lot of spectators as long as the weather's fine enough."

Our next letter from them informed us that the weather on the performance evening had, fortunately, been fine, warm, and sunny but not too hot for comfort. And the crowd watching them had been huge.

The younger children had performed first, Mirabelle and Sylvie had both been part of the older dance troupe and they both sang in the senior choir.

Later, Davie had sung a sea shanty as a solo. It had, apparently, been very well received. Alan and I were pleased for him. 'Right fine voice he has," our long letter had informed us

The youngsters continued to perform for the rest of the week, they were fortunate enough to have had good weather with only one day of rain. On that day they put on their acts in the Pavilion building where, they enthused, was a splendid dance floor plus a large spectators' gallery and tea rooms. "It's lovely," their letter said,

"I'm pleased this trip has been a success for them," I said to Alan, after we had read their letter, both of us smiling as we did so.

"So am I," Alan agreed. "It's probably done them good to gain a bit of independence."

Their final day had been free. But we learned that David had taken them to see the model boating pond with its model sailing boats. The girls had liked this.

That evening they'd gone to a town restaurant for high tea. Afterwards they had embarked on an evening cruise on a paddle steamer called 'The Ivanhoe' that belonged to the Caledonian Steam Packet Company.

In the evening the captain of the 'Ivanhoe' wearing a gold braided uniform had welcomed the children on-board. Alan and I were amused by their comment that he had been 'glittering.' The deck hands had apparently, been dressed in white shirts with navy blue collars.

A German band had played popular tunes and led sing songs with the children. One of the band members had gone round with a hat afterwards for financial contributions from the customers. Our girls had each dropped a coin into this hat.

David had taken quite a few photographs while they were there.

"I'm pleased they've enjoyed themselves while they've been away," Alan said. "But I'm looking forward to having them back home again."

I smiled. "So, am I, they'll be dying to tell us all about their adventures, won't they?"

"You bet," Alan agreed. "Expect they'll be blethering away nineteen to the dozen too."

"And to return to Douglas' music hall," I added.

Alan grinned. "Love their billing as 'The Sisters Fergusson, Charming Junior Dancers and Duettists.'"

"They'll be in 'The Era' next," I said.

"Soon, probably," Alan agreed.

CHAPTER FIFTY

Two weeks later on the Monday, the twins received a letter from David, much to their surprise and pleasure as well as Alan's and mine. They showed it to us, Alan and I both believed they might have wanted it to be kept private. "This is Davie's letter," Sylvie said, handing it to Alan.

"It's interesting," Mirabelle stated. Alan and I managed to hide our smiles.

The letter read:

"Dear Mirabelle and Sylvie

My mother has told me that my father has gone to Perth where he wishes to buy a couple of racehorses as well as going to a few of the races near the ancient Scone Palace."

Bet she's glad about that, even if she won't admit it, openly. I thought privately.

The letter continued:

"You may be surprised by this but I am now living in Brighton with two other fellows around my age, I am nearly 20 as you know, the other two are 21. They are Martin Stirling and Alexander Hamilton. We take part in burlesques at the local theatre. If you're not sure what these are, they poke a bit of fun at some well-known legends and stories. They include singing, spoken dialogue, comedy routines and dancing. I am enjoying this, well, we all do. Martin also writes the odd poem and I write short dialogues sometimes but I feel I need to improve a little in this respect. I still like playing my violin. A few of our fellow performers have appeared at music halls. Expect you two are still thrilling audiences at Mr Phipps' one.

My father wasn't pleased about what I'm doing at first, he would have preferred me to go to university and study for a degree instead. But he was placated a little when I promised I would try to do this at a later date. When I am 21, he won't be able to have much influence over me though he will not like this.

He has not visited me here yet. He'll probably think the house we're sharing will not be the kind he would approve of. However, I should love you and your parents to visit us at a convenient time in the not-too-distant future.
Very much hoping that you are all in good health.
Yours truly
David Irvine."

"What a nice letter," I said, after it had been put back inside the envelope.

"It is," Alan agreed. "You two are lucky."

"Papa," Mirabelle entreated with her most winsome expression. "Can we all go and visit them soon?"

Alan hesitated, taking a deep breath. Then, he smiled. "Aye, I've decided we can. But I'll go there on my own first and find us a suitably priced hotel. I'll stay in it for two days just to make sure it's suitable for us all."

I smiled as the girls cheered.

Alan returned after his two-day holiday and said "Everything's fixed for us for next week in Brighton. Hewitt will be driving us there on Monday and I'm allowing him to stay there for one night too."

"When we will come back?" Sylvie asked.

"The following Monday, Hewitt can come and collect us then."

We were all excited by this news

But during the following weekend, I caught a heavy cold.

"Sorry but I don't think I'll be able to go to Brighton," I said. "Don't feel well enough."

"You wouldn't enjoy it the same," Alan remarked.

Seeing the disappointment on our daughters' faces, I said, "But the rest of you should still go."

Alan frowned. "That would be selfish of us."

Shaking my head, I stated, "No, it would be more selfish of me to insist on you staying at home."

"But you're unwell," Alan protested. Wouldn't be fair of us to leave you while you're feeling like this. And we'd feel guilty about leaving you alone."

I shook my head. "Wouldn't be completely on my own. The maids will be here."

"Aye, they're efficient enough but it's not the same as having family around you."

I sighed. "Look, I'll be disappointed if you don't go. If I start to feel worse, I'll send you a telegram."

After further arguing throughout the week, at the end of it, Alan agreed, albeit somewhat reluctantly, that he would go to the seaside resort with our girls while I remained at home.

"But promise to let me know if you, Heaven forbid, take a turn for the worse but it could happen Isabelle. Do I have your word about this?"

"Yes, of course."

CHAPTER FIFTY-ONE

Three days later I was feeling much better and sent one of our maids to see Lucy Wilson and ask Lucy if she would like to meet me and have tea in Jenson's Department Store. The girl returned with the message that Lucy would like to do this. She was pleased to agree with this idea. We had always found Jenson's department store interesting. So, I caught the omnibus to meet her there.

"In Alan's letter," I said to Lucy, once we were seated in Jenson's Restaurant with a plate of cakes and a pot of tea on the table before us. "He's described what the house is like where the young men are living. Would you like me to read it out to you?"

She nodded. "Yes please."

I read. "The drawing room is clean but jumbled. There's an almost threadbare carpet on the floor plus a fireplace and a piano and a harmonium in the corner. David's violin is propped up against the wall. A bed's in the opposite corner with a patchwork quilt thrown over it and there's a sofa and two easy chairs. The wooden table in the centre of the room is covered by a linen cloth. on top of which there's an aspidistra. And a few copies of the 'The Era.' Plus a few sheets of lined paper with untidy handwriting, hand drawn musical notes and illustrations on them with some of them crossed out. There's a few pictures on the walls and some books on the shelves."

Lucy laughed. "Sounds interesting but typical of untidy young fellows."

But as we were walking towards the bus stop, we saw a poorly dressed boy and girl in the street, talking to each other. The boy looked about twelve or thirteen, the girl around ten years of age. "Wonder if they're brother and sister," I said.

"Don't think so," Lucy commented. "They don't resemble each other much."

The next minute we saw the boy snatch a small purse out of the girl's hand. She started to cry. We managed to reach them shortly afterwards. Lucy caught hold of the boy's collar. "Give that girl her purse back," she ordered in a commanding tone of voice. He started to run away but I managed to grab hold of him and drag him back. "Go on, you heard the other lady," I snapped. "Give it back."

The boy obeyed as the girl's face lit up when her purse was handed back to her. She ran off. But to my surprise, the lad began to weep.

"Ye'll tell the polis aboot me," he stuttered. "And I'll be in trouble with them again."

"So, you've done this before," I stated in a softer tone than the one I'd previously used.

"Aye," he said, miserably. "Ah'm hungry and thirsty."

He was wearing a thin, slightly ripped dark blue cotton jacket over his grey shirt and grey trousers, frayed at the hem with an old cap over his brown hair.

"Surely your mother feeds you," Lucy frowned.

He shook his head. "She's deid," he said.

"What about your father?" I asked. Does he make sure you have enough food? I hope he does, of course."

The lad shrugged. "Sometimes when he isnae too drunk, he does."

Lucy and I were both shocked. We both opened our own purses and gave him some coins that he almost snatched from us. His brown eyes widened.

"Get yourself fed and watered with that, don't waste it on things you don't need," Lucy said, firmly.

"What's your name?" I asked him.

"Ian, Ian McFarlane."

The wisp of an idea occurred to me. "How old are you, Ian?"

"Thirteen nearly fourteen."

"When will you be fourteen?"

"In aboot a week's time."

Small for his age I thought but didn't voice it. "What would your parents think if they knew you'd been stealing?"

Ian shrugged his shoulders. "Naething, my ma died after she got a fever. And ma faither's in the jail."

"What for?"

"Oh, he's a crook, pinches watches, jewellery, clothes and a'that."

"Do you have any brothers or sisters?"

"No, used to but they died of the fever, same as Ma."

So, you were lucky to survive, I thought, or were you, really, considering you seem to have already become a petty criminal? On impulse I handed him a piece of paper with my address on it. Foolish maybe on my part but there were enough staff at home who would make sure I was safe.

"Can you read and write, Ian?"

"Of course, I can," he replied, indignantly. "Cannae spell everythin' though."

"All right, read aloud what's written on that paper to me."

He read my address correctly although haltingly.

"Well done, Ian," I said, thinking a little praise might cheer him. "Come to this house next week, go to the back door and my husband might be able to fix you up with a job, helping him."

Ian looked stupefied as if he didn't know what to think as Lucy stared at me in amazement. Ian blinked his brown eyes, almost the same colour as his unkempt hair.

"Come on, Isabelle," she said. Or we'll never catch our bus."

Almost reluctantly, I did as she asked. "See you then, Ian," I called over my shoulder. He nodded in agreement.

"Are you sure you've done the right thing, Isabelle? That waif might tell others of his sort where you live and they might try to break into your house."

I shook my head. "Understand you thinking that, Lucy. But our house is well guarded by the staff. Only I couldn't help feeling sorry for him." I hesitated before I spoke again. "I *have* thought of a way Alan could employ him."

Lucy's hazel eyes widened. "Alan could very well be annoyed with you when he comes back home with your lassies."

I nodded. "Yes, I'm expecting that myself but if Ian does turn up next week and things go as I'd like them to, Alan might, given a bit of time, come around to my way of thinking."

"Hope so for your sake," Lucy said. "Though to be honest, I'm doubtful."

I changed the subject by asking Lucy about her family. She seemed relieved to be talking about them instead.

When I reached home, however, I did start to feel apprehensive about what Alan's reaction would be like when I told him about Ian.

CHAPTER FIFTY-TWO

My husband and daughters returned one early afternoon from their trip with colour in their cheeks and sparkling eyes. I had missed them and was pleased to see them, they also appeared to be happy to be reunited with me again although they'd only been away for a short period of time, we were happy to be back in each other's' company.

After he had embraced me, Alan said, "How are you now, Isa? Do hope your cold's a lot better."

"It's much better, thank you," I replied.

"That's a relief, we were a bit worried about you while we were away."

I smiled. "There was no need to, fortunately."

"We had a lovely time while we were away, Mamma," Mirabelle enthused. "We went on the beach and paddled in the sea."

Alan grinned. "Aye and I heard you both screaming when you started splashing each other."

"We were laughing not screaming," Sylvie protested.

"It was still noisy," Alan corrected her although he was smiling. "Didn't mind though as long you were enjoying yourselves."

"We thought the burlesques we watched were brilliant too," Mirabelle said. "Wish you could have seen them."

"I've taken some photographs of them," Alan said. "Your mother will be able to look at them when they're developed."

"I'll like that. Tell me about the stories, Belle."

She described them to me. How one had used the fairy tale of Cinderella with Martin playing her part in the story and David and Alistair playing the Brothers Grimm who had collected a lot of old folk tales from their native Germany. David and Alistair had told the tale in a poetic form and added a few of their own jokes.

"We saw Davie with his pals, Alistair and Martin afterwards," Sylvie remarked. Then, she frowned. "But we didn't see Martin for very long. Davie told us he goes out a lot on his own. We asked him where Martin went but Davie said he didn't know. Seemed a bit strange to Mirabelle and me."

I noticed Alan looked a little concerned. Taking a deep breath, I told them all about Ian.

Alan's face became a little red. He and I didn't argue a lot but he could become passionate at times about certain of his beliefs.

"Somewhat foolish, Isabelle. What was the point of you asking him to come here? If he's rough and ready, he could look around our house and bring possibly wretched friends of his here to rob us if we're not careful."

I felt that I needed to make an excuse for what I'd done as well as wishing to placate Alan. "It was an idea I had because I felt sorry for him."

"Obviously but perhaps, he was telling fibs."

"Didn't think that about him." An impulse struck me. "I wondered if you might like to have an apprentice in your studio. He could possibly be an errand boy, could deliver orders to people who've given you custom."

"Might also steal from me, run away with the goods," Alan snapped.

Understanding Alan's point of view, another idea occurred to me. "Maybe if he's sent out with Hewitt to begin with on the days when we don't need the man to drive *us* anywhere, we'll find out if Ian *is* trustworthy."

"H'mm, a bit unlikely in my opinion but I'll give it some thought. He smiled after hesitating for a few minutes. "I can just imagine Hewitt's face when he's told he'll be accompanying a young whippersnapper around the city."

I breathed a mental sigh of relief.

After we had all gone to bed, Alan said to me, "Sylvie seemed attracted to that Martin."

"Don't you like him?"

Alan sighed. "It's not exactly that I dislike him but there are certain men who have … well, different tastes I suppose you could call them, to others."

"You mean the ones who prefer to love others of the same sex rather than women."

Alan started. "Aye, you're aware of them, then?"

"Of course, after I ran away from home in Paris, I knew some of their kind."

"Were you shocked by it?"

"Not completely, to be honest, though I knew a lot of people were. Provided they didn't force anybody or attack children, I could tolerate them."

"Fair minded lady, I admire you for it but let's not let on to Sylvie just yet. We can tell her when she's a bit older and probably more worldly wise."

"In the meantime, try to encourage her to meet other boys, you mean?"

"Aye, talking of which, I think we ought to invite the lads Sylvie and Mirabelle saw recently, to a return visit. I know we can't really put them up in our house."

"Not that we don't have the room," I commented.

Alan sighed. "Aye but we do have our reputations to consider. And we'd be the subject of possibly unpleasant gossip. He hesitated for a few minutes. "But we could find accommodation for them while they're here, couldn't we? Would you be agreeable to this?"

I nodded. "Yes, of course."

Alan smiled. "Good, that's settled then." Talking of young men generally, wonder if this lad you met *will* turn up in the morn."

"He will, I'm sure," I insisted although I couldn't help wondering about this myself, hoping my confidence wouldn't prove to be misplaced.

CHAPTER FIFTY-THREE

To my vast relief, Ian did arrive the next day looking even shabbier than the first time I had seen him. I couldn't help wondering if I had done the right thing but it was too late to change now. Our head housemaid showed him to our parlour. I could see she disapproved of him but was making a valiant effort not to show it. I had wondered whether I should be present when Alan spoke to Ian but Alan said he would prefer me to be there with them.

I asked Ian to sit down and noticed him looking around the room with interest. It made me feel nervous. So, I asked our maid to bring him a glass of lemonade and a biscuit. His eyes lit up.

"Do you desperately need work, Ian?" Alan asked him after Ian had told him where he lived. I thought the question a little blunt but Ian didn't seem to mind.

"Aye, because ma faither hasnae got a job the now."

"What did he do when he was working?"

"Ma faither worked on the docks but he had a row with another man when he was drunk and they had a fight. And he'd picked the other feller's pocket. So, he got the sack."

"Not surprisingly. Did he find another job afterwards?"

"For a wee while but then he lost it."

"I see, so you needed to earn some money to help you both. Am I right about that?"

"Aye, sir."

"Are you fourteen yet?"

"Aye, ma birthday was two days ago."

"Good, you're of age for paid work now Well, you've been honest about your circumstances. I'm wondering if you'd like to work for me. I take photographs of people and Mr Hewitt, our chauffeur, takes some of them round to folks' houses. So, would you like to help Mr Hewitt?"

Ian blinked, looking startled. "D'ye mean, sir? …

Alan smiled. "What I mean is, Ian, I'm offering you a job going around with Mr Hewitt and he'll probably sometimes ask you to go on errands for him. Would you do that for a weekly wage? It won't be a lot of money, mind but it should help you and your father a bit. So, what's your answer?"

Ian's face lit up in a beaming smile. He wasn't a particularly good-looking boy but at that moment he looked radiant. "Aye, sir."

"Well, Ian, that's been settled quickly. You'd better thank this lady though," he indicated me to the boy. "She's the one, really, who's done you this favour. So, what do you say to her?"

Ian looked at me, gratefully. "Thank ye very much, mistress."

"I'm pleased about what's happened today, Ian," I replied. "You will work hard for my husband and do what Mr Hewitt tells you to without arguing though, won't you?"

"Aye, mistress."

Alan handed Ian a ten-pound note. The boy's eyes opened in wonder.

"That's to buy food and some decent clothes with what's left over but make sure they're suitable for work. Get some warm ones because the winter will be coming on soon. You'd better leave us now. Come back at nine o'clock next Monday morning. Don't be late."

"No sir, I won't."

After the grinning lad had left, Alan said. "Are you happy I've rescued your lame duck?"

I smiled. "Think you've taught him to swim a bit, thank you."

Alan looked thoughtful. "I'll try not to let him drown."

"Seriously, I hope I didn't do the wrong thing inviting him here. I did wonder."

"Ah, you did it out of the kindness of your heart, Isa. I do realise that."

That evening, while we were eating our evening meal, I told the girls about Ian. "Hope I did do the right thing; I've begun to wonder."

"Many would say you didn't," Alan said. "But I know you acted out of kindness."

"You were just being good to an unfortunate, Mamma," Sylvie said.

"Like we've been taught to," Mirabelle agreed.

Her sister nodded in agreement.

"All the same," I remarked. "Can't help wondering if he'll be no good at the job your father's been good enough to offer him"

Ian proved to be a good, eager worker much to my relief. Alan and I both had our doubts about whether Hewitt would like Ian but we kept them to ourselves.

The girls were excited about the forthcoming visit of David Irvine and his two companions. They'd received a letter informing them of the day the young men would be arriving.

"We'll be inviting them to see us at Doug's music hall one of the days," Sylvie said. "You won't mind them doing that, will you?"

"Please say it's acceptable," Mirabelle added before Alan and I had had a chance to answer the question.

Alan held his hand up halfway in mid-air. "Aye, of course and they'll probably be impressed."

"Hope you won't be too nervous when it happens," I said. "Although you should be all right."

"We will," Sylvie said, confidently.

"Surely," Mirabelle agreed.

The three young men arrived the following week and were settled into a reasonably priced hotel. It was comfortable rather than luxurious.

On the girls' day off from the music hall, they begged me to accompany them on their first visit to see them David had sent us a letter, inviting us to have lunch with them one day.

Alan was not attending as he didn't want to have too much time away from his business. "You three go, though," he had said. "Don't want to spoil things for you."

We had all thanked him, feeling grateful although I felt that the trio would probably have preferred to have seen our twins on their own but for the sake of what would be considered propriety I agreed, especially as Alan and I knew some of our acquaintances disapproved of us letting them appear on stage especially that of a music hall even though it was a respectable one. But we ignored them. I didn't really care what others thought about it. We were living our lives on our own terms.

When we arrived at the hotel where the young men were staying, we found the food and drink were good, of a better standard than I had expected.

"How have you found this city?" I asked the lads.

"We've enjoyed it," Alistair said. "Davie's been kind enough to show us around some interesting places he knows, some off the beaten track."

"It must have been a bit strange to you at first, Mrs Fergusson, coming from France, as you did," David said. He was wearing a loud checked jacket with a high white starched collar, the other two were dressed in tweed suits.

"It certainly felt different at first," I admitted. "But I'm used to it as my home now and would miss it if I left."

Before anyone could answer, I added. "I like it fine now and don't ever wish to move away from it."

"Your husband must be relieved about that," David said, making us all laugh.

"Yes, fortunately," I agreed.

I noticed David giving a fond look at Mirabelle.

Martin said "But poor Davie's not been able to see his parents yet."

David scowled. "They disapprove of me, well of the life I lead. My father's worse than my mother, though. You know that."

"Give us all a laugh, Davie. Do your impression of them," Martin said.

"I'm pretending to be him now," David said. "When he's talking about me to other people."

He put on a pompous expression and spoke with an exaggerated drawl. "Our family may not be the oldest noble one in the land. But we still have a proud and worthy name." He frowned. "Unfortunately, our eldest son has been a disappointment to us. Never liked hunting though he's a good

196

rider. Yes, he has musical ability but he mixes with the wrong sort including our miners too much and is, I can hardly bear to say this, an entertainer of the common type. His mother and I wouldn't object to him performing privately at home but on public stages, not even theatres some of them, watched by common ... well ... words fail me."

"Wouldn't think they did entirely, not after a speech like that," Alistair said, making us all laugh.

I looked admiringly at his tall figure with his auburn hair worn slightly long, blue grey eyes and fair skin although I knew I would keep this opinion to myself.

"My parents are both dead, unfortunately," Martin said.

"Sorry about that," I sympathised. "You must miss them."

Martin looked resigned. "Naturally, I did at first but I've now got used to them no longer being around."

Wishing to introduce a lighter note to our conversation, I said "Sylvie and Mirabelle can't wait for you all to see them on stage."

"We're all looking forward to that," Alistair said, eagerly.

When we arrived back home, we saw Ian outside our door with his outdoor clothes on, looking dejected. He was looking as if he was trying not to cry.

"Is something wrong, Ian?" I asked, wondering if Hewitt had upset him.

He glanced at the girls in a nervous way. "Can I tell ye on yer ain, mistress?"

"Very well," I sighed, indicating to Sylvie and Mirabelle that they should enter the house. They looked disappointed but didn't argue with me about it.

After they'd gone, I asked, "What's the matter then, Ian?"

"Ma faither's in Calton Jail."

"What did he do?"

"Broke into a jeweller's shop three nights ago and pinched watches, necklaces and stuff like that. But he was disturbed afore he could get oot o' the place so ye'll no be wanting me to go on workin' here."

197

I shook my head. "You're not responsible for what your father did, Ian. But I'll have to see what my husband says about letting you to go on working for him."

Ian's face fell.

"Look," I said. "I'd like you to stay. I'll ask Hewitt to drive us to the prison and you can visit your father for as long as they'll allow."

Ian looked grateful. Thank ye, mistress."

"Wait here while I go in and tell the girls we're going out for a little while but I shan't tell them where, yet. I'll also find Hewitt though he won't be pleased."

Ian began to shrug his shoulders then thought better of it.

CHAPTER FIFTY-FOUR

As Ian and I reached Calton Hill near Princes Street, I understood why visitors to the city often mistook the prison with its castellated design for Edinburgh Castle.

I shuddered as I remembered Alan telling me the tale of Burke and Hare, the notorious pair of Irish body snatchers and murderers in the eighteen twenties, how they had killed lodgers in their home after they'd invited them in to have a drink with them. Their victims were totally intoxicated before being murdered. Burke and Hare were believed to have slain about sixteen people altogether and sold their bodies to a Dr Robert Knox, a lecturer at the University, and his students to experiment on. Burke had been hanged but Hare had given so much information about the pair's activities to the authorities that he had been set free much to a lot of the public's annoyance. He had been put on a coach but another passenger had recognized him. So, he had alighted from it but then disappeared.

"Come on, Ian," I said, noticing he was looking nervous. "Your father will be pleased to see you."

Ian gave a brave nod while Hewitt tried to hide a scowl as he held the car door open before driving to a nearby street.

We were shown to McFarlane's cell. He was dressed in a white cap, jacket, and, trousers with a blue stripe and heavy boots. He looked surprised to see us. Then he looked at his son affectionately.

"Ye look as if ye're keepin' well, right enough, son. "Was a wee bit worried aboot ye."

"Why did you do this, da?" Ian burst out, angrily.

I thought this question a little ironic considering the circumstances under which I had first encountered Ian. But then I decided he probably considered his father's crime a more serious one.

McFarlane had the grace to look a little shame faced. "Know I was stupid, shouldn't have done it. But what's done is done. And who's this with ye?"

He looked me up and down, I couldn't help wondering if he would have liked to steal my red velvet jacket and skirt, I wore warmer clothes now that the autumn weather was growing colder and it would soon turn to winter. His gaze made me feel uncomfortable.

"This nice lady and her man have give me a job."

"Are ye' gettin' wages for it?"

"Of course," I snapped. "Ian's not a slave. My husband pays him,"

"Good, glad to hear it. I get miserable wages in here. Just a pittance. "What's happenin' wi' the hoose, Ian?"

"It's aw'right, far as ah ken. Havenae been back there since I left."

"Do you own the house?" I asked McFarlane.

He shook his head. "No, ah rented it. Sometimes needed to borrow off pals to pay it."

I guessed they were talking about a tenement building rather than an actual house. And money for the rent was, in my opinion, more likely to have sometimes been stolen but I didn't comment on this. McFarlane would probably have denied it in any case.

"What do ye have to do in here every day?" Ian asked, looking slightly embarrassed.

"Get up at six in the mornin,' do some work around the place, mainly cleanin,' surgeon comes twice a week to inspect us. I've no needed treatment so far, thank God. Chaplain gives three services on Sundays and blethers borin' prayers to us other days. There's also school teachers, master, and mistress what learns us readin' and writin.' Didn't like that at first but I do now I've got better at it. Go to bed at nine o'clock."

The last statement of McFarlane's had given me an idea.

"I'll leave you two on your own here for a little while," I said.

I then sought the company of the Prison Governor, James Harris. He had given me the impression he was a decent man who was most likely firm with the prisoners when necessary but also fair.

"I'd like to help the school master and mistress with their teaching of the prisoners if I may," I said, boldly.

He smiled. "You'll be more than welcome."

I breathed a mental sigh of relief, at the same time, I couldn't help wondering what Alan and the girls would think of my decision.

When we had our evening meal, I was proved right.

"Don't think it's a good idea, Isa," Alan said, firmly.

I was disappointed, it must have shown in my face.

"Don't get upset," Alan said.

"Can't help it," I remarked.

"Mamma," Sylvie said. "When Ian's father gets released, he could try to persuade Ian to try to rob us."

"They could try to break in at night while we're all asleep," Sylvie agreed. "Especially if he's lost his lodgings."

I shook my head. "Doubt they'd try to do that. McFarlane wouldn't wish to be caught a second time. He'd know he'd get a longer sentence next time."

"Some criminals get used to prison terms," Alan said, darkly. "Become hardened to them."

"I'm sure this one won't," I disagreed, mentally praying I would be proved right.

CHAPTER FIFTY-FIVE

The arguments with my husband and daughters went on over the following week but finally Alan lost some of his patience.

Alan had also said to me at bedtime one night when we were out of the girls' hearing. "Prostitutes are said to run races with each other down the pavements outside of the prison. You might be mistaken for one of them."

"Doubt it, anyway if they did, I'd certainly prove them wrong by denying it."

"And how would you prove them wrong?"

"Could carry a little handbell with me. Hide it under my clothes."

Alan laughed. "Imaginative but my answer's still 'no.'"

I turned on my side, feeling frustrated but making no further comment.

However, the following week, Alan took me by surprise saying, "I'm tired of seeing you with a long face, Isabelle. Well, I've decided if you really want to help these prisoners, I'll agree to it but on condition that you only help teach the female ones."

He frowned. "But if any of them tries to attack you, you're to stop going to the jail. What do you say to that?"

"Thank you," I said, gratefully although I was feeling a little apprehensive about this, myself. But I wasn't going to admit this.

However, upon my arrival at the prison the following week, Mr Harris smiled when he saw me enter his private quarters saying "Welcome, Mrs Fergusson, take a seat. We're right glad to have you here. Would ye like a cup of tea afore ye're introduced to some of our …" He hesitated. "Guests though they're not really that. It just sounds better than ruffians or inmates."

"Yes please, I should like a cup of tea very much." I hoped it would calm my nerves.

"Feeling a bit uncomfortable are ye?"

"I just can't help wondering if …"

"Ye're doing the right thing. Understandable at first. But if you don't like it, you needn't come again. A matron looks after our female prisoners. Our school teachers will do their best to help ye settle in to begin with, anyway."

"Thank you."

"Ye've come at a good time for us. There's six girls from the Dalry Reformatory School been brought before the Police Court because they tried to escape from it but got caught. Two of the lassies tried this trick twice and they've been sentenced to 40 days in jail. Another two were found on Calton Hill in a man's company. Don't think I'd better tell ye what they were doing."

I smiled, thinking it was possible I wouldn't have been shocked but I didn't voice this opinion.

"They'll be here for fourteen days," Mr Patterson continued. "And a further two who stayed absent from the reformatory all night, have got to spend ten days in our company. Don't believe that lot will be all that aggressive towards you. And I've got a suggestion for you. Why don't ye talk to them about France. Doubt they've ever been there so they'll probably be interested."

I fervently hoped this was a true statement although I began to start thinking it was a good idea.

"I'll not put ye with the school master and mistress today," Mr Patterson said, kindly. "Better if ye have a chat wi' the lassies first. Is that acceptable to ye?"

"Yes," I answered, swallowing.

"That's the spirit. Let me take ye to meet them now."

There was no need for me to have fretted so much, to my great relief, because the girls did prove interested in what I told them about my home country. I told them that my father had wished for me to marry a man I disliked so I refused. I didn't mention that I'd run away from my home, merely saying that I hadn't in the end, wed him. I described Montmartre with its artists and said I had become friendly with a particular artist, not mentioning Leon by name. They were particularly interested in the Moulin Rouge and the Folies Bergère. I said I had been employed by them both, causing them to become wide eyed when they looked at me.

"Ye're makin' us all want to go there," one girl said, wistfully.

"Well, perhaps one day you will be able to," I said although I secretly had my doubts about this "As long as you keep out of trouble in future." After a moment's hesitation, hoping I hadn't sounded like a preacher with my last remark, I said. "My two daughters perform at a music hall on three evenings a week now. They used to only appear there in the afternoons. It's a respectable one owned by my husband's friend."

"I'd like fine to be able to go to one of them," another of the girls said.

"You probably will, one day," I remarked, trying to sound encouraging in view of my earlier comment.

I was both proud and amused that they seemed to have the impression that the twins were engaged in something glamourous.

"Do they have laddies?" one girl asked me.

"Yes, but just as friends at present," I replied.

"We all ken ye got caught wi' one, Eleanor," one of the girls said, making the others laugh.

I smiled, thinking it might be prudent to change the subject. "Well, let me tell you about the Seine River, it's a famous one. People go for rides on boats on it."

When I was due to go home, Mr Harris was smiling. "Very well done, Mrs Fergusson, when I passed by discreetly once or twice, I could see ye were keeping the lassies spellbound."

His glowing praise warmed my heart.

I had been happy with Alan and my daughters but upon occasion I had felt there was something missing from my life as I had wanted to do something in my life that would help others. Now my wish had been fulfilled.

204

CHAPTER FIFTY-SIX

I began to learn all about the crimes most of the prisoners had committed.

A poisoner had added arsenic to his wife's porridge. I heard that suspicions had been aroused when one of their neighbours' dogs died after eating it. Another man always wore an expensive gold ring with an embedded diamond. The diamond flew back after a tiny spring was pressed. There was a concealed cavity with opium stored in it. Another prisoner had killed his wife by lacing slices of orange she had eaten with opium. He had studied medicine and boasted that he could poison her without the doctors knowing. But they had known and reported him to the authorities.

These cases disturbed me because they reminded me of Leon, bringing back unhappy memories. But then I mentally chided myself because that was a long time ago and I now had a different sort of life.

A nursery maid had attacked another servant she'd had an argument with in the home of a wealthy grain merchant, causing her serious bodily harm. The merchant had reported her to the police.

A tall, beautiful blonde young woman had hired a car and went on a shopping spree. She had filled her lodgings with goods from drapers, jewellers, and wine merchants. She had said she was related to the Earl of Roseleans but he had furiously denied this. I could well imagine this. Warehouse company detectives had followed her movements and she was found to only have ninepence on her person. And she had no aristocratic relatives at all. Her debtors had besieged her lodgings. She had also defaulted tradesmen she had flirted with. She was sentenced to twenty days for having committed fraud to the value of twenty pounds.

To my surprise I found that I liked her although I had naturally disapproved of what she had done. However, she was an entertaining speaker, I guessed that after she had been released, she would probably find a male protector.

Some young apprentices in a printing office had stolen sheets of printed text for books and sold them as waste paper. They were only confined for a few days.

Two months later Ian informed us that his father was due to be released from prison the following week, his term had been shortened due to his good behaviour.

"Expect that was welcome news for you, Ian," Alan said.

Ian's face lit up. "It was. He was talkin' aboot findin' a place for us both to bide," "Have you any idea where he'll be looking?"

"Not yet, no. But he was bletherin' on aboot flittin' to Glasgow. Thinks there might be better chances of us both findin' work there."

"He may well be right, Ian. It probably would be good for you both to have a change of circumstances and go to a place where nobody knows you. Not that I wouldn't wish you to meet new people and make friends. Keep out of trouble though."

I smiled. "Try to make sure they're respectable too. Do you promise us that?"

Ian nodded. "Aye, we'll do that."

"Well, whatever is decided between the pair of you, we wish you both the very best of luck with it," Alan said.

"Thank ye. But he's said I'm to tell ye how grateful he is that you, mistress, took me in and helped me when I needed that. And he's watched ye aboot the jail and admired what ye do there wi' the lassies."

Even Alan smiled at this last comment. "Have you told Hewitt about this yet?" he asked.

Ian shook his head, "No." He grinned, mischievously. "The old bugger will be pleased as punch when I do tell him."

Alan and I exchanged secretly amused glances although trying to look disapproving. "Don't swear, Ian," Alan said.

"Sorry, ken I shouldnae have said that."

"Never mind this time. Just be careful in future. We all need to think sometimes before we speak," Alan said.

And before we act, I thought but didn't say so out aloud.

"Will you be replacing Ian after he leaves?" I asked Alan in bed that night.

"Don't think so, he was useful as an errand boy but Hewitt will be able to cope with deliveries on his own."

"Probably prefers that situation," I said dryly.

Alan laughed. "Aye even though it means a bit more work for him."

CHAPTER FIFTY-SEVEN

David had written to Alan to inform him that he was coming back to Edinburgh soon because he wished to try, eventually, to open a department store like Jensen's. But in the meantime, he would look for a smaller shop even a tiny one where he could sell things like photographs, stationery, and postcards.

"Bit ambitious of him to want to get to open something on the scale of Jensen's," Alan said.

"Where would be the best place to search for one of them, do you think? What would *you* advise?"

"Not sure yet but I'll have a look around the place and if I do come across somewhere that I believe would serve his purpose, I'll let him know."

"Do you think he'll want to borrow any money off you?" I asked, tentatively. While I didn't wish for Alan not to help David financially at all, I wasn't sure that it would be wise for him to be too generous in this respect.

"Not sure but I would be willing to give him a small loan to begin with."

I was relieved. "Good of you but you won't let him take advantage of you, will you?"

"Don't think he's the type to do that."

I sighed. "You're probably right but sometimes I'm naturally cautious."

Alan laughed. "Not all the time, sometimes you can be impulsive."

"Can't we all behave that way on occasion?"

"Aye, ye're right there. Oh well, time will tell. Shouldn't like Davie to discover he's made a grave mistake though. Still, if that does unfortunately happen, I'll give him a job helping me in my studio. It would be a temporary one though."

"Expect he'd love it while he's gaining the experience. But maybe we're counting our chickens before they're hatched."

Alan smiled. "As long as we don't all start clucking, I've a feeling Davie *will* succeed."

"We can only hope and pray about that. Do you believe he'll be living with his parents again?"

Alan laughed. "Some hope of that, I would think. Let's face it, he's been off their leash for some time now. He must have become used to his independence. And I also think the lassies will like having him around."

I nodded. "Completely agree with you about that. Believe they've both got a soft spot for him."

"Well, it's certainly better than them having one for someone unsuitable." Alan said.

I hesitated before I spoke again. "Must admit I worry about them a bit sometimes while they're out at night, performing. In case they're taken advantage of by undesirables."

Alan tried to reassure me. "Oh, I shouldn't fret too much. Doubt that Douglas would allow anything improper to take place. I'm sure he keeps a keen eye on everything that's going on there. He's an observant chap. Too fly to let people take a lot of advantage of him."

"Needs to be in that place though I must admit it's one of the nicest ones there are."

Alan grinned. "You got around a few places in your hometown when you were younger, don't forget."

"That's true," I smiled, wryly.

David returned to Edinburgh a week later and came to see us all one evening. "I've found some quite comfortable lodgings near your house," he said.

"Pleased for you," Alan said. "Like to share your supper with us tonight?"

"Delighted to," David beamed. While we were consuming it, he said, "I've found the ideal wee place that I need to start up my new business. It's an old tobacconist's shop. I'm excited about it."

"But what's happened to your burlesques?" Alan asked.

"Oh, they were doing well for a while but then Alistair got a job helping the stage manager at the Brighton Theatre and Martin … well," David hesitated. looking slightly embarrassed. "He had to go away for a short time."

I was tempted to ask why Martin had had to do this but in view of David's apparent reluctance not to talk about it, decided not to do so.

Alan was looking thoughtful. After a pause he said. "Presume you'll be working on your new venture during the daytime."

David nodded in agreement. "Aye."

"I'm willing to give you a small loan to help you start up," Alan said. I couldn't help hoping Alan wouldn't be over generous, I had seen David's eyes light up. But I felt that David was honest.

"You're most helpful, can't describe how grateful I am."

"Glad you think that. But bear in mind it's a loan not a gift, Davie though when you start paying me back, it can be with instalments."

Alan paused before he spoke again. "Another thing, it seems a shame to me to waste your musical talent but while I'm naturally hoping you'll do well with your new business, how about if I ask Douglas to let you play your violin at his place a couple of evenings a week? It would also give you a bit of extra income to help you get started with your new project."

David looked delighted. "I'd like that very much. Thank you for suggesting it."

Alan smiled. "Good, in that case, I'll go ahead and ask Douglas soon."

"Have you seen your parents yet?" I asked, wondering if the earl might have offered his son some financial assistance.

David's face fell momentarily. "Yes, but the atmosphere was icy to say the least. My father was still trying to lecture me about my duties to his estate and said he was horrified about my descent into becoming a tradesman. Told me I probably wouldn't succeed with what I wanted to do anyway. My mother tried not to cry when she said she wished I still lived with them. I pointed out that it was more sensible for me to bide near my workplace. We had quite a row about it. I think he'd like to have another son and disinherit me. But it's not very likely I'll ever now have younger brothers."

I sighed, shaking my head. "Families and their problems."

"Are you still determined to go ahead with your plan?" Alan asked. I guessed he wished to change the subject.

"You bet. And I'll be eternally thankful to you for helping it proceed."

Alan smiled again. "Let's all drink a toast to that, then."

We all took pleasure in this.

CHAPTER FIFTY-EIGHT

David continued to visit us frequently. His new business had started off slowly but gradually more and more people had become interested in it and he began to make a profit, paying back small sums to Alan until the loan had been fully repaid.

I was relieved about this, it wasn't that I hadn't believed David had been insincere when he said he would repay the loan, I had wondered if he might not be able to do so.

He eventually earned enough to manage to buy himself a car. It and his violin were his equal prides of joy. David liked discussing the mechanics of it with Alan and the pair of them took different photographs of the vehicle.

"I've even given my car a name," David said, one day.

"Oh, what's that?" Alan and I both asked, amused.

"Ivy, after one of the singers at Dougie's. She's what I'd call the 'in-between act.' Not the star but more than a chorus player. She is a good performer but not quite as popular as she thinks she is."

"There's always people like that," I said, dryly. "Certainly, came across some of them when I was younger."

Alan grinned. "Including me."

"Didn't mean you." I was smiling and shaking my head,

On the evenings that David and our girls were performing at the music hall, he began to bring them home in his car so we didn't need to send Hewitt out to do this. I noticed that a great attraction was growing between David and Mirabelle. However, I could see in Sylvie's expressive face that she was also strongly attracted to him but trying valiantly not to show it. I could hear the longing in her voice whenever she spoke about him.

My heart reached out to her in sympathy. I wondered how I could go about maybe introducing her to other suitable young men who might be interested in her but unfortunately, I drew a blank here. I certainly wouldn't have wished her to become involved with any of the prisoners at Calton Jail.

One morning when she had risen before Mirabelle, Sylvie said. wistfully, "Mamma, when Davie brings us home from Doug's, Belle always waits for me to get out of his car before she does."

"Don't like to tell tales normally but it seems to take her a little while before she eventually comes in, quietly, almost creeping you could say."

Feeling a little apprehensive about this, I tried to dismiss my suspicion that they might be making love after Sylvie had entered the house. Aloud, I merely said. "Perhaps they feel they have a lot to talk about."

Sylvie looked sceptical. "Cannae see what's so important that they dinnae include me in their conversations."

"Maybe they believe you wouldn't be interested in what they're saying to each other." This sounded doubtful even to my own ears.

That evening Alan said to the girls. "Your mother and I will come to a night at Doug's next week when you're all on including Davie," I looked at him, knowing he had said this, impulsively.

"That will be wonderful," Sylvie enthused.

Mirabelle didn't look as if she were as pleased about the idea, merely giving a little smile in response to Alan's comment. I noticed she looked paler than usual and she had put on a little weight.

We went to the show and all of us *did* enjoy it. Sylvie and Mirabelle both looked enthusiastic, putting a lot into their performances with great enthusiasm. I knew Mirabelle well enough to know she wasn't "faking it."

"They were wonderful tonight," I enthused to Alan.

"You can say that again," he agreed. "We can feel proud of them both. Lovely lassies who take after their mother."

"Oh, get away with you," I said, laughing although I was flattered by his comment.

He smiled. "Was only telling you the truth."

CHAPTER FIFTY-NINE

The following week Alan said to me, "Davie's said that his friends, Alistair and Martin are coming to stay in the city for a couple of weeks afore the weather gets colder."

"That'll be nice for him and for the girls," I commented.

Alan nodded. "Davie says he'll ask them if they'd like to go to Dougie's place when the lassies are on. He said he thinks the pair of them will love seeing them again both in person and on the stage."

"Hope they won't be disappointed when they do," I remarked, a little dryly.

Alan shook his head. "Sure, they won't be."

"Admire your confidence in them. I know they're used to performing and coping with stage fright but they could well feel more nervous with those three watching them."

"They'll cope, they always have."

I still felt a little anxious, it was instinctive on my part. "Know I'm maybe sounding too pessimistic but there's always a first time when things can go wrong."

"Think you *are* sounding over anxious. Try to cheer up a bit."

I smiled. "You're right. Things probably will go well and I'll wonder what I was concerned about afterwards."

Alan nodded. "That's the spirit."

The twins were excited when we told them the news.

"Hope Davie helps them enjoy themselves," Sylvie said.

"He will, I'm sure," Mirabelle agreed, I wondered why there was a slight blush in her cheeks.

The twins asked if they could show the three young men the sights of Edinburgh. Alan shook his head. "No need, surely. Davie will be able to do that. And they had a good look around the last time they were here."

"But what about Davie's shop, Papa?" Mirabelle asked.

Alan frowned. "He's the owner not an employee, Belle. He should be able to take time off whenever he likes. The last time I spoke to him, he led me to believe that even if he wasn't making a huge profit, he was doing reasonably well."

Mirabelle's face lit up. "He deserves to with all the ideas he's got for it. He's hoping it will mean his business will get bigger so that he can extend it with maybe some new premises after a while."

"So, he confided in you, did he?" I asked.

"He certainly did," Sylvie confirmed. I couldn't help wondering how she knew this and spoke. "You also know this, then?"

"Hard not to. I heard him talking about it nineteen to the dozen when we were both in his car. He's keen to get on."

"Have a feeling that even though not *all* of his dreams in this respect will come true," Alan said. "He *will* get on, given time, I am convinced about this."

"We'll all hope he does," I confirmed.

We decided to invite the three young men, David, Martin, and Alistair to have an evening meal with us one night but David said. "Martin thanks you for your kindly asking Alistair and myself to dine with you but unfortunately, he has a prior engagement."

"Never mind, that can't be helped," Alan remarked.

"Have to admit I'm disappointed," I said because I sensed that Sylvie had affectionate feelings for Martin.

We had engaged a cook, a Mrs Spicer. Alan had winked at me before she started working for us, saying. "Hope she won't be as spicy in her behaviour as she her name might suggest."

I smiled. Mrs Spicer proved to be a good cook, one of her specialities was casseroles. She was aided in her endeavours by our youngest maid. I thought this experience would do the girl good.

"Hope a restaurant won't find out about Mrs Spicer and steal her from us," I said.

Alan smiled. "Not yet I shouldn't think."

Mrs Spicer's beef casserole was a huge success after David and Alistair arrived and partook of it. "I've had some good meals here before," David approved. "But this one has been out of this world. Thank you so much for inviting me to it."

"The best I've tasted for a long time," Alistair agreed, his dark blue eyes lighting up. "I'm sure the players I know would have agreed with me if they had been able to come too. Your cook could manage a banquet if necessary."

"Did you get to know any famous actors?" Sylvie asked, wide-eyed.

He nodded. "A few, yes. They're not all particularly nice people though."

"That's surely true of any profession," Alan said.

"I tended to be a bit more interested in the technical side." Alistair commented. "Lighting, sound, stage effects, all that sort of thing."

"Does sound interesting," Sylvie agreed. "But *I'm* still more keen on the performing side. Want to be in the glow of the lights rather than making them work."

Her comment made us all laugh. I was pleased the atmosphere round our table was light hearted.

But the next time I went to the prison on a visit, just before seeing a couple of the female prisoners, I was shocked to see Martin there in the jail. When he saw me, he looked both surprised and ashamed.

"What are you in here for?" I couldn't help asking him.

He looked shame faced. "Indecency. I was caught in the act with another man."

"Oh, Martin," I sighed.

He blushed. "Expect you hate me now."

I shook my head. "No, I don't."

"Thank you for your understanding."

"Wasn't saying I approved but I don't dislike you for it as long as you've never forced anyone, especially children."

"Wouldn't dream of doing that."

"Good, I'm relieved to hear it.

Then there was another shock a week later when Mirabelle said on one of the nights that she usually performed at the music hall, "Don't want to go there tonight, Mamma. Don't feel very well."

"What's wrong, love?"

Mirabelle glanced nervously at her father. "Can I tell you on your own, Mamma?"

"All right," I said, looking at Alan, wondering if he felt annoyed by her question. But he looked a little concerned. "Let's go to your bedroom, you can tell me there."

"I believe I'm having a baby, mamma," she said, bluntly while we were sitting on her bed.

Unable to stop myself sighing, all I could say was, "Oh, Mirabelle, did you miss your last monthly?"

She nodded.

"David's child?"

"Aye," she whispered as her tears started to fall once again. She looked down at the floor. "I'm sorry."

I was dismayed and was sure Alan would be as well. "It's a little late to be sorry, Belle. Your father will have to be told too; you know. I'll try and break it to him as gently as I can."

Mirabelle was crying again.

"Well," I said, briskly. "Before we do anything else, you'll have to be examined by our doctor."

Sniffing, Mirabelle nodded in agreement. So, I put my arms around her as she began to sob on my shoulder.

"Come on now," I said, firmly. "Wish we didn't have this problem even if we're not sure about this yet. I'll arrange a private meeting at our doctor's house where he can examine you and confirm if you are … what we would have called in France *enceinte*".

"Papa will probably be furious if I am, won't he?"

"Not necessarily," I said, with more hope than conviction. "He's not a hard man as you know."

"Aye but this is a bit different to most things."

I sighed. "We'll just have to manage as well as we can. Think you'd better go to bed now and get some rest."

Mirabelle wiped her eyes with a handkerchief. "Thank you for not being angrier with me."

I sighed. "Can't say I'm pleased to put it mildly but we'll cope somehow."

"I'm grateful, Mamma."

Alan thought I was going to the prison as usual when I went to see our doctor with Mirabelle. He believed she had gone out earlier to meet one of her friends. Our doctor confirmed that my daughter, was indeed, pregnant.

CHAPTER SIXTY

I broke the news to Alan about Mirabelle one evening after Sylvie had gone to the music hall as usual. Mirabelle had told her sister she wouldn't be accompanying her as she wasn't feeling well. Sylvie said she wished for Mirabelle to get well soon. Mirabelle had smiled, wanly.

"Know she's in bed but send one of the maids up to tell her to come down here for us to have a word with her," Alan said.

I was alarmed. "You're not going to hurt her, are you?"

He shook his head. "No, not physically but she'll have a few questions to answer."

Mirabelle came into our parlour, wearing a dressing gown over her nightdress.

"You've got a bit of explaining to do, young lady," Alan said. "Is this bairn you're expecting David's?"

Mirabelle nodded, bursting into tears at the same time. I handed her a handkerchief and after a short while, she wiped her eyes.

"I love him, believe he loves me too," she said, defiantly.

"For your sake, I hope he does and faces up to his responsibility," I couldn't help remarking.

"He will," Mirabelle confirmed.

"We don't know that, for definite," I protested.

Alan put his hand on her shoulder and spoke to her more gently. "Hope you realise his parents may not acknowledge him or her, they'll just think of the kid as David's bastard."

"We don't know that yet," I commented.

"No, we don't," Alan acknowledged. "But knowing the nobility, where marriage is concerned, they stick to their own kind."

"They'll probably support the baby financially though, won't they?" I asked, hopefully.

"They should but look, we'll all go to see David at his workplace tomorrow. He'll have some explaining to do as well."

Mirabelle was concerned. "You won't attack him, will you, Papa?" she asked, fearfully.

Alan shook his head. "Must admit it's what I feel like doing but for your sake, I won't.

You'd better go back to bed now and get some sleep."

"I've been stupid," she said.

"Too late to worry about that, now," Alan said, bluntly. "Get some rest."

I couldn't help thinking she would probably have a disturbed night although I did not wish this for her.

Alan and I sat up late, discussing, sometimes disagreeing about what our next course of action should be but we were both determined to confront David.

We went to his shop the next day, having left Mirabelle in bed and asking Sylvie to keep an eye on her and make sure she was as comfortable as possible. I had told Sylvie about Mirabelle's condition.

"Davie's bairn is it, do you know mamma?"

"Yes."

Sylvie looked sad, I felt sorry for her but didn't comment on it.

When we reached David's shop the following day, Alan immediately asked him. "Are you proud of yourself?"

I noticed he was frowning with his hand balled into a fist. He wasn't violent by nature but like most placid people, when he was annoyed, he really was angry. I put a restraining hand on his sleeve and he opened his fingers, much to my relief.

David looked puzzled. "What do you mean?"

"Our daughter's in the family way and we believe you're the bairn's father."

David turned pale.

"Well, do you admit it?"

David sighed. "Yes, I'm prepared to marry her. I do love her."

"Whether you're telling the truth about that or not, at least you're prepared to do the right thing by her," I said. "But I think *we* are the ones who we should ask her how she feels about this first. Are you agreeable to this?"

218

David looked taken aback. After a slight pause he said, "Very well, I agree. But I'd like to see her soon afterwards."

But when we told Mirabelle about this, she shook her head, saying "No, I don't want to see him ever again. If we married, he'd only grow to resent me."

Alan, Sylvie, and I both protested that this would probably not be the case but Mirabelle was adamant that she did not wish to have any further contact with David.

"We'll have to accept it, we can't force her to change her mind," I said, wearily.

"You're right but …" Alan shrugged his shoulders.

A month later, one afternoon when Mirabelle had stayed in her bed longer than usual, we heard her give a piercing scream.

Alan, Sylvie, and myself rushed into her bedroom. "Maybe a stupid question but what's wrong, hen?" Alan asked. "Are ye in great pain?"

Mirabelle nodded. "Look at my bedclothes, they're covered in blood and I haven't stopped the flow yet."

We all gasped.

"Right," Alan said, "I'm going for the doctor's immediately and he'd better come back with me. Isabelle, make Mirabelle a cup of tea and Sylvie, you stay here and talk to her."

We did what he asked but I had a little difficulty in persuading Mirabelle to drink her tea. But Sylvie managed to persuade her to do so.

We stayed with her until Alan and the doctor arrived. He examined Mirabelle thoroughly after we had left the bedroom.

Afterwards he told us. "I'm afraid Miss Fergusson has lost the baby she was carrying. She's been in pain and had a nasty shock. But she's young and should recover in time. However, I'm leaving you a tonic I've prescribed for her."

"Thank you for what you've done," Alan said. He paid the doctor his fee and the man departed.

During the following few weeks, Mirabelle was depressed. She rose very late and had lost some of her appetite. Alan, Sylvie, and I were all worried about her. But then an event occurred on a world scale which changed everything.

PART FOUR: WAR

CHAPTER SIXTY-ONE

In August war broke out. A ragged urchin boy waving a newspaper broke the news to Edinburgh citizens in a theatre.

"Apparently also from what I heard," Alan said. "The audience sang 'God Save the King' at the beginning of the evening. Other songs they particularly like are 'Pack up Your Troubles in Your Old Kit Bag' and 'If You Were the Only Girl in the World'"

Some people were saying that the war would probably only last until Christmas but Alan and I were not so sure about this.

Some outlying farms were offering rehabilitation for wounded soldiers, fruit and vegetables were being sent to the Royal Navy and some private gardens were turned into allotments while some chickens were kept in back gardens. Conscientious objectors to war tended to work on the land.

Our daughters decided to travel to my home country, France, to entertain the troops stationed there.

"Many folk believe this war's only going to last till Christmas," Alan said, shortly after hearing about this. "I'm not so sure, myself. "David's told me he's been accepted as a war photographer."

Alan only saw David occasionally now but the atmosphere between them was different, it was more civil even if not as friendly as it had formerly been.

"What's the reason for this war, Papa?" Sylvie asked. "Why is Britain involved?"

"It's a bit complex love but basically it's because the Germans invaded Belgium."

"Sylvie's applied to become a nurse, hasn't she?" Alan said next.

"I'm proud of her for doing that," I remarked.

"I am going to do that too," Mirabelle said. She had by now fully recovered.

But when Sylvie came back from her interview, she was looking disappointed. "They've turned me down," she said. "Said I'd be better staying as an entertainer to cheer our boys up."

"Perhaps they're right," Mirabelle said, thoughtfully.

"They would probably have the same attitude towards you, Belle," Sylvie remarked. But why don't you apply to be an entertainer too."

"I'll think about it," Mirabelle said, cautiously. I hoped she would do so although I was determined not to put pressure on her about it. Neither did Alan. However, she still applied to become a nurse.

"They've turned me down for a nurse too," she told us, looking disappointed after she returned home.

Sylvie smiled. "Never mind Belle, become an entertainer and we'll still be together, hopefully."

Mirabelle sighed then looked pensive for a few minutes. "I might just do that," she said. Alan and I exchanged relieved looks.

I had now started to engage some of the female prisoners at Calton Jail to start sewing shirts for the troops.

We were visited soon afterwards by Eloise and John. We had invited them to lunch with us as we had only seen them occasionally in recent years. But I now hoped we would be seeing more of them in the future. John's printing and publishing business was doing well. He wanted to include some of the photographs of families that Alan had taken in a new book John was publishing after the family members had given their permission for him to do so.

"It's admirable what you're doing, Isabelle," Eloise said. "Visiting the female prisoners and sewing shirts." I was grateful that she and John were looking at me with what I could tell was genuine admiration. As we were both by now bi-lingual, we conversed in English to be courteous to our husbands. "And what your daughters are trying to do, too," she added. I was gratified by this.

Finally, a month later, the twins were delighted to be accepted by Miss Daisy Farmer's choir who were due to travel to my home country, France, to entertain the troops there.

"There's strength in numbers," Alan said. "I'd rather our lassies are amongst others instead of on their own."

"I couldn't agree more," I stated. I was able to tell that Alan and I were pleased by our girls' decision although we would both miss them.

When the day of their departure finally arrived, Alan and I went to the railway station to wave them off. I managed not to cry in front of them but as the train pulled away my tears began to fall. Alan squeezed my hand in sympathy.

CHAPTER SIXTY-TWO

"We're always relieved when we receive letters from our daughters," I commented when John and Eloise paid their next visit to us a few weeks later.

"That they're still safe," Alan said. He put his hand on his heart. "But unfortunately, their circumstances could change any day soon."

"Heaven forbid, they won't," John remarked.

"In their last letter," I said. "They told us that they were performing in the open air where there's audiences of huge crowds of men who sit or stand if they can on the lawns of chateaux that have been converted to hospitals. Now and again, they play in a huge marquee. And occasionally in actual hospital wards they play to unfortunate men who've lost their arms, legs or even their eyes."

"Poor souls," John said.

I continued speaking." There's other entertainers in different theatrical companies with them, including singers, comics and even jugglers and acrobats."

"Hope there's at least one magician waving a wand over them, to keep them safe," Alan joked.

We all smiled but I added a serious note. "We've also been told that the landscapes surrounding them are often shattered with broken trees and pock marked earth."

"Not a pretty sight then as you can imagine," Alan remarked. "Still, they're taking part in a grand effort. My heart could swell with pride, hope it won't burst."

"Don't believe it will do that just yet," I smiled.

"We've also received a letter from our friend David," Alan said. "Much to our surprise I confess in which he informed us that he had witnessed the unfortunate results of the battle of Gallipoli in Turkey, involving several regiments of Australian and New Zealand forces."

"Brave young men," John said. I've heard that quite a few from our city are eager to sign up and join the forces."

"Hope most of them will be able to return home after the war ends," I couldn't help saying. "Although I have my doubts."

"Me too," Alan agreed.

After our meal was finished, Alan said. "I'd like to go to my club now, would you be happy to come with me, John? If your lady wife agrees of course."

I saw John glance at Eloise who gave an almost imperceptible nod of agreement.

Alan turned to me. "You don't mind too, do you, Isa?"

I smiled. "You should know by now I never object to that. Anyway, I've got some sewing patterns I'd like to show to Eloise while you two are out."

"Thank you both," John said.

"In that case, we'd better go and beard Hewitt in his den," Alan grinned.

Eloise looked puzzled.

"We'll go to his room, don't think he expected to go out today but I'll give him a different day off this week, believe he'll accept that."

To Eloise's and my surprise, Alan and John returned to our company earlier than we expected both looking slightly unkempt and red in the face.

"You won't be seeing Hewitt again, Isa," Alan said.

"Why not?"

He and John both grinned.

"Because on his day off," Alan said. "His friend, Avery, visited him and I overheard the two of them discussing how they could break into a department store at night. But they couldn't quite agree on the methods they'd choose. So, we gave him this opportunity to have a different sort of choice."

John grinned. "We could have contacted the police about him". "What we did," Alan said. "Was force him to drive us to The Army Recruitment Office, making sure he couldn't escape. Several young men have been keen to join the Forces Bet Hewitt won't be their most enthusiastic recruit, though."

Eloise and I stared at them both for a few seconds then all four of us started laughing, heartily.

"He did put up a bit of a struggle," Alan said, after we had calmed down.

"But it was two against one so fortunately, we managed to overpower him in the end," John added

"But," Eloise stated after we had calmed down. "You should be on your guard because Hewitt probably has friends and contacts who could cause trouble for you if you're not careful."

"Aye," Alan nodded. "We found a letter that fell out of his trouser pocket, to this fellow named Hector Avery, it had details of a plan for the two of them to rob a warehouse."

"Don't you think you should inform the manager of this warehouse?" I asked.

Alan shook his head. "No, I believe we ought to let sleeping dogs lie. And only wake them up again if the worst comes to the worst."

Following this comment, we all laughed again before drinking a glass of wine each.

But. luckily, we found out later that we didn't need to contact the warehouse manager or his staff anyway because the place had closed not long afterwards.

"How did you find out about the war, Alan?" John asked.

"I heard that a newsboy, he was barefoot and ragged, poor soul, broke into a theatre." Alan grinned. "He was wearing a cap but it didn't fit him properly because it was too big for him. He was shouting "Buy the paper, see the news. We're at war now."

"How did the audience react?"

"Differently, some even clapped but they earned some disgusted looks. Others looked horrified and frowned. There was some shaking of heads and there was also a small amount of shrugging of shoulders."

The war that several people had thought would only last for a few months, dragged on for four years in total, the Americans declaring war on Germany on 6 April 1917. Britain with the aid of its Empire had been involved in it right from the start.

Alan and I went to church more often now and when we did, we prayed for our daughters' safety.

225

We received letters from Sylvie and Mirabelle, one in which Mirabelle wrote:

"Dear Mamma and Papa
We are still alive and well for which we thank God daily but we feel sorry for the servicemen who have died or been wounded while fighting for our country, Britain's, safety.

We heard about Louisa Garrett Anderson and Flora Murray the well- known female surgeons who founded the Women's Hospital Corps and recruited other women to staff it. They offered their assistance to the French Red Cross who accepted it and provided them with a newly built hotel in Paris as a hospital. Sylvie and I admire them a lot.

To our surprise, we met Alistair again, he was performing with the Pierrots but unfortunately, they were attacked by some unruly troops who accused them of being cowards because they haven't enlisted. But Alistair calmed them down a little when he told them that he had been turned down for active service because on a trip to Dover with two friends before the war, they had climbed a cliff but he had fallen and broken his wrist. Although it had mostly healed, the authorities were not sure how capable he would be of handling weapons."

"Sylvie and I have missed you and hope to see you again once this horrible war is finally over. Hoping and praying you two, Uncle John and Aunt Eloise will keep safe and well.
Sending all our love,
Mirabelle"

Tears fell from my eyes as I stood up from my chair and handed the letter to Alan to read. He took me in his arms and pulled my head on to his shoulder. "Is it bad news?" he asked me, anxiously.

I managed to lift my head up and shake my head. "Not the news we were dreading, it's just that this letter has touched me."

After he had read it, Alan said. "It's made me feel exactly the same way too."

"I've heard what happened was, a newsboy, he was barefoot and ragged when he broke into a theatre."

A lot of folk believe it could be over by Christmas but I'm not so sure," Alan said, his brow creased in thought.

Not long afterwards we received a letter from David Irvine. He had sailed with the British infantry from the 29th Division under the command of Sir Ian Hamilton and they had landed at Cape Helle. The Anzacs were situated north of Gaba Tepe, an area that would later be called Anzac Cove.

David informed us that he had taken photographs of the infantry disembarking into a rowing boat from the troopship in preparation for their landing at Cape Helles. Later, he photographed the 29th Division's line at Cape Helles and the Royal Field Artillery, the forward observation post in the British lines at Cape Helles.

"I have become horrified by the trench warfare as the casualties have begun to mount up and then increase," he wrote. "The summer heat was oppressive and sickness was rampant. Some of the food became inedible and black flies hovered around. I was only allowed to take certain photographs with the officers' permission. Their decisions sometimes irked me to be honest.

In August we heard that a new assault was launched north of Anzac Cove against the hills around Chunuk Bair. And there was a fresh landing at Suvla Bay.

That December a decision was made to evacuate Anzac Cove and Suvla Bay followed by evacuation from Cape Helles in January 1916. The Americans entered the war in April, 1917.

David informed us that he was extremely grateful that he had managed to stay alive but he felt sad when he remembered all the servicemen who had lost their lives or been maimed. Many of them were people he had liked. He no longer believed in the old saying "All is fair in love and war."

CHAPTER SIXTY-THREE
SPRING 1918

A telegram had been sent from the War Office to announce the end of the war and it led to the demobilisation of troops. Alan and I were highly relieved. We were also looking forward to our girls coming home for a longer stay with us than usual. They would be travelling on a train mainly filled with servicemen.

But shortly afterwards, the first wave of what was called 'The Spanish 'Flu' began. The sick had chills, fever, and fatigue. Most of them recovered after several days. The second wave happened in the autumn. This time, several victims died within hours or days. Their skin turned blue and their lungs filled with fluid causing them to suffocate.

Our family was not affected by it although we pitied the victims with all our hearts.

"Lots of young people have caught this illness," Alan said, sadly, to me

"Not ours, fortunately," I said.

"Thank goodness for that," Alan stated. "However, it's a shame that schools, theatres, and businesses including ours have had to close. And the children can't go to school. I'm glad our two aren't affected by that, not that they're still children of course."

"I don't like wearing a mask whenever I go out," I said.

"Nor me. But we need to, don't we? And we don't go out all that often now, do we?"

I nodded in agreement. "Probably just as well."

David sent us a letter in which he stated "I went to my parents' home after my return from the war. It was a warm afternoon in both senses of the word."

"My mother had tears running down her face as she said. 'You've done us proud, Davie,' as she gripped me in a bearhug.

I had to laugh when I remarked. 'Let me breathe, Mother, please.'

"She said that she and my father were very proud of me, I remember my father nodding with a thin smile.

After our welcome tea, I showed my parents some of the photographs I had taken while I was away but not the more gruesome ones.

I eventually showed them a few photographs of the SS River Clyde at the beach named the 'V' beach and the British infantry from the 29th division disembarking into the rowing boat.

My father said 'Most interesting, David.' Mother said they were wonderful and thank goodness they hadn't lost me like so many other poor parents.

"Another interesting thing that's happened to me was meeting a Swiss chap called Otto Pfenniger when I went to Brighton with a soldier, I became friendly with, who comes from there. Anyway, this Pfenniger also lives in Brighton. He's developed an interesting method of colour photography. I've also seen a three colour lantern slide he made of children playing on the beach. I was fascinated by this.

Finally, I am so looking forward to my visit to your house, I'm grateful that you always make me feel welcome."

"It will be nice to see him again," I said, after putting his letter away.

Alan nodded. "I agree. And I'll be interested in hearing more about this Pfenniger fellow."

CHAPTER SIXTY-FOUR

Sylvie and Mirabelle returned to us after travelling on trains filled with returning troops. Alan and I were delighted to welcome them home.

But I felt sad when one of David's letters to Alan informed him that Martin who had joined the Navy after he had been released from prison, had died when his ship was sunk by the enemy.

"Dear Mr and Mrs Fergusson, Sylvie and Mirabelle

I expect, like me, that you are highly relieved the war is over. Truly hope it has not affected you too badly, I have been lucky in this respect myself and know I am one of the fortunate ones.

What I have been doing since the end of the war is visiting a lot of towns and having a look at their theatres. My reason for doing this is because it is my dream to have a theatre of my own one day. I think I gained valuable experience with the Pierrots despite the bit of trouble we had on that one occasion.

However, I hope to come to Edinburgh soon and will be pleased if you allow me to visit you. Can you recommend a reasonably priced hotel near to your house where I could stay?

Hope to see you all soon.

Yours sincerely

Alistair Patterson"

Alan handed me his letter "Read this then tell me what you think about it, Isa," Alan said. I did so.

Smiling, after I had read it, I handed the letter back to him "I'd be happy to see him again. Don't know why, exactly but I sense he has a soft spot for Sylvie."

"You could well be right enough there. But maybe she hasn't got the same feeling towards him." Alan sighed. "Oh well, time will tell."

I replied to Alistair's letter explaining that our girls would shortly be coming home from France, giving him the date and saying Alan and I were sure that they would be delighted to see him again.

But Alistair then sent us a further short letter saying he was very busy and would not be able to pay us a visit as soon as he had hoped. However, this certainly did not mean he didn't intend to pay us a visit at all, it would just be later than he had hoped. In the meantime, he hoped life was treating us as fairly as possible.

Alan and I met the girls at Waverley railway station. There was mutual laughter, tears, and excitement after they had alighted from the train. We embraced each other, uncaring of any bystanders who might have disapproved of such a public display of affection.

"Oh, it's so good to be home again," Sylvie and Mirabelle said together.

"And we're delighted to have you two back," Alan said. "Don't you agree, Isa?"

"Of course," I agreed.

Not long after we had arrived home, our staff did us proud with the hearty meal they had prepared for us. We spent the next few days relaxing, even Alan taking a few days off from his business.

But not long afterwards the 'Spanish flu' epidemic struck. It was called this because the first cases of the illness had been reported in Spain.

The Earl of Roseleans had allowed his house and land to be turned into a convalescent home for wounded servicemen.

"I wish to go and visit the injured at Roseleans," Mirabelle said, enthusiastically.

"So do I," Sylvie added. "We've discussed it together, Belle and me."

"What do you intend to do there?" I asked. "It's not as if you've been trained as nurses."

"We know," Mirabelle said. "What we'd do is talk to the sick people there and give them little presents of things like small embroidered handkerchiefs that we could make."

Alan frowned. It's a kind idea but I'm not sure about it being a good one. And you could become victims of the disease yourselves."

Their faces fell, I felt a small amount of pity for them although I could understand Alan's fear as to what their fate could be if they followed this course of action.

Alan turned his gaze on me. "And I'd like your mother to stop visiting the prison."

"I'll do that," I agreed, a little reluctantly. "But on one condition. I wish to make one last visit there and after I've seen the prisoners, I'll let the Governor it will be my last visit to his - er- premises."

Alan sighed. "Very well."

"And I'd like to go to Roseleans with the girls."

Alan shook his head. "No," he said, firmly. "You deserve a rest."

The prison governor looked disappointed when I told him what Alan had decreed. "I understand how your husband feels, Mrs Fergusson but I should like you to know how grateful I and my staff are to you for what you've done here. We'll surely miss you. Wishing you all the best for the future."

"Thank you," I said, turning away to wipe the tears from my eyes.

David Irvine wrote to Alan to say he no longer wished to be involved with running the shop. He said he was leaving it entirely up to Alan whether he wished to continue running it or to sell it.

"I think I'll sell it," Alan said. He advertised in the local newspaper and received enquiries from a couple of unsuitable applicants but a short while later, made a successful sale to a respectable businessman.

After a week of arguing Alan capitulated about the twins intended visit to Roseleans. "I'm tired of seeing your long faces," he said. "Well, I've been thinking things over." He indicated the girls "I'm willing to let you two go to Roseleans but not every day, just two or three days a week."

Their faces lit up. "But if either of you starts showing symptoms of a cold or maybe more seriously, coughing, you're to stop visiting there immediately. In fact, even one cough should make you both ready to leave."

"We'll be careful to always wear our masks and to wash our hands a lot, won't we, Belle?" Sylvie said.

"Of course," Mirabelle agreed.

But after they had gone to Roseleans for two weeks, the countess became a victim of the pandemic and died a week later.

The twins returned home to us. "Davie's sore upset about it," Mirabelle said.

"Naturally," I remarked.

"His father must be grieving too," Alan said. He sighed. "Like lots of other folk at present but fortunately not ourselves."

"Thank the Lord, hope it continues," I added. "We can only hope and pray for this."

"I think Davie's sweet on Mirabelle," Sylvie confessed to me a day later.

"Do you believe she feels the same about him, especially after what happened to her before?"

Sylvie hesitated. "Yes, but she seems to be a bit wary of him."

CHAPTER SIXTY-FIVE

Alistair was true to his word and visited us a month later. He had booked a room in a small hotel near our house and sent us a note telling us about this.

"We should invite him to dinner with us one evening, don't you think?" I asked Alan.

"Aye, of course."

When Alistair arrived, while we were dining, I noticed him giving quick, admiring, yet discreet glances at Sylvie. She looked away demurely but I could tell she was pleased by this.

"Have you heard from David Irvine?" Alan asked him.

Alistair nodded. "Yes, shame about his mother. Davie said he'd like to meet me soon but not just yet."

"He's in mourning though, isn't he?" Mirabelle asked.

"Aye," Alan said. "But a discreet meeting with Alistair shouldn't really matter that much. How have your theatre visits gone, Alistair?"

"They've been most interesting; I've visited a lot of them and gained ideas."

"Bet that's cost you a lot of money," Mirabelle said. I saw Alan begin to frown.

"A fair amount, I admit," Alistair said. "But I managed to save some up before I started on my travels. And I also wrote a play that was performed at one of the tiniest theatres in London that I've ever seen. Although I didn't make a fortune from it, it was more successful than I expected it would be. Can't fully describe how relieved I was about that."

"Well done, Alistair," Alan said, I could tell he was impressed while the girls were wide eyed with admiration. "And at least a London theatre was willing to take a risk with your play."

"What is it about?" Sylvie asked.

"Oh, an imaginary country where the people are living under a cruel ruler. He declares war on his neighbours' land but he's defeated in battle and dies. The king of the winning country marries the princess of the defeated land and they rule together. But their rule is kind and fair."

Alistair glanced down at the table, looking almost embarrassed. "Does it sound daft? Please be honest."

Alan shook his head as Sylvie, Mirabelle and I all said "No," together.

"It can't be that silly if it's been put on by a theatre," Sylvie remarked. Alistair looked both relieved and pleased.

"I felt a bit scared to mention this," he said. "But I've been thinking of trying to write another play with a fair amount of music included in it."

"You didn't need to be scared," I protested. "I'm sure we'll all wish you every success with it."

Alistair looked at me, gratefully. "Thank you."

"As long as you're not sick and tired of other theatres to the one that put your play on," Alan said, with a twinkle in his eye. "Would you like it, if we all went to our local theatre on one of the evenings next week?"

"I'd like nothing better; I'm honestly not just saying that."

"Good, that's settled then, I'm happy to say," Alan said. "Why don't we all drink a toast to Alistair's continuing enterprise. A glass of wine should go down nicely."

We all enjoyed the play, a comedy, when we went to the theatre. I believed that Alan had deliberately chosen something light hearted after all the recent sadness there had been.

I noticed that Alistair was engrossed in the activities on stage but he also now and again, cast shy yet affectionate glances at Sylvie. She gave him a discreet smile in return. He also had a good look around at the other members of the audience as well as the theatre's furnishings and seating.

During the following week when Alistair visited us, he looked pale and drawn. We all wondered what had happened to him but were not sure about asking him about the reason for this. However, he told us himself. "I've had a letter from David, there's been a terrible accident at his father's mine. Four men have been killed there."

"Do you know how it happened?" Alan asked.

Alistair nodded. "The main gist of it, yes. The canary birds they keep in carriers with the small oxygen bottles attached to revive them began to show more actual signs of distress than the miners themselves. They're sensitive to small amounts of gas and usually quicker to react than humans. The canaries were the first to provide the warning to exit the tunnels."

"Clever birds," Sylvie said.

Mirabelle nodded in agreement. "I agree."

"Think we're all impressed by them," Alan remarked.

"Let us visit Roseleans now, Papa," Mirabelle pleaded.

But Alistair shook his head before speaking quickly again. "If you don't mind, Mr Fergusson, I believe I should be the one to go there, the first anyway."

He glanced apprehensively at the twins before adding. "No disrespect to Sylvie and Mirabelle but after all, as a male, I'll have more of the physical strength to help carry the bodies,

Alistair looked deep in thought for a moment. "Or any heavy items that may be left lying around," he continued. "I'll also try to assist in other necessary physical tasks."

Alan smiled. "I agree and admire you for what you've just said." He looked directly at me. "I'm sure feel the same way too, don't you, Isa?"

"Yes, I do," I answered, even though I could see and to an extent sympathise with the girls' disappointment.

"Thank you for your understanding, I'd better be on my way there now," Alistair said.

"Hope it won't be too distressing for you," Alan stated.

"Realistically, it's bound to be but I'm prepared for that," Alistair confirmed.

CHAPTER SIXTY-SIX

Alistair returned to his hotel two days later. The following evening, he called on us unexpectedly. Alan and I were pleased to see him. The girls, especially Sylvie were delighted. We noticed he was looking drawn and tired.

"I'm so happy to see you all again," he said. "It's a great relief."

"We're grateful to see you once more too," Alan remarked. "Mind you, we hope it won't be the only time you come here."

"Thank you, I had wondered if I might be calling on you at an inconvenient time."

"No, you're not," Alan consoled him. "If I dare ask, how did you get on at Roseleans? We'll understand if you don't feel like talking about it."

Alistair shook his head. "I wasn't quite prepared for all the death and destruction I saw there. A few of the bodies of the dead men not yet buried, the smell of destruction and the air of hopelessness of the survivors. The most terrible thing of all was when one of the miners, Williams, I think his name was if I remember correctly, was so overcome with grief at losing a couple of mates that he pushed the earl into the mineshaft."

We all gasped in horror.

"It may be a stupid question," Alan said. "But was the earl killed outright?"

Alistair frowned. "No, although crippled, he survived for another week, his doctor did what he could for him but the earl died at the end of the seven days."

"Not wishing to sound heartless," I said. "I'm sorry the earl was killed but I doubt that he would have wanted to live as a disabled man when he'd always led an active sort of life."

"Papa," Mirabelle said. "I really believe now that Mamma, Sylvie, and I should go to Roseleans to help the wives of the dead and injured men. Will you let us go?"

Alan frowned slightly. "I'll think about it." He hesitated then he smiled. "I've come to a quick decision. "Aye, you can all go there as long as you don't wear yourselves out."

Sylvie, Mirabelle and I cheered. I was pleased to see Alistair smile again. "That will be much appreciated," he said, gratefully.

*

So, we all went to Roseleans in order give whatever help we could to the injured men. We knew it would mainly consist of wiping their faces, holding their hands if they still had them, talking to them as quietly as possible and the girls singing softly to them. Alistair had decided to come with us, he lifted them up gently so that we could tend to the men.

David beamed at us when we arrived, his eyes lit up when he looked at Mirabelle. "Cannot thank you four enough for what you're doing for us here." He sighed. "Though as I'm sure you already know some of the sights, you'll see … well, they'll be horrific."

"We are prepared for that," I assured him.

"I'm grateful," David said, simply.

"Alistair's already prepared us for this," I said.

David gave Alistair a grateful look.

It was heartbreaking to see the conditions some of the poor men were experiencing. Some were blind, some had lost their limbs, others were feverish. But fortunately, there were others, more fortunate who were recovering. David arranged for the dead to be buried.

One day at Roseleans a month later after some of the men who were recovering from their injuries were sent to their homes or to hospital. Alistair returned to London where he bought and converted a previous large warehouse into a theatre in a side street.

"He's enterprising, I'll certainly say that for him," Alan remarked.

"Done well for himself," I agreed.

But Sylvie was bitterly disappointed, Alan and I felt sorry for her although Alistair corresponded with her on a regular basis.

"Alistair's told me a lot about his new theatre. Seems very keen on it," Sylvie said. "But I think he sees me as just a friend."

I gave her what I hoped was a sympathetic smile although I felt for her. When I confided in Alan, he said. "Shouldn't worry too much, I'm sure if it's not to be with Alistair, I'm sure she'll meet somebody else."

"Hope so," I said.

But Mirabelle was now being invited to special occasions at Roseleans. These were mainly small, discreet parties attended by a few relatives and close friends of David's.

CHAPTER SIXTY-SEVEN

Alistair wrote to us soon afterwards to invite Alan, Sylvie, Mirabelle, and myself to go to the opening night of his play. He said he would send us free tickets if we were interested

"Of course, we are," I said. I looking at Alan. "As long as you agree." He frowned. "I might put my foot down with a firm hand and refuse," he remarked. There was a tiny pause then he smiled and said, "Can imagine the hell on earth you'd all put me through if I did refuse."

The girls cheered although Sylvie looked a little apprehensive.

Alistair had also stated in his letter that he had sent an invitation to David Irvine as well. "Not sure if he'll be able to make it," Alistair had written. "But hope he can because I think it will do him good after everything that's happened lately."

He recommended a small, nearby to the theatre hotel where he had checked that we would be able to stay for a short stay of three nights. Alan accepted on our behalf, I was pleased, the girls were excited although in Sylvie's case I could see that it was tempered with a little wistfulness.

Alan drove us to London himself in the new car he had bought. He had allowed our new chauffeur some deserved time off.

After we reached our destination, after our evening meal we were all feeling tired so we went to bed early. The following day we went sightseeing and, in the evening, we went to see the play. We all enjoyed it very much but the icing on the cake for Mirabelle was seeing David Irvine sitting in the audience. He waved to us.

Afterwards we met Alistair backstage and congratulated him.

"We all loved everything tonight, Alistair," Sylvie said, a little shyly.

He beamed at her. "Delighted to hear it. Thank you all for coming. I hope you'll agree to play parts in our next major production, Sylvie, and Mirabelle."

"It's kind of you to offer, Alistair," Mirabelle said. "But I'd like to have a rest from performing for a while."

"I understand. "Do you feel the same way, Sylvie?"

Sylvie shook her head. "Not at all, I can't wait to be back on a stage again."

"That's a relief because I know the very role that will suit you down to the ground in our next production."

Sylvie blushed slightly although I could tell she was elated.

"Once I've got changed," Alistair added. "I'll meet you all at the restaurant. But can I have a private word with you first, please, Mr Fergusson? It's important what I've got to ask. I'll be having a word with Davie too."

"All right," Alan said, looking a little mystified. "The rest of you can wait downstairs for us."

"Take a seat there," Alistair said. "The rest of the crowd should have gone by now."

The men rejoined us fifteen minutes later. "Wonder what they're blethering about," Mirabelle had said. "Like to be a fly on the wall," Sylvie added.

Just after she had said this, Alan drew me aside for a quick private word.

"Not sure how you'll take this, Isa. It could come as a shock. But Alistair's asked me if he can propose to Sylvie and David wishes to do the same thing with Mirabelle. How do you feel about it in both cases?"

Too startled to reply immediately, I took a deep breath Then I allowed a slow smile to spread all over my face. "I'm thrilled for them both."

"Good, thought I could rely on your reaction. I've invited both Davie and Alistair to come to our favourite restaurant next Friday night, they'll be asking the lassies themselves."

"Can't wait for that night," I said.

Alan nodded. "I'll explain to you what my plan is for then."

The restaurant was busy, the tables were covered with white lace cloths and white candles in silver holders had been placed in the middle of them. The waiting staff were rushing around and a pianist was playing traditional tunes.

David and Alistair both had an air of suppressed excitement.

We saw an elderly, well dressed man at a nearby table with two other men. There was something vaguely familiar about him but I was still surprised to see him wave to us. Alan looked even more startled when he walked over to our table. We could see that he had probably been a handsome man in his youth. We noticed him look at the twins with obvious admiration.

"Excuse me," he said to me. "I heard your French accent, Madame and wondered which part of that country you came from."

His voice was deep and cultured.

"She was a Parisienne," Alan said, not looking very pleased.

"Ah, I remember the great Sarah Bernhardt playing Hamlet at the Theatre Sarah Bernhardt in Paris in 1899."

Perhaps that's why he looked a bit familiar to me, I thought. Probably saw him at that theatre with my family at some time in the past, not that I can remember it now.

He turned to Alistair. "You're doing well for yourself now; I hear my laddie."

Alistair looked slightly embarrassed. "Try to do my best, Mr Brewer," he said.

Wish you every success, you deserve it," Brewer said. "Well, hope you all enjoy this evening, I certainly intend to do so myself. I'd better get back to my place or the staff here will think I've left."

After our meal we were sharing a large bottle of red wine. "Save some for a bit later," Alan said. "Sylvie, Mirabelle, David, and Alistair have something important to ask you both. You two go into the lounge first. But don't be too long, please." He nodded to David.

David was grinning as he and Mirabelle withdrew. They returned with their hands clasped together.

"Now you two," Alistair and Sylvie went to the lounge and came back to us with a visible lovelight in both pairs of eyes.

Many of the other customers had been watching us, a few of the more straitlaced ones a little disapproving but the others were curious.

"There's going to be two weddings in the near future then," Alan said before everyone else who was still in the restaurant clapped and cheered. The twins blushed to the roots of their hair but we could tell they were pleased.

CHRISTMAS EVE 1919

Alan and I were relaxing in the evening after different preparations had been made for decorating our house. "Our lassies have done well for themselves, haven't they?" Alan said, proudly. "Sylvie an actress and singer in London and Mirabelle a countess, never would have expected that, even in my wildest dreams."

"I admire the way Mirabelle's organised treats for the miners' wives and children," I said.

Alan nodded in agreement. "Aye and Sylvie positively shines on the stage." He grinned. "Didn't do so badly when I married you did I?"

I pretended to hit him. "No, you didn't, you cheeky so and so. You were lucky even if I'm saying this myself. I'm looking forward to visiting Colette. She wasn't affected by the recent war, glad about this as Italy was neutral."

"A terrible war, thank the Lord it's over and done with." Alan stopped looking sad as his face brightened and he gave a contented sigh. "Not long now until we're in a new decade, wonder it will have in store for us."

I smiled, happily "The sun will be shining over us, "Can't help feeling that in my bones."

Alan grinned. "Hope we'll be shiny too."

I shook my head although I was grinning at the same time. "Think we'll sparkle like the stars," I said as Alan nodded in agreement.

The end

Milton Keynes UK
Ingram Content Group UK Ltd.
UKHW020717311024
2488UKWH00040B/282